FATAL BLOW

A classic British whodunnit

JANET NEEL

A Wilson and McLeish Mystery

Originally published as *Death's Bright Angel*

JOFFE
Ostara
CLASSICS

Revised edition 2024
Joffe Books, London
www.joffebooks.com

First published in Great Britain in 1988
as *Death's Bright Angel*

This paperback edition was first published
in Great Britain in 2024

Cover art by Dee Dee Book Covers

ISBN: 978-1-83526-006-7

For my mother
Mary Neel

CHAPTER 1

The elderly little man in the old navy suit looked ill at ease tucked away in the corner of the big fashionable pub in Little Venice. Not that the rest of the customers were particularly homogeneous, but they had in common the particular ease that comes with the possession of a high income and the willingness to spend it freely and with the maximum of display. This man was plainly from a different world, one where you counted the coins in your pocket and piled them up carefully when paying for a drink. He rose from his corner and went over to the bar to order another half of lager.

'Is there another pub here with a similar name?' he asked apologetically. 'I've been here twenty minutes and there is no sign of the person I came to meet.'

The barman pointed out briskly that it would hardly be possible to confuse the Pig and Whistle with the Royal George or the Crown and Anchor which represented the choice locally available. Seeing him look downcast and assuming instantly that it was a woman who had stood him up, he volunteered that there were, however, a great many pubs just the other side of the canal, many looking much the same as each other, and that it would be easy to get confused.

The man, appreciating the courtesy, smiled his thanks, finished his drink and walked out into a very dark evening. It was only just past seven but the whole of the November day had been grey and rainy, and a depressing drizzle still fell. He walked briskly across the bridge, turning into one of the featureless little streets off the Edgware Road, full of small bed-and-breakfast houses. Not an attractive area, he thought disapprovingly; rubbish in the streets, mean cold houses, and not a trace of anything green. No wonder London schoolchildren grew up delinquent. Not enough street lighting either. He decided that it would be simplest to go back to the unattractive house where he was staying and to use the phone in the hallway, supposing it wasn't jammed, to find out what had happened to the man he was meant to be meeting. Then he would ring his sister in Yorkshire to find out how their mother, just out of hospital after a hip operation, was getting along. He sighed as he thought about his mother; had his wife still been alive the phone call would have been unnecessary, since she would automatically have been round to the nursing home with flowers from the garden. His sister, however, had grown from a careless girl to a scatterbrained and feckless grandmother, prone to forget her husband's tea or the existence of her grandchildren, never mind her mother. He brightened as he was reminded of his own grandchildren and felt in his pocket for the miniature teddy bear he had bought for his treasured three-year-old grandson and the little plastic rattle for the child's six-week-old brother. The strap on the expensive gold watch slipped down on his wrist as he fished in his pocket, and he adjusted it patiently, admiring the face of the watch as he did so. It was a good watch, received only last week from the hands of his Chairman to mark his forty years' service with the company, starting as a boy of fifteen in the war. It was a pity he hadn't been able to enjoy the presentation ceremony, worried as he had been by the thought of the interview to come, but he loved the watch, and he still had the presentation box in his briefcase.

He stopped to check that he had enough coins for the phone, and lifted his head, surprised by the sudden silence. He realized that, unconsciously, he had been aware of someone walking down the street behind him and he glanced back, but there was no one. Must have turned off into one of the houses, he thought, and bent his head again short-sightedly to sort out coins. He heard the sodden dead leaves on the pavement squeak, and an indrawn breath, and as he turned just saw an upraised arm, elongated by something held in the hand; but before he could cry out, his head exploded and he felt himself falling.

His attacker, moving with desperate speed, knelt beside the fallen body and prised the fingers away from the briefcase. Cursing with panic he reached under the coat, took the man's wallet, considered for a second and tore off the watch. He laid a gloved hand against the pulse in the neck, swore, and glancing round the deserted street, picked up the hammer and smashed it down twice more on the side of the skull. He froze where he was crouching as a car came slowly down the road, obviously looking for a place to park, and he breathed out carefully as it speeded up again, discouraged by the solid lines of parked cars. Covered with cold sweat, he stood up and started to walk quickly away from the body, gloved hands dug deeply into his pockets and chin tucked well down into his scarf so that between the scarf and the flat, peaked cap only a small, unidentifiable part of his face could be seen.

It was not more than five minutes later that a young West Indian secretary, coming home after supper with a girlfriend, walked past.

She hesitated by the dishevelled bundle of clothes huddled against the hedge, and, true to a sound Baptist upbringing, bent bravely to see if help would be kindly received, or whether, like other derelicts in this area, this one would merely curse her. Her enquiring gaze met a sight that was to give her trouble for the rest of her life; the last two savage hammer blows had pulped the left eye and pushed the skull out of all human shape. The intensity of her screams, even in that area where people mind their own business, brought the street out to her aid. In that time, however, the murderer had rejoined the Edgware Road, pausing under a streetlamp to quickly check his clothes for signs of blood; satisfied, he climbed sedately on to a bus going up toward Notting Hill Gate, still carrying the nondescript briefcase into which he had thrust the wallet and the watch.

* * *

Ten minutes away, in one of the CID rooms at Edgware Road police station, Detective Inspector John McLeish and Detective Sergeant Bruce Davidson were considering going out for supper. They had each done three hours of virtuous paperwork well after normal office hours, and both were hoping to get home before any more work came in.

'Better get some dinner in, then.' Davidson at twenty-eight was a stocky, dark-haired, black-eyed Scot from Ayr, the force of his native accent undimmed by five years' service in London. A misleadingly benevolent and comfortable figure with a hint of a beer belly, he was highly intelligent and a legendary womanizer.

'Coming.' John McLeish at thirty-one was also a Scot — the Metropolitan police force, like the armies at Waterloo, could not function without the Scots in their ranks — but there all resemblance ended. He had only a trace of accent, having been brought up in the South, and as he unfolded himself from behind a desk his head, as usual, narrowly missed the hanging light. The electrician had not reckoned with a detective inspector six feet four inches tall and springy on his feet as befitted a rugby forward who had been in the Scottish international squad, and had just missed a cap in an unusually strong year. As Bruce Davidson had observed to a colleague the first time he saw McLeish, it was in its way a pity not to keep him in the uniformed branch. Add a helmet on top of that lot and you had a sight to strike terror into any number of villains.

The phone rang at the desk which McLeish had just left.

'Will we run?' Davidson enquired, faking a dash to the door. McLeish cursed but reached automatically for the phone.

'CID.' He jerked his head back, setting the light swinging. 'A murder? That's a bit better than the rubbish you've been sending us.' He listened.

'Does sound like drugs, doesn't it? — using a hammer. Can you get the usual set up? We'll be with you.'

'I must eat,' Davidson said plaintively, following his chief down the stairs. McLeish was, as usual, jumping them five at once.

'So must I, don't worry.' Anyone working with Davidson knew that you kept him from his dinner at your peril. He really did need to eat every three hours or, as he mournfully observed, nothing worked.

They swept into Pindar Road still chewing on greasy kebabs in pitta, and stopped well away from the scene of the crime to finish their meal. They were both in unspoken agreement that decent reverence in the presence of the dead was absolutely required, and both had survived years in the Serious Crimes squad with this conviction undimmed. They finally arrived on even terms with the police pathologist and the photographer. Two of the uniformed branch, a sergeant and a constable, were already there, their car parked beside the body with the blue light flashing. The street was full of people, hanging out of windows and lining the doorsteps. McLeish knelt by the body in one swift economical movement, and looked without touching, lost in concentration, while the photographer worked. He sat back on his heels finally, and produced a piece of chalk to draw round the outline of the body.

'Got the weapon?' he asked, getting up.

'Hammer. Standard claw type. No prints.' The man from forensic was evidently one of the strong silent ones. He jerked his head. 'Over there, in the gutter.'

McLeish considered the hammer, blood congealed on all its surfaces.

'Anything in the pockets?'

'Haven't looked yet. You want to, you go ahead.'

McLeish signalled to Davidson who slid a hand into a plastic glove, then felt delicately inside the coat and jacket.

'No wallet,' he reported.

'No watch either,' observed the uniformed constable who was adjusting the screen round the body, and McLeish glanced at him consideringly. The CID recruits from the uniformed branch, and is always on the look-out for competent people.

'How do you know he wore one?'

'Deep mark on the left wrist.'

'Good, well done. What have you got there?' This to Davidson who was extracting a small plastic-covered card case which he handed gingerly to the forensic man. The group bent silently over it.

'"William Fireman, Purchasing Manager, Britex Fabrics, Towneley, Yorkshire",' Davidson read, squinting to see through the plastic.

'Staying in one of these places, probably,' McLeish observed. 'Get asking, Bruce. Take the constable here with you if he can be spared.'

The constable gave him a swift pleased smile, seeing it as a reward.

McLeish was amused that the boy did not apparently realize that anyone in uniform would have been sent — the presence of a uniform saved a lot of time in explanations on a house-to-house trawl.

He waited to see the screens set up and to check that everything at the scene of the crime had been collected, noted, bagged or photographed as appropriate, under the charge of the scene-of-crime officer. The sheet covering the body snagged as they shifted a screen, momentarily revealing the frightful misshapen head. We'd better find this one, McLeish thought grimly; that sort of savagery should not be walking the streets.

The routine swept smoothly on, eating up the hours of the night.

One of the little bed-and-breakfast places was quickly identified as the place where the late William Fireman would have spent the night. He came apparently to London every two or three months and always stayed there, but the West Indian proprietor knew nothing about him personally. The sub-routine which has to do with notifying the next of kin and getting the body identified had been put into action. The personnel officer of Britex Fabrics had been roused from the family television, and, greatly to his credit, on being told the nature of the injuries had immediately volunteered to come himself to identify the body, rather than ask the family. He had scrambled on to a late train and been taken straight from King's Cross to the mortuary, where he had been offered the least injured side of the head to identify, and white-faced but stolid, had confirmed that it was indeed the late William Fireman. Women police constables in Towneley had been dispatched to break the news to his sister and mother, waiting till 7 a.m. to do so, in a well-established compromise between telling next of kin as soon as possible and not adding to the shock by waking them in the middle of the night to break the worst news of all.

'What kind of firm is it?' McLeish had drawn the task of organizing the Yorkshire police to notify next of kin, and thought he might as well get some background information from them.

'Textiles. Sheets, duvet covers, thermal clothing, some industrial clothing. Biggest employer by a long way up here, although the gossip is that they aren't doing very well. My brother works there. What happened to your body? No, don't you try and wish it on us, lad, we've got the Moors Rapist to cope with, and the nuthouse specialists here reckon him for another go come full moon on Friday. If this chap's head was bashed in and his wallet and watch are gone, it's a London special, isn't it? One of your drug addicts?'

McLeish had had to agree that this was much the likeliest solution, and had gone on to talk to the pathologist.

'One blow, delivered from above by someone taller and right-handed. The other two, which killed him, delivered when he was on the deck. Mind you, the first blow would have knocked him out, and if he'd survived it might not have left much of him worth having, but it didn't kill him. So the murderer finished him off, for some reason. Be worth finding a chap like that and putting him away.'

McLeish had confirmed as equably as possible that same was in fact his intention, shared by the entire Edgware Road CID, and had set in motion the routine check of all locals with a record of violence, whether accompanied by robbery or not. His chat with the pathologist, however, had left him uneasy. Why had the murderer struck two extra blows when the victim could not have been offering any resistance at that stage? The classic answer would be that the victim knew the attacker. On the other hand, he thought wearily, if the murderer was an addict, logic simply did not apply. Under the influence of hard drugs, who knew what considerations applied. He resolutely went on working his way down the checklist of procedures, until Davidson put his head in.

'Coffee? Or breakfast?'

'Breakfast, knowing you. Let's go to that caff in Wellcome Street.'

It was still cold and dark although it was past 7 o'clock and they were glad to huddle in the plastic-coated warmth of the café in Wellcome Street, along with what appeared to be the labour force of a medium-sized building site. As it got close to 8 o'clock the café emptied, and reluctantly McLeish and Davidson got up to leave too. They were both pale and irritable after the long night, but both felt better for breakfast.

'Extraordinary, this street,' McLeish observed, as they walked towards the car. 'Middle of a slum, really, but every other house has got a skip outside, or scaffolding all over it, or both. It's coming up, as the agents say. I really ought to try and get a flat up here; Ealing's too far out. Cost a bomb though, I expect.' He and Davidson paused to look at the brightly coloured front doors and window-boxes that had appeared on three or four of the little Victorian houses.

'See the lassie over there?'

McLeish glanced over following Davidson's gaze, and was just in time to see long elegant legs stamping up the steps of a little house with a new dark-green front door.

'She's been up and down those steps three times,' Davidson observed, amused. 'Getting gey irritated, too.'

The girl burst out of the house again, stopped on the doorstep and stood, visibly reciting a list of things she needed, ticking them off on her fingers, concentrating hard. She banged the door shut, and started down the steps, then stopped half-way down, looking horror-stricken and scrabbling in her handbag.

'Forgotten the keys. And left the radio on,' Davidson said, grinning.

'Not her day.' The girl across the street raised her head and looked at them both despairingly.

'Lost your keys?' called Davidson.

'I can hardly believe it, but I've locked them inside.'

McLeish followed Davidson across the road, reflecting with amusement that his sergeant would probably find good-looking women in the Sahara. He arrived to find that Davidson, drawing on his vast experience, was gently urging her to turn her handbag out and see if the keys were not, after all, with her.

'Oh. They are here. You are clever — how kind to come and help.'

Davidson moved to one side to let McLeish come up beside him, and the girl smiled at him too, radiant with relief. McLeish stopped in his tracks, and just stared at her.

'All part of the service. We are police by the way — plain clothes branch. I'm Sergeant Davidson and this is Detective Inspector McLeish.' Davidson had no objection to doing a bit of neighbourhood public relations work.

McLeish was still stuck looking at the girl. Not really pretty, he thought, except for the dazzling dark-blue eyes, that short helmet haircut a bit severe combined with the straight nose and well marked eyebrows. She was no longer smiling at him, he realized, but was considering him as seriously as he was considering her.

'I'm Francesca Wilson. Sweet of you both to stop,' she said, turning to Davidson. 'I can at least now go to work. I too am a civil servant.'

'You've left the radio on too, lass,' Davidson pointed out.

'Not the radio, it's a tape and it'll stop; but thank you.'

'"The Lost Chord",' Davidson observed, listening with interest. 'Don't hear that much now, but my dad used to sing it.'

'It's my brother singing.' She listened for a minute, then sang softly and unselfconsciously along with the tape: *'It may be that Death's bright angel, Will speak in that chord again. It may be that only in Heaven, I shall hear that grand amen . . .'* She smiled at Davidson. 'That's it, finished. Oh God! Is that the time? Thank you again.'

'Which department do you work for?' John McLeish finally found his voice.

'Trade and Industry. In Victoria Street.' She smiled at him, and he pulled himself together with a mighty effort and wished her a good day. She slid into a Mini, carelessly parked outside the house, and shot off, with a little wave to both of them.

'Left it unlocked,' Davidson observed, disapprovingly, studiously not looking at his chief.

'Do you think she lives there, or was she visiting?' McLeish was watching the car disappear round the corner.

'Lives there, surely?' Davidson, fascinated, observed him out of the corner of an eye.

'I expect she's married, mind you. I've reached the age where all the pretty ones are.' They had walked across the road and got into the car, with Davidson not daring to speak. He sat in the passenger seat and slid his eyes sideways to observe his chief who was gazing moodily through the windscreen. He was an impressive sight, all six foot four of him folded behind the wheel, the huge shoulders making the car look dangerously small. And a good-looking bloke with it — dark, almost black hair, brown eyes, and surely not short of women in his life.

'I've seen you with a few pretty ones. Are they all married then?'

Curiosity finally overwhelmed Davidson.

McLeish did not reply but continued to look out through the windscreen, lips pressed tightly together. Without looking at his sergeant he reached a huge hand for the car radio.

'Karen. Would you get a name and address on KYU 123X please.' He put the microphone down, and sternly avoiding looking at Davidson, put the car into gear and drove off. Davidson sat silently beside him, deeply amused and somewhat awestruck. All policemen know the rule that the address of the registered keeper of a particular car may only be sought from the computer if some criminal act is suspected.

So ingrained is this knowledge that a policeman asking for a trace always adds the words 'suspected violation' as automatically as 'amen' at the end of the Lord's Prayer. McLeish was widely recognized as a punctiliously straight copper, having survived five years in the Flying Squad without cutting corners. It was like the man, thought the more flexible Davidson, not to add the words 'suspected violation' nor to ask for Davidson's discretion. That formidable Puritan conscience would probably make McLeish feel, if he got caught out, that justice had been done. What had that girl done to him?

The microphone crackled. 'Detective Inspector? The registered keeper is a Miss Francesca Wilson, 19 Wellcome Street, W.10.'

'Thank you.'

McLeish drove steadily for the police station with Davidson silent beside him. They stopped at a light and McLeish glanced sideways.

'Say something Bruce, even if it's only goodbye.'

'We could go and have breakfast in that caff every morning. She's bound to lose her keys again,' he offered, and McLeish's face relaxed into a sheepish smile.

'You did but see her passing by?' Davidson, who had a good Scots education, asked seriously.

'That's right. I may be off my head, but at least she isn't married. Back to the grindstone.'

CHAPTER 2

Four hours later and three miles away, the November sun shone on a scene of simple but expensive comfort. Three men in their fifties were gathered in comfortable chairs at one end of a huge room, otherwise furnished only with a huge desk, a table to seat twelve, and six large paintings of ships all in full sail bursting indefatigably across uniformly stormy seas. The Civil Service does not provide its employees with grand offices but the Permanent Secretary to the Department of Trade and Industry had maintained, successfully, that he needed an impressive office in which to receive the captains of industry who constituted the Department's clientele. His contention that these gentlemen, seeing the average accommodation accorded to a Perm. Sec., would simply not take him seriously had finally and reluctantly been accepted by the Treasury.

'Most satisfactory. All the Assistant Secretary postings fixed,' observed Sir James Campbell, KCB, Permanent Secretary to the Department of Trade and Industry, leaning back. His audience agreed fervently. The Assistant Secretary grade is where the main weight of responsibility falls in the service and mistakes in this area are expensive and difficult to sort out, since no established civil servant can be sacked for less than gross misconduct or incompetence of truly appalling proportions.

'After this hard morning, I hesitate even to mention a Principal posting.' William Westland, CB, DSO, Principal Establishment Officer for the Department, sounding not at all hesitant, leaned his full fifteen stone on the back of his chair and smiled on his two colleagues.

'What have you done, Bill?' Campbell, a small, dapper, dominant fifty-year-old who had known Westland since they were at university together, raised both eyebrows. However dedicated to staff relationships a Permanent Secretary may be, given that the Department boasted on that day, in descending order of grandeur, six Deputy Secretaries, forty Under Secretaries, 110 Assistant Secretaries and 260 Principals, he does not normally expect to concern himself with a Principal posting, unless it is to a Minister's private office.

'The Principal in question is Francesca Wilson.'

'Ah. Oh dear. Remind me, Bill.'

'Our Ambassador to the United States asked that she be withdrawn from the Embassy where we had sent her for her final year as an HEO(A). We posted her there because, apart from the fact that she is ferociously bright and very quick, she had suffered an extremely painful divorce and we — I — thought a change of scene would be valuable.'

'Surely she is too young to be divorced?' Geoffrey Catto, the third man in the room, a senior and desiccated official, enquired in horror.

'We have all led a sheltered life by comparison with this generation, Geoffrey. Francesca was married at twenty-two — I went to the wedding, and I must say it didn't look like being a success even then — and they were divorced by the time she was twenty-six. She's just twenty-eight now. Anyway, the Ambassador wanted to send her home because she was having a security-threatening and embarrassing affair with the Junior Senator for West Virginia.'

'Michael O'Brien?' There was a general pause for reflection on the reputation of the Senator. 'Was she indeed? So what did we do? Or rather, Bill, what did you do? Is she not a godchild of yours?'

'Indeed yes. I am a man of peace, but I was going to Washington anyway, and with very real heroism I tackled Francesca, taking the line, you know, that there were other chaps in the world with whom she could have a walk-out without getting right up the nose of Her Britannic Majesty's Ambassador to the United States of America, and couldn't she find someone else? Maybe even someone not currently married?'

'I long to know what she said.'

'I think in deference to my grey hairs she did not explain why she was having an affair with this one rather than another, but she was wholly unrepentant. She took the line that it was HM Ambassador who was being unreasonable, and suggested that the real problem was that, like all his family, he simply couldn't bear people being invited to smarter parties than he was. In which, of course, she has a point, but, as I told her, my sympathies are entirely with the Ambassador. Not exactly conducive to the dignified conduct of affairs of State to have a junior member of your staff in the *Washington Post* every other day, and the security chaps reporting to you in those tiresome Tennessee accents. And then her brother didn't help.'

Sir James concentrated, and recalled with some triumph that there were four Wilson brothers. Westland nodded.

'This is Peregrine, aged about twenty-four, number three in the clan. You may well not have noticed, but he has had some success as a pop star under the name of Perry Wilson. In the middle of trying to convey official displeasure to Francesca I had to break off to solicit Peregrine's autograph for my daughters. It would not have been worth my returning home without it. He was doing a series of concerts there, and according to the Head of Chancery — a sensible man and not given to exaggeration — used to paralyse operations at the Embassy by appearing with his associates in one form of fancy-dress or other. Surrounded, moreover, by nearly as many bodyguards as Francesca's admirer.'

Sir James sighed. Like most of the Department of Trade and Industry, he shared the view that the Foreign Office was so called because the bulk of its personnel was working for the other side. He could nonetheless see that the Department had been poorly placed to resist a demand that this particular stormy petrel should be recalled to base.

'So we had to bring her home.' Bill Westland agreed with his thought.

'But I made them keep her for a full year, and we brought her home on promotion just to show the FCO they can't push our people about. In fact, the Commercial Attaché says she did an excellent job, handicapped or assisted by her various adherents. Her father, of course, was an industrial star even by the time he died at thirty-seven.'

'Where have you put her? Or are you seeking guidance?'

'No, no, I thought we'd give her the liaison job with the Industrial Development Unit, looking after all those accountants and businessmen seconded in to help us form industrial judgements. She'll stop them irritating Ministers, will introduce the odd note of political realism, tell them the facts of life and so on.'

'Being used to doing the same for four younger brothers,' Sir James observed drily. 'I suppose you've got that right, Bill? To put her in with all those City people, mostly her contemporaries and all men, seems to me to be asking for trouble. These aren't respectable career civil servants, you know, used to working with women, broken in to it as we all are. They've probably never seen a girl who isn't a typist.'

'Oh, I think things are changing, James, even in the City.' Both men spoke of the City of London, not more than a mile away geographically, as if discussing the waters of the moon.

'You've actually decided, have you?' Geoffrey Catto enquired. 'Might it not be worth consulting with Mr Blackshaw, our tame industrialist? He is to be head of the IDU after all. He has now met the Secretary of State and even so seems to be willing to come to us for two years.'

Bill Westland observed that this confirmed a previous view that Henry Blackshaw's Chairman had offered him the choice between two years' secondment to the Department of Trade and Industry in a prestigious job, or a walk to the nearest

Labour Exchange. Assuming, he added, that labour exchanges still existed, following recent cuts in public expenditure.

'So, you thought you would give him Francesca Wilson as a surprise?'

Sir James was far too experienced not to stick to his original question.

'These industrialists, you know, they're not like us. They don't just get issued with whatever staff the company has in stock. Out in the world they choose their own staff and fire people — revolutionary stuff like that.'

'No. I did raise this particular post with him, James. He took the line that the whole place seemed to be full of earnest young men and that a pretty girl would cheer the place up.'

Geoffrey Catto put his glass down sharply, and pointed out that the good Mr Blackshaw probably envisaged something blonde and cuddly; while recruitment to the fast stream of HM Government service as presently constituted was not bringing blonde cuddly ones into the Department in any great numbers, some nearer equivalent than Francesca Wilson could surely have been found?

'When I last saw her she was looking like a hawk in a bad temper.'

Sir James was laughing. 'Impressive, but not exactly cuddly. Oh well, Bill, provided he has had warning . . . Given the public reputation of the civil service, he probably expects a hard-bitten intellectual in a brown cardigan at best. No, leave it, Bill, we'll all watch with interest. She'll probably seduce him. I must go to lunch.'

'I have something else to raise, Secretary.' The formality caused Sir James to stop looking for papers and to give Geoffrey Catto his full attention.

'Britex Fabrics. Frank Jamieson had a word with me last night at the Cordwainers' dinner. The Managing Director himself warned him that they are not far off real trouble. Jamieson is in a twitch because it is 1400 jobs which they cannot afford to lose.'

Bill Westland observed that surely Britex Fabrics was Darlington and as such not Jamieson's constituency.

'No, but a lot of his constituents work there. Most, indeed, of those who do work are employed there. The constituency MP is Williamson — F. not C.E. — who has a huge majority. Jamieson's is marginal, he won by 1500 votes last time, which is not comfortable. Some of those votes come from Britex employees.'

'We had better warn Ministers.' The Civil Service attempts at all times to be professionally omniscient, and Ministers in the Department of Trade and Industry would, very reasonably, be displeased to hear of a major industrial failure from the Press rather than from their own civil servants.

'Oh, quite. I am only mentioning it now because I believe you will see Mr Blackshaw at this lunch, as well as other textile people. It would be very useful to get him here a week or so early, to get his mind round this. Someone will be doing a note for Ministers for tonight and we will put it through you in case your meeting at lunch adds anything.'

Sir James nodded at this piece of automatic professional competence and joined the hovering private secretary who was waiting to take him down to his car. The young man gave him a short brief as they reached the car and he skimmed it. It was depressingly familiar material. The textile industry, in all its manifestations from thread manufacturer to little factories making up clothes, was being squeezed by cheap imports from the Far East and from the Comecon countries desperate for hard currency. In an attempt to contain costs, labour was being shed at all levels but turnover was continuing to drop faster than costs could be cut. Britex's troubles would be repeated in many other firms over the next year; the pattern was already there to see. However clearly this had been explained to Ministers as a consequence both of policy and the economic facts of life, they were never keen to accept it when the consequences were job-losses in their heartland. Not an easy lunch today.

CHAPTER 3

It was also a bright day in Yorkshire and the sun shone on the roofs of the four giant buildings that housed Britex Fabrics. Peter Hampton slid his big Rover into the parking space labelled 'Managing Director', and the small group gossiping outside the big weaving shop dissolved swiftly.

'Morning Mr Hampton.' The security man at the office desk beamed at him as he pushed through the swing door.

'Excuse me.' A solid dark man, practically square, with a boxer's broken nose and hair on the back of his square hands, had followed Hampton through the door. 'Mr Peter Hampton, the Managing Director? I have a writ to serve on you. Thank you.' He pushed a brown envelope into Hampton's hand, nodded contentedly and disappeared through the swing door, leaving the two Britex people staring after him.

'I'm ever so sorry, Mr Hampton, I didn't see him. Where'd he spring from?' The security man looked round wildly, visibly rattled. 'I don't usually let people like that through the door.'

'I'm sure you don't.' Hampton spoke heavily. 'That's why he followed me in. Not your fault, lad.'

The security man watched him run lightly upstairs and reflected that he must tell the manager of the firm he worked for that all the rumours about Britex were right enough.

Management did not seem to be panicking, but someone must be having real difficulty getting paid if he was using that particular bunch of heavies to serve a writ.

Peter Hampton, carrying two briefcases under one arm, waved the writ in greeting to a pretty secretary he passed in the corridor, and she looked wistfully after him. Like most of the girls in the building she found him extremely attractive, and in particular she wished she were working for him rather than for the distinctly middle-aged and portly Sales Director. She watched him covertly as he stopped to talk to one of the accountants, whom he topped by a head, and smiled involuntarily to herself as he laughed at something the man said, the bright blond hair and blue eyes very vivid against the clear pale skin.

He clapped the man on the shoulder and swung round to go into his own office, with the easy fluent, all-in-one movement of the good athlete.

Hampton dumped both briefcases on his desk and tore open the envelope. The writ was from their second largest supplier, Alutex, who were by no means their largest creditor or the one whose bill had been outstanding longest. It took the form of a petition to the court to wind up Britex Fabrics PLC. Peter Hampton swore; this was not, of course, a serious attempt to bring down his company, indeed no one would be more horrified than the Directors of Alutex if the Directors of Britex were to respond by putting the company into receivership, but it was an effective way of getting a bill paid. He dropped the envelope on the Chief Accountant's desk in the office next to his own, anchoring it with a substantial glass ashtray; irritated beyond measure by this particular demand, he added a scribbled note suggesting the supplier be told to put the writ where the monkey put the nuts.

He went back to his own office and stood gazing out of the window, thinking about his empire. The buildings were freshly painted and shone in the clear thin air; a detached eye would have judged it to be a German or Scandinavian factory. The impression of bustling efficiency faded on closer inspection: inside, the main spinning and weaving areas the labour was thin on the ground. Only about one-third of the looms were working, and those minding them were not fully occupied. Small gossiping groups could be found at the end of the long rows of looms, lifting one earmuff, in strict defiance of all regulations, and leaning close to each other to talk. Close up, people looked anxious and sullen, oppressed by the silent looms and the lack of light. Only half the factory was lit, a logical but depressing piece of economy.

In the equally modern and sparkling office building there was less obvious anxiety. The clerical workers did not have before their eyes the silent looms. Nor had their ranks been reduced to the same degree as the manual workers in the factory. When a manufacturing concern falters it is the people engaged in making the goods who get sent home first, laid off but not made redundant in the hope that their hands will be needed again quickly. The office staff, particularly salespeople, are slower to feel the draught. It is only when the managers have perceived that they cannot sell their goods that real inroads are made into staff numbers. It is also true that staff as opposed to manual workers cost more to make redundant; and it is a fact of industrial life that managers are slow to waste money, as they see it, on redundancies even where these would be useful and productive.

Hampton sighed, common sense superseding rage, and rescued the writ and his note from the Chief Accountant's desk. Once writs were issued they could not be ignored, and he would have to negotiate. He picked up his phone, but was distracted by his own secretary, a pretty, bossy, cheerful girl, well married to the local bookmaker and unimpressed by Hampton's considerable attractions.

'Excuse me, Peter. Is what the girls are saying about Bill Fireman right? Has he been in an accident?'

'Oh Jesus. Is the news round already? It's worse than that, Jenny — I'm afraid he's dead. I understand he was mugged, in London, near where he was staying, and died in hospital apparently. Barry went down and identified him

— I didn't even know until midnight because I was on my way back here in the car, and the phone's on the blink again — get Fred to take it away and fix it, will you, while I remember? Oh hell, I'd better get an announcement out, then; I was going to tell the Board first at the noon meeting. What time is it? Well, that lot won't be out of bed by now, will they?'

'Shall I get Mike and Jim?' Jenny did not make the mistake of taking Hampton's strictures as applying to the executive members of the Board.

'Yes please, Jenny, now. Oh, and Les as well — the Chief Accountant has to know. Barry isn't in yet, I assume — he must have come back on the morning train.'

He got restlessly to his feet as Jenny left the room to round up the rest of the top management, who arrived looking anxious and enquiring. Peter Hampton rarely summoned people to his office, preferring to discharge some of his restless physical energy by walking round to their offices. He nodded to them all.

'Sorry, just before we start . . . Jenny, get William Blackett on the phone, ask him to get here about twenty minutes before the meeting — I want a word first, tell him. Then find out where Simon Ketterick is and say I want to talk to him on the phone in about half an hour. Thanks.' He waited till the door had closed behind her.

'I have bad news, which some of you may have heard. Bill Fireman died last night in London — he was mugged, I understand, and died of his injuries. Barry went down to identify him, and he'll tell us more when he gets here. I was only told very late last night, and I decided not to get you all up to hear that kind of news.' He went on incisively to delegate responsibility for getting out a notice to the work force, and to appoint Fireman's deputy in his place. The group round the table were shocked, but not, he noticed, particularly grieved.

Fireman had been ten years older than any of them, and his meticulous, pernickety conscientiousness had annoyed more than one harried man round the table over the last year.

'What a thing to happen just after he got the gold watch, though,' Michael Currie, the Sales Director observed, as the meeting broke up.

'When was it — Friday, the presentation? The watch must still have been in its box.'

'No, he put it on straight away. Pleased as Punch he was. Didn't you notice?'

'Did they find it?' Mike Currie had spoken idly, but blushed scarlet as he heard what he was saying.

'Dunno. Can't ask for it back, can we?' Hampton was grimly amused.

He waved the group out of his office, and the phone buzzed as the last of them went through the door.

'I have Mr Ketterick for you.'

'OK.' He waited, unmoving, while the box on his desk said it was just putting him through and he got Simon Ketterick on the line.

'What are you bastards at Alutex doing putting in a writ on the September bill? Do you want to lose the order?'

'Peter, for Christ's sake, I'm having difficulty telling the Directors the order's worth having. Not much point in an order if the customer doesn't pay. And you know as well as I do, I don't see a penny till you pay.' Hampton, well familiar with the principle that a salesman does not draw his commission until the customer has actually paid, observed impatiently that he had been in textiles for the last ten years.

'In any case, Peter, there's something up here . . . strangers around, you know what I mean, and meetings where only the blue-eyed boys are invited. My bet is the shareholders are trying to sell while there *is* something to sell, know what I mean?'

'So they don't want too many old debts. Won't help them much if we go bust, though, will it? What are we, 20 per cent of your turnover?'

'Close,' Ketterick's flat Yorkshire voice reluctantly confirmed, and Hampton mentally noted that Britex must then be nearer 25 per cent than 20. 'Anything you can do, Peter, and I'll try and get the writ withdrawn. Half of it? £100,000, then?'

'Maybe.' Hampton considered the desk in front of him. 'You heard Bill Fireman died last night, as a result of being mugged in London?'

'Did he now? Sorry to hear, of course.'

'That invoice. Maybe we are in dispute with you about it, that's why it's not paid?'

'It's three months old, Peter, and you've not said a dicky bird. It won't wash with my guv'nors, know what I mean?'

'Yeah. I'll do what I can.' Hampton pressed the cut-off button, and sat, mouth compressed. He might find £100,000 to keep this particular creditor at bay, given a bit of indulgence from the bank, but it was time and beyond time for the meeting of the full Board arranged for later in the day. It would inevitably cause gossip to have a meeting so soon after the last one, attended by all eight directors; and there was no hope that the outside non-executive directors would have the sense to arrive quietly. They would, as usual, arrive in the Rollers, with the best and most conspicuous table in the local hotel booked afterwards.

Little pleasure as there was in the situation, there would be some to be derived from watching those plump and privileged burghers face a future without fat directors' fees for doing not very much and without their dividends. And, he thought with particularly malicious satisfaction, all their wives, mothers, cousins, aunts, ex-wives moaning at them because they too would have to do without the dividends that had kept them in decent houses and the children at good schools without Daddy doing too much by way of hard work. On the heels of this thought, William Blackett, son of the present Chairman, presently Sales Director of Alutex and, for historical reasons, non-executive director of Britex, was announced.

'Wheel him in, Jenny.' Hampton rose to greet his visitor, in order to give himself the momentary advantage conveyed by his six feet three inches. William Blackett was a stocky five foot ten and at forty-three, only five years older than Peter Hampton, he looked a good ten years more. Black haired, thinning from the crown, skin reddened with livid patches over the broken veins on the cheekbones, the whole face was cast in the sullen, downward lines of the depressive who also drinks too much. Hampton, shaking hands, decided the man was looking fatter and more out of condition even in the three weeks since the last Board meeting.

'I've been talking to Simon Ketterick,' he said as Blackett disconsolately accepted the offered coffee, having looked all round the office in vain for something stronger. 'As you should bloody well know, we can't pay that bill just yet. You're his Sales Director, you tell him. It'll look pretty odd if Alutex brings this company down, when you are a director of both companies. And it won't do any of us any good.'

'Why the hell can't we pay?' The livid colour in the cheeks flamed, and Hampton observed with interest but not surprise that Blackett, although a director, had really not understood the depth of Britex's difficulties.

'Because the bank would bounce the cheque if I was fool enough to write one.'

Blackett gaped at him. 'You mean we can't find £300,000? But Hampton — bloody hell, I'm not supposed to tell you this and you'll have to treat it as confidential — but our shareholders at Alutex want to sell. To Smith Brothers, who won't want any of the senior management. So I won't have a salary from there pretty soon.' He stared at the desk, unseeingly. 'I need a drink,' he said abruptly, without apology. 'Where are they?'

'In the boardroom. Just wait a minute, will you? That's not the only news — Fireman was mugged last night and died of his injuries.'

'I'd heard.' William Blackett rubbed both hands down his face. 'Sad loss, of course,' he added, perfunctorily.

'Where did you hear from?' Hampton asked, casually.

'The old man. Barry whatshisname told him — rang him this morning.'

Hampton nodded, resignedly. Feudal habits ran deep in this part of the world, and it did not amaze him to hear that his Director of Personnel had taken it upon himself to inform the Chairman, rather than leaving that task to the MD. He considered, exasperatedly, the fidgeting man the other side of the desk.

'You worked here long enough, William; you should have known what a shambles the place was when you got me here as MD.'

'When my father got you here, you mean. When I was here, we could sign the fucking cheques without worrying whether they would bounce.'

'So you borrowed in the good years, and we're paying the price now.' Hampton, who had been determined not to be riled, felt himself going red.

'You and my father got me out of here, and you can get us out of this fuck-up. I've got to have a drink, bugger it.'

'I'll get Jenny to take you to the boardroom, I've got to go through the numbers.' He looked with exasperation at the sodden figure opposite him. 'I've done better than you had any right to hope, Blackett. You drank yourself out of a job here, and I came at a drop in salary because I was given share options. At 25p — and the shares haven't been above 13p since the day I could exercise the options. I know when *you* sold, and I wish we'd all been as lucky.' He stopped abruptly, angry with himself for whining, and pressed his bell. 'Jenny, will you take Mr Blackett to the boardroom, and see he has everything he wants? Call me when Sir James arrives.'

Left alone, Peter Hampton finished the summary of the Chief Accountant's figures. He had got rid of this man's predecessor a year ago. The young accountant who had replaced him was not yet on the Board, though he had been promised a seat within the year. Hampton reflected sourly that Les Graham had not recently sought to remind anyone of this commitment; no one, of course, wanted to be a director of a company when it went into receivership, the personal risks as well as the problems of explaining in the future being far too difficult.

He double-checked the figures and considered them again, tight-lipped.

His secretary put her head in to tell him that the Chairman had arrived, plus the dim local solicitor and a Blackett cousin who sat on the Board to look after other local investment interests. She volunteered to fetch Michael Currie, the Sales Director, and James Finlay, the Production Director, who made up the rest of the Board. Hampton waited a deliberate few minutes before going into the boardroom. Like the rest of the building, it was pleasant, furnished well but without extravagance: a large board table made by a local firm, a few reasonably pleasant portraits of past chairmen, and a magnificent view of the surrounding Yorkshire hills. He nodded to the Company Secretary, a bright local boy in his late twenties who was there to take the note.

'Morning, Sir James, morning again, William.' He shook hands with Sir James, who at sixty-eight was in better shape than his son, less red, thinner and, in Hampton's view, a great deal more intelligent.

'Shall we start, Chairman, if you are ready?' The courteous formality pulled William Blackett up, and drew prompt attention from all the executive directors.

'Always means trouble, when you start saying "Chairman" in just that way,' Sir James volunteered, helpfully.

'It is trouble, I'm afraid. First, I should tell those members of the Board who have not already heard that we have suffered a sad loss. Bill Fireman, our Purchasing Manager, died last night, as a result of a criminal attack.' He paused to allow explanations and condolences, and for Sir James to move that a message of sympathy be sent to Fireman's daughter, sons, mother and sister. 'And flowers, of course, Hampton — Jane and I will send some personally, but I imagine the Board will want to send some from all of us. Let me know about the funeral arrangements.'

These niceties exhausted, Hampton, at a nod from Sir James, went on to the main business of the meeting, addressing the Board as a whole. 'I spoke last night to Sir James and he felt we should meet this morning. Morningtex have withdrawn — Mike Reece spoke to me yesterday afternoon.'

'Why for God's sake? What have you been saying to them?' William Blackett heaved himself up in his chair, flushing even redder with indignation and surprise, leaving Hampton silently noting that Sir James had not forewarned his son before this meeting. Well, he could deal with the situation now, blast him. Hampton turned deliberately towards Sir James.

'Well, Willie, they have.' Sir James was unflustered. 'I spoke to their Chairman myself just before this meeting, to make quite certain that this was not simply a negotiating position. They have decided that they don't really want the thermal-wear business at any price, or at least not at any price that would be useful to us. At a price of less than about £6m we can't make the sums add up, can we, Hampton?'

'No. The bank has a charge on all our assets for £10m. The assets involved in the thermal-wear business are in the books at £7m. The bank might have agreed to release the assets if they got £6m. At £4m odd, Morningtex's last suggestion, there is no chance.'

'The bank won't pull the rug just because that sale hasn't gone through. If they do, they won't do much business in Yorkshire from now on.' William Blackett spoke confidently, and Peter Hampton reflected that William had all sorts of enlightening experiences coming his way if that was what he thought.

'I agree that the bank would hold the position, provided it did not get any worse,' Sir James said judiciously. 'Unfortunately, as I understand it, the position does get worse.' He raised his eyebrows at Hampton, who nodded.

'Yes. I have a cash flow here — it's handwritten, for obvious reasons.'

He handed round sheets of paper and waited patiently while his Board worked their way through it, confirming as he waited a previous view that William Blackett had no idea how to read the document, and indeed appeared to be trying to add the final income line to the final expenses line.

'How far are we behind on VAT and PAYE?' Sir James was scowling at the large sums postulated to go out over the next four weeks.

'VAT is already four months overdue and the PAYE three months. Both lots — HM Customs and the Inland Revenue — are threatening actions.'

'Bloody ridiculous!' William Blackett fulminated. 'Little Hitlers, trying to drive us out of business. We've been supporting the Government for over a hundred years by paying taxes. Let them support us for a bit.'

Peter Hampton glanced at him. 'It's not our money, William. We collect the cash from our own employees by withholding a percentage of their pay, or from our customers if it is VAT, as agents for the Government. They won't want to push the company over the cliff in a hurry, but in the end they'll put in a writ.'

'Any good news from Sales?' Sir James was methodically considering the options.

The Sales Director frenziedly assured the Board that all his sales force was working night and day. These assurances went on for some minutes, giving the main protagonists a breather, as he inveighed against the unseasonably warm weather which meant that the population of England and Scotland had massively refrained from ordering thermal knickers. 'If we could just have a cold snap, we could do a million in sales, easily,' he mourned.

'Better do a snow dance, Currie.' Sir James knew a hopeless cause when he saw one. 'Would a quick increase in sales do much for us, Hampton?'

'No.' Hampton spoke flatly. 'We should have closed the household-textile operation in the spring and gone to the bank for the cash to pay the redundancies. That's where we are bleeding to death.'

There was a reflective and resentful silence round the table. Peter Hampton had indeed fought for this plan in April, but the non-executive Board members had not been prepared to accept it, coinciding as it did with a period of exceptional and misleading buoyancy in the household-textile market. Hampton spread his hands.

'That's twenty-twenty hindsight. I could have pushed harder, I suppose.' He could have, indeed, he reflected, except that he would have been in absolutely no position to resign if the board had refused his advice.

Sir James cleared his throat. 'As it happens, I may have found another way round this problem. I may have found a purchaser for the household-textiles side.'

'Who?' demanded five people at once.

'Connecticut Cottons. Americans. Had a word with their Chairman yesterday.'

Peter Hampton shook his head. 'Chairman, I don't believe they can be serious. We did talk briefly in May. They have far too much capacity in the US and in Birmingham already.'

'Yes.' Sir James looked smug. 'You've forgotten the quotas. They can't cover the UK market by expanding in the US since the July agreement on imports, and the factory at Birmingham is uneconomic if they don't get more through it. So, it's either get more orders or close Birmingham.'

Peter Hampton nodded slowly. It made sense for the American firm to buy their order book. It might even pull their chestnuts out of the fire if the Americans were prepared to put up some cash and take over the liabilities. In any year the thermal-wear business was profitable, and given time, without the drag of the loss-making household textiles, Britex could trade out of its difficulties.

'Had another idea, too,' Sir James volunteered, justifiably pleased with himself. 'Met one of the high-up civil servants last week at the Cordwainers' dinner — not the top man in the Department of Industry, but close. He seemed to think we might get some cash out of the government to help with redundancies and reorganization to preserve the jobs we'll have left, because we are in an Assisted Area. Must be worth talking to them. I'll have a word with Williamson — the MP. Time he earned the vast salary we taxpayers find for him.'

Peter Hampton considered his Chairman with reluctant respect. In terms of social justice there could be no reason for paying this old man approximately three times an MP's salary, but there was no doubt that this week at least he was earning his money. The range and depth of contacts that had enabled him to talk informally to two chairmen of major companies and a senior civil servant inside a week, and find at least a glimmer of hope for a hard-pressed company, was well worth paying for. At the same time he felt the familiar bitterness about the way the country was run. Start with the right school or university, and above all the right family, and you were made. Start without and it was nothing but hard graft all the way, and no net to catch you when you fell — as, short of a miracle, he was about to.

William Blackett, who had been silenced, presumably by shock, came back into the meeting like a loud-hailer. 'What's Hampton here been bloody doing, for God's sake? We hire ourselves an expensive Master of Business Administration to run a perfectly good business and in three years you're telling me we are bust.' He stopped under his father's minatory stare.

'I'm not here to make excuses, but we aren't the only ones.' Peter Hampton, who had been expecting this attack, spoke evenly. 'Even Allied had to close five factories last year, and they took write-offs of £150m. They can carry that — just. Brown Ashmore and Williams have gone. It's a holocaust. Three years ago, in this very room, all the people who are here now agreed that we should invest and put in *more* spinning and weaving capacity, on the basis that this was a £100m turnover business. Three years later we can only sell £40m and that's not for want of trying. We can't cut our costs fast enough, and we are stuck with interest on the money we borrowed.' He paused for breath, and waved down William Blackett. 'I'm sorry for all of us and particularly for the people who work for us, but some of you have had an easy living out of this firm for years. William, happen your dad has found us a way out, but it'll be a very long haul, and we don't need bloody fools like you, who've put nothing into the business, whining.' He stopped, shaking, and thought calmly that he would probably be out on the streets a few weeks earlier than otherwise after that, but Sir James surprised him again.

'Shut up, both of you. We have to pull together or we may as well ask the bank to put a receiver in right now. Hampton, you and I go and see the bank and then the DTI. William, you do the MPs, Williamson and then Jamieson. He met that civil servant too. Tell them they can both come down with us, earn their pay.' He bent an eye on the rest of the meeting. 'The rest of you, get out there and keep the business running, that's what you're there for. And look cheerful!'

CHAPTER 4

Henry Blackshaw looked with pleasure at the Thames, glinting in the brilliant unseasonable November sun that was causing such dismay to the sales force at Britex, and stopped to lean on the parapet and to look up towards the City. A slightly built Yorkshireman of fifty-four, he was also a victim of the recession. Until July that year he had been Managing Director of two large subsidiaries of United Textiles, the second biggest textile group in the UK. One of his companies and four other major subsidiaries had been closed over the last eighteen months, leaving two managing directors markedly surplus to requirements. Rather than a job at head office, imprecisely specified and working to a younger man, he had chosen to accept his Chairman's alternative offer, that of a secondment to the Department of Trade and Industry.

'We'll pay you same as you've been getting plus a cost-of-living supplement for London, we'll keep up the car and pay reasonable expenses,' the Chairman had offered. 'The Department pays us a Deputy Secretary's salary for you. We make a loss of about £20,000 a year on the deal, but it's worth it to us in favours owed and in what you learn about how their minds work and the friends you make. In two years' time you come back to us, and with any luck this recession will have eased and we can give you a decent job. No guarantees, mind; it might have to be redundancy in two years' time. Go and see them,' he had suggested blandly, ignoring Henry's open reluctance.

'We're not putting you out to grass — we're trying to do a favour where we can when we've got time. I can't send Derek Barlow there, he has no finesse, and these civil servants are clever buggers. I've got to send someone who knows how to see them off.'

So Henry had gone to see them and had been reluctantly impressed.

He had been received by the Deputy Secretary, Bill Westland, and a very smooth Indian called Rajiv Sengupta, who had interviewed him once, then asked him to come back. The second time they had given him lunch, and Bill Westland had been both direct and friendly.

'We want you to come, Mr Blackshaw — Henry, then, if I may. We particularly need your expertise in textiles to enable us to sort out which firms we should be helping. If any.'

'What sort of help are we talking about? Soft loans?'

'Mostly grants, in fact. Where we are trying to save jobs at risk in a collapsing company, every case is special, and we will do what we have to, subject to Ministers' views of course. We do not have a fully developed policy in this area. We are still building up a body of practice, and that's why we need people with specific experience of financing industrial companies and projects.' Westland had passed menus to him and to Rajiv, and was rapidly and expertly scanning his own.

'As William is not saying, he and the present Permanent Secretary practically invented the Industrial Development Unit, always called here the IDU,' Rajiv observed.

'It is probably my only lasting and effective contribution to sensible administration,' Westland agreed with a trace of smugness. 'Dealing at high speed with a lot of applications for assistance requires a level of numeracy and a body of expertise which we could never have recruited in a hurry by conventional means. In theory, a civil servant is supposed to be able to attempt any task, but, as Rajiv and I have cause to know, that is in practice neither possible nor desirable. The IDU, therefore, consists largely of people seconded to us for periods of up to two years, plus a small civil service staff.'

'I am most of the small civil service staff,' Rajiv offered, and Henry thought about him while he chose a meal. He was used to elegant Indians in the textile trade but had not expected one in the Civil Service. This was a particularly elegant version, attired in a beautiful dark-blue suit which Henry, to whom it was second nature to assess any wool cloth in his vicinity, mentally priced at a month's salary for this particular civil servant, even before you took the Hermès tie and Gucci shoes into account. Or the made-to-measure plain pale blue shirt. Disconcertingly, Rajiv read his mind.

'Two of my uncles run businesses in Delhi. My father has several companies which make steel tubes in the Midlands and which I am thankful to say are not candidates for assistance from the Government.

'The remaining two uncles are senior civil servants in the Indian Civil Service, and since my father has no particular need of me in his business, I taught at Cambridge for five years and then joined the Civil Service here. The day may come when I have to take over from my father, but it is not here yet.'

'Lucky man,' Henry said, deciding not to be rattled. 'How big is the whole Unit?'

'One director — you, we hope. Four deputy directors, two of whom are partners in major accountancy firms, and two from industry. Twelve case officers, mostly young accountants or merchant bankers, aged about twenty-eight.'

'Do you have difficulty recruiting?'

'No, no, people have been very good about letting us have their chaps.' Westland made a swift selection from the wine list and caught Henry's eye. 'You are quite right, of course, it's good business for them. Civil servants are very conservative people: once we know someone, we go on using him or her for everything. And people seem to enjoy their time with us.'

Henry had been taken on, after lunch, to meet some of the other members of the IDU, uniformly tall, healthy, public-school twenty-eight-year-olds, virtually indistinguishable from each other at first sight. Examination of their curricula vitae had, however, confirmed the Department's boast; most of the top firms of accountants had indeed been very good about subscribing their best people. It would be a real pleasure to work with people of this calibre.

That lunch seemed a long time ago, though it was only four weeks, he thought, as he worked his way through helpful but muddled reception staff at the Department's glass palace in Victoria Street.

This obstacle passed, he was welcomed by Rajiv Sengupta, introduced to his secretary, to the messengers, to the clerical workers and to his high-priced staff, still looking uniformly healthy, young and keen.

'Finally you will wish to meet the Principal who will be working with me on the political side. Her name is Francesca Wilson,' Rajiv offered. Henry noted the use of Civil Service jussive, with interest.

'You will wish', his Chairman had told him, grinning, means 'you had better, soonest'. He decided to go along with it for the moment, but to alter the programme slightly.

'My motor does not start in the morning without coffee,' he announced, uncompromisingly. 'Might I have some, and perhaps Miss Wilson can join us after that?'

Rajiv stopped short in the dingy corridor. 'My dear Henry, I do beg your pardon. So like the private sector have we become here that we seem completely to have missed out on the morning coffee. There is a machine, the products of which are virtually indistinguishable, but there is certainly a button marked "Coffee". It does produce a liquid more like coffee than, for example, the button marked "Soup".'

Henry was just opening his mouth to indicate that there were some privations up with which even the beleaguered private sector did not put, when he became aware that someone in a nearby office was reading the riot act in no uncertain terms.

'Peregrine, for God's sake, we are not working class.' The beautifully pitched female voice made it sound like an important plank of party policy. 'If mystery voices ring us up in the middle of the night offering threats, we go the police. We do not sit shivering or working out who we can enlist on our side; we advance smartly to the nearest nick and tell them all about it. What's the matter with you?'

The party in the corridor, rooted to the spot, was wholly unsurprised to hear no response to this trenchant enquiry.

'What do you mean, embarrassing?' The clear, superbly produced voice rendered every word fully audible in the corridor. 'You mean that you, or Sheena, will find it difficult to explain to the police that you are receiving threatening telephone calls from her ex-husband — sorry — estranged husband, is it? Perry, get yourself together, ring up the police — it's Edgware Road for you, same as me — and they will send some decent bored detective who has heard it all before, and will doubtless have some method of dealing with the problem. More embarrassing to wake up dead, won't it be?'

Henry and Rajiv, by mutual consent, moved to tear themselves from this fascinating conversation, and retreated, fast, to Henry's office.

'As soon as Francesca is off the telephone I will bring her to meet you,' Rajiv offered.

'The young woman offering her views on the proper behaviour to adopt when being threatened by ex-husbands?'

'That is Francesca. Not short of views on the proper conduct for most situations. I'll get coffee,' Rajiv volunteered and disappeared again into the corridor. He returned carrying two paper cups of pale brown liquid, calling over his shoulder to someone in the corridor, 'Now, please. Do the submission later.' He put the cups down carefully, and Henry and he gazed sadly down at them.

Henry picked one up gingerly, found it too hot to hold, and put it hastily down again, slopping it. As he looked round for something to mop up with, he became aware of someone new in his room, and straightened up to find himself face to face with a distinctly compelling presence. Straight off a tapestry, he thought, as he looked into dark-blue eyes under straight eyebrows and a solid dark fringe.

Add a helmet with a nose-piece to shield the long straight nose, and you would have any one of the nameless Norman foot-soldiers who marched through the Bayeux tapestry. He noted with fascination the way the straight uncompromising lines in the face broke up as she smiled in greeting. A tall girl, slightly taller than he in her shoes. He straightened unconsciously to his full five foot eight as he shook her hand.

'I'm Francesca Wilson. How do you do,' she said, not making it an enquiry. 'You can't drink that muck. We all have illegal kettles here, and make our own.'

'Illegal kettles?'

'All kettles are illegal in this building. The wiring dates from before the Second World War, if not from before the First, and minutes come round every week pleading with us not to overload it — by switching on lights, for example. The coffee and tea provided by the management are so unspeakable — you drank some? — that we all have kettles and make our own. One day there will be a terrible bang and the whole building will combust.' She sounded notably unperturbed and wholly authoritative, producing a Kleenex and briskly mopping up his spilt coffee. 'Your secretary has a kettle, don't you, Mary?'

His secretary, a solid middle-aged lady of reassuring competence, confirmed from the outer office that she did indeed, and would produce coffee at once. Henry invited Francesca to stay and asked her cautiously what project she was engaged on.

'I don't work on projects in that sense. I translate the views of the IDU on a particular project to Ministers and vice versa. I could use some help, actually, on a particular case. One of Martin Bailey's, Rajiv; should I call him in?'

'If you feel the need of him.' Rajiv sounded slightly acid and the girl glanced at him doubtfully, but summoned, apparently from thin air, a tall earnest blond young man whom Henry recognized as one of the respectful group of young accountants who had been presented to him that morning. He noted sardonically, as the little meeting composed itself round his table, that this particular young man was obviously dazzled by Francesca, who was completely unconscious of her effect. He stumbled over the opening explanation and Francesca took over at once.

'This is not yet a project Mr Blackshaw — you are kind, Henry, if I may — in the sense that the Department has not yet been formally asked for assistance, and so we are not yet doing a case paper. It is just a cloud on the horizon. There is a textile company in Yorkshire called Britex Fabrics which we know to be in difficulty. It employs 1400 people, Yorkshire is an Assisted Area, so theoretically we have power to give financial assistance to preserve or safeguard those jobs.' She paused, courteously, to make sure he was following. Henry decided it must be his surroundings that somehow made Yorkshire sound like the headwaters of the Amazon, but nonetheless found himself irritated.

'I know them,' he said shortly.

'Oh, good. Well, that will help. We hoped you might, since to be honest, we are all a bit out of our depth.'

'How do you know they are in trouble? I am *sure* they are, but it's my trade. How did you find out?'

'We have a branch which is supposed to know everything about the textile industry, and it has heard rumours. We really know because the company appeared on the Bank of England's list which we get every month.'

'What is the Bank of England list?' Henry was beginning to feel and sound dogged.

'Ah. If a clearing bank gets worried about a big loan — say £5m plus — it goes and whinges to a couple of chaps in the Bank of England, who then put the company on their "At Risk" list. We get a copy; so does the Treasury.' Henry waited for further elucidation, but Francesca appeared to feel she had told him all anyone could wish to know.

Martin gave him a look of cautious sympathy but did not seem inclined to speak so Henry tried again.

'What do you do with this list?'

Rajiv stirred from his elegant languor. 'No, no, Henry, we don't do anything, except open a file — which is all Francesca and Martin have so far done. The real point is simply that we know where there is a problem. It enables us, and our Ministers, to say that yes, this company has been causing them serious anxiety. And until we are asked to intervene, we can't do anything. One can't really creep up on chairmen of companies and ask if they would like a little assistance, special rates for you only.'

'Is it worth even having the information?'

'Henry, you are impugning every principle on which HM Government service is based with that question. We can *Be Prepared*.'

'Not very prepared,' Francesca pointed out fair-mindedly. 'All Martin and I have been able to assemble so far is five years published accounts, an Extel card, and a brokers' circular now nearly a year out of date. I suppose it is better than not being prepared at all. Oh, and half a page on market conditions from the sponsoring branch. Roughly speaking, they say it's all terrible.'

'That's about right.' Henry spoke evenly, and the blue eyes widened.

'I beg your pardon, Henry, I forgot it was your trade and it must be miserable for you. Sorry Mary?' This last was addressed to Henry's secretary who was hovering.

'The Private Office would like to speak urgently with Mr Sengupta or Miss Wilson.'

Francesca nodded, and went out to the outer office, leaving Martin to show the other two the accounts they had collected. She reappeared, looking very slightly harassed. 'Here we go. The Chairman and Managing Director of Britex plus two MPs are booked in to see the Minister at 3.30. He was nobbled in the House this morning. Please can he have a brief and suitable official support. I'll do the brief; it won't take ten minutes to recite every single fact we know about Britex from the files. Who goes — Rajiv, Henry and which of us?'

Henry held up his hand. 'The Minister is not capable of seeing these people by himself?'

'Goodness, no!' Both civil servants spoke at once. Rajiv silenced Francesca with a look and went on. 'The polite way to put it is to say that it is simply inefficient for a Minister to see them alone, because he isn't going to work on the case, officials are. It also wouldn't be safe. All politicians are eager to please — it goes with the job — and get themselves into frightful messes promising things they can't deliver. I think Henry and Martin should both go. You can go, Fran; you don't need me unless the Secretary of State is intending to come?'

'No, he ducked.' She caught Henry's eye. 'By convention, Henry, the Secretary of State in this Department would expect to have an Assistant Secretary or above present at his meetings. A Minister or a Parliamentary Secretary is expected to be prepared to put up with a Principal. Since you rank to Deputy Secretary you are really a bit too good for this meeting, but you need to meet the Minister.'

Henry nodded, feeling dizzily that the morning had really gone on quite long enough. He noticed that Francesca seemed to share his thought, and was visibly fidgeting.

'Could I go and get the brief done?' she asked. 'If it will fit in, I am committed to go and have lunch with my brother.'

'Is Perry in a mess again?' Rajiv asked, carefully.

'Yes, the poor idiot. I need to get round there to make sure he and that bunch of comprehensive-school dropouts which constitutes his backing group don't come up with anything really silly. He is sending The Car, however.' She vanished economically from Henry's room, leaving him blinking slightly.

'Tell me about Francesca's family,' he said to Rajiv.

'Mother is a widow, and there are four boys younger than Francesca. Father died young.'

'Are they all like Francesca.'

'They are precisely not all like Francesca. All four of the boys are trouble one way or the other. The one she was sorting out on the telephone is Peregrine, who is a pop star.'

'Really?'

'Well, an embryo pop star. He is a superb tenor, and before that was a superb treble — the St Joseph's Cathedral choir treble to be precise.

'People have been getting very excited about him since he was about eight. Recently he recorded a couple of ballads and one of them stands third in the best-sellers' list now. Called "The Wrong Road", or similar; musically trivial as Perry would confirm; but I believe he is just about to get a Golden Disc. He is splendidly good looking, idle to a degree, and not nearly as clever as Francesca. The youngest two are twins and have both been asked to leave at least two schools despite their splendid singing voices. The next in age to Francesca, Charlie, is the most nearly normal and he keeps a bit clear of all this lot. Francesca has been up to her ears in trouble with those boys since she was about ten.'

Henry regarded him curiously. 'You've known her a long time?'

'Ten years. I taught her at Cambridge. And no, Henry, I do not feel the urge to rescue her. I like them a bit feminine and clinging, and Francesca is neither. In addition to her good degree at Cambridge, achieved by doing three hours' work a day, if that, the dear girl has, as far as I can see, the stamina and emotional temperament of a granite cliff. I love her, but it would take a stronger man than I. Ah, I believe that is The Car. In keeping with Perry's new status, the recording company to whom he is contracted has provided a car and driver for his use. Look.'

Opposite the Department's building, on the other side of Victoria Street, a vast brown Rolls Royce, being driven like a Mini, bumped two wheels on to the kerb and halted just in front of a bus. A head as dark as Francesca's appeared out of the back window.

'He's come to fetch me himself, the good boy,' Francesca observed from the door with sisterly complacency, her earlier strictures evidently forgotten. 'I've dictated the brief and Martin is going to check it for me so it can go up. Come and see Perry, Rajiv. Do come too, Henry, you need to go down to the canteen anyway.' She beamed on Henry, evidently pleased to be conferring this treat. In practice, he thought, following her down the corridor, she did right to be confident. Even after only a morning of Francesca he had to see what a younger brother looked like, particularly one who moved in such raffish circles.

Coming face to face with Perry in the Department's glass entrance hall, he sustained a small shock. Perry, he recognized, was a dazzler.

Not all that tall, perhaps three inches more than his sister, and graceful with it, he had Francesca's straight severe features in a longer face, Francesca's wide blue eyes set further apart than hers, with eyelashes a good deal thicker and longer than hers. While Francesca was dressed in a good grey Jaeger suit, in a style too severe for her, and a plain white blouse, Perry wore perfectly cut navy leather trousers and a pale blue silk shirt under a slightly darker cashmere sweater with two thin gold chains at his neck. They would have been recognizable anywhere as brother and sister, but they were as different as a kingfisher and his subfusc mate. Perry greeted him with courtesy and even with warmth, and Henry was charmed, though deciding that the boy was just a bit too conscious of those wonderful looks. He felt a pang for Francesca, so overshadowed.

'What you been at then?' the object of his pity was demanding, with affection. 'I'll have you know, Peregrine, we've always kept ourselves respectable, never had the police in the house till now.'

'Well I know,' Perry agreed, looking gracefully helpless. 'I suppose it was that sort of thought that made me hesitate to call them.'

'The fact that the chap from whose bed you have removed her is her husband must have given you pause as well.'

'Frannie,' Perry said indignantly, and glanced towards Henry and Rajiv both of whom were blinking at this trenchant approach. 'You're hardly one to talk, come to think of it.' He looked severely at Francesca who was slowly reddening.

'Children, children,' Rajiv intervened, and Henry hastily took his leave of them, reminding Francesca that he would need to talk to her that afternoon before they saw the Minister. He watched for a moment as the two graceful creatures left hand in hand and scrambled into the back of the Rolls.

'Rajiv, whose husband did Francesca steal?'

'That's not very fair of Perry. The cases are not analogous. Fran had a very much publicized affair with a US senator while she was over there, but there was no question of his leaving his wife. Perry, as I understand it, has actually abstracted a top model who is married to someone else, and has moved her into his house. Her husband seems to have taken exception to this and threatened retaliation. As we both heard, Fran has advised calling in the police.'

'And has gone along to hold his hand while he does it?'

'Evidently.'

Henry followed Rajiv down to the canteen, deciding reluctantly that it would be in poor taste to ask more questions, but that it was all a very long way from the vicissitudes of the textile industry.

CHAPTER 5

At Edgware Road police station, three miles away from where Henry Blackshaw was being introduced to his new colleagues, McLeish and Davidson were organizing their day.

'Right then, Bruce, let's go through the card for this morning. Peter Hampton, the Managing Director: he was in London on Monday and he told me that he saw Fireman at 5 p.m. and had a chat with him. The next candidate, William Blackett, was also in London. But they are the only two people from the company who were, is that right?'

'Yes. Two more Board members were at a Round Table dinner in Towneley with their wives, nae bother there. The Chairman and the local solicitor were both at a Hunt Ball.'

'Right. And we're visiting these two characters for a friendly at their London offices, just by Paddington?'

Davidson explained that it had seemed easier than inviting them to the station and McLeish agreed.

They were shown straight up to Hampton's office on their arrival, and offered coffee.

'I'm not sure how I can help you,' Hampton said discouragingly, passing the sugar. 'As I said on the phone, we finished our meeting around 6 p.m. and Bill went off — to get some dinner in, I assumed. I never saw him again.'

'I just need some background. Can you tell me why Mr Fireman was in London at all? Was he often here?'

'No, in fact hardly ever. He'd come down to talk to a possible new supplier — as you know, he was in charge of our purchasing function — and he came on to talk to me after he had seen them. He arrived about five and left at just after six. I am sure about the later time; I'd been trying to get him out of the office for half an hour.'

'What were you talking about.'

'Oh, Christ. He was boring on — I'm sorry to say that but it's true — about whether he should give this new supplier a chance.' He hesitated.

'I imagine all this is strictly confidential? The reason it was a bore is that the company is going through a very bad patch and we're having all the trouble we can handle keeping the suppliers we have. It just isn't realistic to take on a new supplier in our circumstances, but I could not make old Bill see it. Of course, to be fair, he doesn't — didn't — quite know the full strength. He isn't on the Board, and I thought they should be told before anyone else.'

'So it was a nuisance that he wanted to change suppliers?'

'Yes, but it wasn't going to happen unless I said so. Anyway, I daresay he would have gone on for another hour, but William Blackett came in.'

'Does Mr Blackett take an active part in the company?'

'Not really, he is non-executive here. He is the Sales Director of one of our suppliers, and of course he is full time there. I don't see a great deal of him in the ordinary way.'

'What did you talk about?' McLeish was working through a routine, his mind not wholly engaged, but his attention was snagged by the slight pause before the answer.

'I can't really remember — nothing important, it was the end of the day. We just chatted. I wasn't going to tell him too much about our difficulties until I could talk to the whole Board. Giving non-executive directors bits and pieces of information is always a bad idea, in my experience.'

McLeish went patiently on, eliciting the information that Blackett had left about 6.30 and Hampton about 7 p.m., vouched for by the building's security man.

'What time did you say Bill was killed?' Hampton asked, suddenly.

'He was found at 7.45, but the girl who found him was too upset to be clear as to whether he was dead then. He wasn't long gone when the ambulance got there. He was probably killed around 7.30.'

'You haven't asked me, but I went to the McDonald's on the corner about 7 p.m. — it was crowded and I had to queue, and I should think I got out about 7.45. I was back in Towneley by 11 p.m., and it's a three-hour drive. I can prove that, because I had a drink with a mate. I'll give you his name.'

McLeish sighed inwardly, reckoning the chances of anyone in a crowded McDonald's remembering an individual customer. He considered Hampton again and decided however that it was just possible that one of the girls would have remembered him. Hampton was a good-looking bloke, and his height made him distinctive as well. As McLeish rose to leave he realized that Hampton was much the same height.

'I'm sorry to hear of your business problems,' he said politely.

'Oh them. Well, we are in trouble and that's why I'm in London again. I'm not usually up and down like a monkey on a stick, but we have to see a lot of people this week. You must excuse me if I've seemed a bit rushed.'

McLeish made civil, comprehending noises, and removed himself and Davidson into an under furnished, slightly dusty meeting-room next door to Hampton's office, where William Blackett was reading the *Daily Telegraph*. As he and Davidson introduced themselves, McLeish felt a familiar tightening of the nerves; Blackett was sweating slightly, his voice was a little too loud in the small room, and he licked his lips nervously before he spoke. McLeish took him patiently through his day, which had seemed to consist largely of lunch at the In and Out starting at 12.30 and ending around 4 p.m.

'Business, you know. That's how you sell,' Blackett explained importantly, the twitching hands steadier now. 'Anyway I then went off to see Simon Ketterick, one of my salesmen for Alutex — we supply for Britex — and I came here about 6 p.m. to have a word with Peter Hampton, take a drink off him, you know.'

Probably much needed, McLeish thought. 'What were you having a word about?'

'Eh? Oh, nothing in particular. It was the end of the day, you know, and we just chatted.'

'And when did you leave?'

'Half six. The security man will tell you.'

'And where did you go then?'

'You're asking about my alibi.' Blackett tried a booming laugh which didn't quite come off. 'I went to the cinema. Alone.'

'Which cinema?'

Blackett hesitated, turned red, but looked him defiantly in the eye.

'Place in Soho. Blue films, you know.'

McLeish, who did indeed know, patiently extracted the name of the cinema, the false name under which Blackett had entered himself as a member, and the fact that he thought he had arrived about 8.15 but perhaps the chap there would remember. McLeish, reflecting that nothing could be less likely, accepted this hypothesis for the purpose of the interview.

'I suppose I could have killed Bill Fireman — I mean Pindar Street is only round the corner here,' he said, with bravado, but he was, McLeish observed, less nervous now that he had brought himself to reveal the evening's programme. McLeish made a suitably non-committal noise and rose to go.

'I expect you'll be very busy just now?' he remarked, making use of one of the useful phrases of farewell collected from his first mentor in the Force.

'Oh, you know about all that?' Blackett asked sharply. 'Yes, we'll be seeing the Minister this afternoon, heaven help us.'

McLeish and Davidson withdrew in good order and sat in the car to compare notes.

'They have a Minister for duff companies?' McLeish wondered aloud.

'Maybe it is a Minister of religion he is thinking of?'

Both policemen considered the likelihood of a pray-in for collapsing companies, and gave it up.

'Well, that's it finished anyway,' McLeish said. 'The rest of the Board are placed in Yorkshire at the relevant time, and so are all the deceased's family. No one remotely connected to him, except for Hampton and Blackett, was here on Monday.'

Davidson cleared his throat. 'We maybe should be considering an unconnected murderer.'

'I know you think it was a straightforward mugging, Bruce, no need to remind me. Let's leave it for now anyway — I picked up a bit of light relief on the way out of the station. Call from some pop star who is receiving threatening phone calls. Just round the corner here, and we may as well do it on the way to lunch.'

* * *

Three streets away the big Rolls took a corner with the tyres screaming.

'There is going to be nothing left of this car, Perry, if it gets driven like this all the time,' Francesca observed, clinging to the strap as the brown Rolls swung round another corner and slammed on all anchors in front of a large early Victorian semi-detached house. A selection of disapproving residents of the quiet cul-de-sac popped out of various doors and retired again, visibly disgruntled.

'Since it belongs to Trio Recording, I should co-co,' her brother retorted. 'We aren't middle-class poor anymore, you know. I am part of the rich *meeja*.'

'Easy come, easy go. Look after the pennies and the pounds will look after themselves.' She thought for a moment. 'That really can't be right, can it?'

'Not possibly. It's part of the Old Scots Lies we were brought up with.' Perry was laughing. 'Fran darling, do you know how much I have earned from "Wrong Road"? One hundred and fifty thousand pounds so far. OK, there is tax, but it pays a few bills.'

'Speaking as one to whom HMG pays twenty thousand a year, it must.'

'Never mind, darling, I expect you'll get married. Again.'

'You're joking. I plan to be Dame Francesca Wilson loaded with years and honours, and to have a long string of lovers.'

'It won't suit you,' her brother warned, with love. 'You'll have better luck next time and a string of children.'

Francesca, looking mutinous, scrambled out of the car, the door held for her by Perry's driver, a hefty young man with a ponytail and a lot of clanking medallions. She knew that he was also a bodyguard for Perry but had never quite got used to his style, and could not manage to believe that he would be any use in a fight. In this she did him a serious injustice; he had been heavily fined and put on probation for half killing a troublesome fan at a pop concert before he had entered Trio Recording's service.

All three of them stood for a moment gazing at the front of the house. It was a mixed and lively scene. Scaffolding ran up to the roof, with men spread out over it at various points. Two transistor radios, tuned to two different stations and both playing at full volume, operated separately at roof and first-floor level. From the ground floor, in effective competition with both radios, the choral passage from Beethoven's Ninth boomed out. As they watched, a dark head popped out of a second-floor window and a clear soprano shriek could be heard above the din adjuring one Frankie to turn the fucker off. One transistor and the Beethoven fell silent forthwith, and Perry glanced uneasily at his sister.

'Most effective,' she said blandly. 'If Sheena could just use a similar approach to get the other trannie tuned out, we could ring Edgware Road.'

'I've done that. They are sending someone round, so I decided I had just time to come and get you.'

'But Perry, they won't want to talk to me. I only came to persuade you that you really did need to call them.' She noticed that he was looking uneasy. 'What is it? Oh sorry, hello Sheena.'

'Hi, Frannie.' Sheena Roberts, who at twenty-one had already been a top photographic model for six years, kissed Francesca ceremonially, as usual managing to make her feel awkward, clumsy and ungracious.

She was taller even than Francesca, weighed about twenty pounds less, had long silky black hair, a clear olive skin and a body which managed to be both thin enough for photographic modelling and voluptuously sexy. That morning she was dressed in skin-tight men's jeans, and a baggy, immaculately clean white sweatshirt, and made everyone else look stuffy and overdressed. She looked full of health and very intelligent, and Francesca, who knew that she was only just literate and suspected that she regularly took drugs, marvelled again. She always felt markedly inferior in Sheena's company, and it was only of limited comfort that she knew Sheena felt the same way in hers.

'Well, that's all right then, Sheena,' she observed, trying for a friendly sisterly approach and, as usual, feeling like a fifty-year-old headmistress. 'If I can take some lunch off you, I'll be away. I'm needed back at the ranch.'

'I done lunch. Come on down.' The group picked its way through the scaffolding and down the stairs to the basement which was recognizably on its way to being an open plan kitchen/dining-room.

On the large table enough lunch for at least twelve people had been expensively assembled.

'I'll call everyone, shall I?' Perry volunteered.

'Perry, you 'aven't told Frannie why she is 'ere, 'ave you?' Sheena, sought after by every agency and photographer in the UK since she was fifteen, had never seen any need to modify her native East End accent.

Perry looked uneasy, but stood his ground, and Sheena glanced at him indulgently. 'It's like this, Frannie. Thing is, my old man, my 'usband, 'e's a stylist.'

'A what, sorry, Sheena?'

'He's a hairdresser, Fran.' Perry evidently felt it would be safer to intervene than to let Sheena explain. 'In fact, darling, he is a hairdresser at Gordon and John.'

'But that's where I go.'

'Exactly. So he knows about you, and in fact the mystery voice has uttered threats against you as well as against me.' Perry considered his sister, who was apparently struck dumb. 'Well I'm sorry, Fran, to have involved you, but I didn't know you went to Gordon and John or I would have warned you, and of course Sheena didn't either.'

'Is it possible, Sheena, that it is your husband who does my hair?'

'No, it's Ted does yours. 'E uses Alexander as 'is professional name, of course. 'E's good. Much better cutter than my old man.'

Something about this seriously expressed judgement amused Francesca sufficiently to make her forget her mounting outrage, and Perry heaved a small sigh of relief as he realized his sister was not going to hit the roof.

'What is the voice threatening to do, precisely?' she asked, just as the front doorbell rang.

Perry picked up the intercom and listened. 'The police,' he reported.

'I'll go. Where do we want to see them? It's a choice of down here or in the bedroom — that's where we are living.'

'The group's in the bedroom,' Sheena volunteered. 'Better down 'ere.'

Perry nodded, took the basement stairs in four strides and seconds later his long leather-clad legs reappeared, followed by two pairs of orthodox grey trousers. Fran was momentarily distracted by Sheena who, with her back turned, was speaking into the intercom, just audibly instructing anyone upstairs who had anything they shouldn't to dump it or get off the premises, since the Old Bill were visiting.

Rattled, she moved swiftly over to the stairs to cover the conversation and almost bumped into the descending group.

'My sister, Francesca.'

Francesca put out her hand automatically, too distracted by trying to hear whether Sheena was still talking to register what the newcomers were like. The sheer size of the hand that enveloped hers startled her, and she looked up at its owner who was staring at her with an expression of pure amazement. The smaller man at his side was visibly suppressing a grin, and saying, 'Aye, well Miss Wilson, we met yesterday. Ye were running up and down the steps forgetting things just round the corner here. My name's Davidson, and this is Detective Inspector McLeish.'

The taller man let go of her hand as if he had been stung, and Francesca, feeling that events were getting beyond her, shook hands with Davidson.

'Detective Inspector McLeish, and Detective Sergeant Davidson, my sister, Francesca Wilson, and Sheena Roberts.' Full marks to that young man, thought McLeish, recovering from the temporary paralysis induced by finding himself in the same room as the girl he had been thinking about for twenty-four hours. Not everyone bothers to give the police their right names and titles.

'It was my sister who felt that we should ask you to advise us on this difficulty,' Perry said helpfully, seeing that for some reason no one else seemed to be going to speak.

'Well, that's what we are here for,' McLeish said heartily, making an effort and sounding to his own ears like a caricature of the local bobby. He glanced despairingly at Davidson who was standing woodenly but unselfconsciously beside him, his gaze resting consideringly on the table. 'If I could start by getting everyone's names and addresses.' He nodded to Davidson who pulled a notebook from his pocket, as Perry urged everyone to sit down.

McLeish sat, squaring his elbows and making an effort of concentration, acutely conscious of Francesca. Beside her brother and Sheena, both phenomena with which as a London policeman he was familiar, Francesca looked as exotic as a hawk in her tidy Jaeger suit. She in her turn, now that her attention was no longer distracted by the possibility of the immediate arrest of one of Perry's henchmen, all of whom she knew from experience took an amazing variety of pills and drugs, was watching him under her eyelashes with interest.

An attractive man, she thought, with the wide shoulders and generally triangular shape of the athlete, dark springy hair above a high brow, rather heavy eyebrows above eyes somewhere between green and brown. Not quite good looking, she thought, the crooked nose and the rather heavy jaw prevented that, but very distinctive. A Scot, of course.

He turned his head suddenly and caught her watching him, and their eyes met. Francesca, who had all the social confidence of her background, went on placidly contemplating him, and he looked back at her equally steadily, deciding that her eyes were more grey than blue. A serious, disciplined face, like no other girl he knew, but somehow deeply familiar.

At his side, Davidson noisily turned over a page in his notebook, and clattered with a pencil. 'Right, if we could start with your details, please Mr Wilson?'

Perry offered his name, address, and occupation and introduced Sheena as Miss Roberts.

'That is your professional name. Miss Roberts?'

'It's my given name. My married name is Sheena Byers, but I never use it professionally. All the agents know me as Sheena Roberts.' A raving beauty, McLeish thought in appreciation, and too confident to bother with changing her given name to anything more exotic. 'I live 'ere, with Perry.'

McLeish glanced involuntarily at Francesca but that serious face gave nothing away.

'My legal name is Francesca Lewendon.' McLeish was conscious only of a violent stab of disappointment. 'But given that I am now divorced, I have reverted to my maiden name, Francesca Wilson.'

McLeish felt Davidson next to him breathe out cautiously. 'I live round the corner, where you saw me yesterday, at 19 Wellcome Street. Damn!'

Davidson and McLeish both looked up startled.

'Soup is burning.'

Davidson, who had eaten nothing since breakfast and who was always hungry, unconsciously licked his lips, and McLeish reflected that it was a pity they had not stopped on the way. He saw Francesca's glance flick across Davidson.

'Could we not all have some lunch?' she proposed. 'It's past 1 o'clock, I haven't eaten, I have to be back in my office for 2.30, and I work very badly without lunch.' She raised an eyebrow at her brother, ignoring Sheena who might, McLeish thought, be presumed to be the mistress of the house and indeed looked irritated by this treatment. Perry seconded her invitation immediately.

'Please do eat. I appreciate you are on duty, but it is after all we who have asked for your help, rather than you who are asking us to help with your enquiries.'

'Thank you,' McLeish said, realizing that he as well as Davidson was tired and hungry and presumably less than efficient. He watched with interest as Francesca served the soup and assembled five plates of smoked salmon and assorted goodies.

'Forty bars silence,' Francesca commanded, and Davidson, his mouth full, gazed at her enquiringly. 'Old family saying, originating with our mother when asked kindly what piece of music she would next like to hear. No one can eat and talk, so let's eat first.'

Davidson beamed at her gratefully and fell to. McLeish watching her out of the tail of his eye as he worked his way through a vast plate, noticed that she was not in fact all that hungry, and that she kept an eye on their plates to see they had enough. Davidson, McLeish noted, obviously felt himself perfectly at home, and passed his plate matter-of-factly for a second helping. He watched, noticing that she had unobtrusively slid another plate of bread over to them both, and was herself sitting companionably eating grapes in order to keep them company, both Perry and Sheena having eaten very little.

'That went down grateful.' Davidson beamed at her, and held out his cup for more coffee. She grinned back.

'Must have. You've gone a quite different colour.'

McLeish felt a moment's murderous jealousy at Davidson's accustomed success with women, but realized that Francesca was in fact wholly unimpressed, merely amused.

'So, everyone,' she said encouragingly, when they had cleared their plates, and she was pouring coffee. 'I've got about twenty minutes before I must go back unless I can have The Car?'

'I'll be happy to take you back, Miss Wilson. I have an errand at New Scotland Yard. Sergeant Davidson can finish up here if there are any loose ends.' McLeish had a well-justified reputation for decisiveness and ability to make the machine work, and Davidson knew better than to ask questions about how he would manage without a car.

'I understand that threats have been made against you, Mr Wilson, and against Mrs Byers and against Miss Wilson.' McLeish, having seized the advantage, pressed on.

'We — I — have now received up to three phone calls in the early hours of the last three mornings demanding Sheena's return forthwith, or unspecified nasties would happen to me and to my sister.'

'No threats addressed to Sheena?' Francesca asked.

'I told you. 'E wants me back.'

Francesca's eyebrows went up and McLeish intervened hastily. 'Did you recognize the voice, Mrs Byers?'

'Never 'eard it. Perry don't like me to answer the phone in case 'ooever it is finks I'm alone.'

McLeish distinctly saw Francesca's lips move disbelievingly, but pushed on. 'And you, Mr Wilson? Did you recognize the voice. Or are there several voices?'

'No,' Perry said, with certainty. 'But I would know it again. It's always the same voice.'

'What does your husband do, Mrs Byers?' McLeish decided to pass on.

''E's a stylist.'

'A hairdresser,' Francesca volunteered, blandly. McLeish patiently extracted his name and address, and the information that Francesca attended that particular salon.

'Or used to attend. I hardly feel I can go back there, in the circumstances, which is a bore.' She gave her brother a hard-case scowl, and looked up to see McLeish looking at her thoughtfully.

'Miss Wilson, if you got Mr Byers on the phone, your brother could listen to the voice and identify it if possible.'

'Would that be evidence?'

'Not by itself, no. But I had it in mind to go and interview him, and it would help me if I could be sure it was he making the phone calls.'

Francesca thought about that for a minute, then went to the telephone, motioning Perry to an extension. She checked his working name with Sheena, and put on a masterly performance of a rather stupid debutante's mother, with a high-pitched county drawl, who had been particularly recommended to him and who wanted to seek his advice on a hairstyle for a gala occasion. The East End accent could be heard clearly through the modish, slightly camp, patter of the man at the other end, and Perry looked up and nodded to McLeish after three or four sentences. Francesca's performance was the more impressive as a piece of imagination, thought McLeish, inasmuch as she had obviously never in her life thought in terms of a hairstyle for a gala occasion. The same thought had obviously struck her brother, who put his extension down at the end of the conversation, grinning broadly.

'It's not funny, sorry Sheena, but I did like the idea of Fran with her two inches of hair done up in Empire-style ringlets for the Feathers Ball. It's the same voice, Inspector, and I feel a fool. We could have thought of ringing up ourselves.'

'Are you quite sure?'

'Oh yes.' Perry spoke with dismissive confidence. 'I could swear to it in Court if necessary.' He saw McLeish's doubtful expression. 'It has to do with being a singer — I'm so used to listening to voices I really am sure.' He reached out for Sheena, and dropped an arm round her shoulders, unselfconsciously caressing one perfect breast.

Francesca looked away, embarrassed.

'Right then.' McLeish rose to his feet, looking very large in the low-ceilinged room. 'We'll take Miss Wilson with us, Sergeant, and I'll drop you off at the station.' Davidson folded up his notebook, collected his coat and reflected that he was lucky to be getting a ride home at all with his superior in full hunting cry. Francesca, both amused and impressed, meekly followed them both to the car. She and Davidson conversed politely about different varieties of car used by the police force, and McLeish observed with pleasure that this formidable girl had no idea which car was which. They left Davidson at the police station and drove off in a slightly constrained silence.

'Very kind of you to give me a lift. I hate being late for meetings.'

'Well, it's not exactly in your day's work I imagine, this sort of thing?' McLeish offered, cautiously.

Francesca made a noise of sheer exasperation. 'We must seem pretty incompetent to you, Inspector, but Sheena and her adherents are a bit outside our experience so far.' She scowled at the windscreen, looking very young and very annoyed. McLeish decided that a note of realism would not come amiss.

'They seem very devoted — Mrs Byers and your brother, I mean.'

There was a thick dismayed silence from his left and he felt a brute. He looked cautiously sideways to see Francesca looking straight forward out of the windscreen, absolutely expressionlessly.

'Sorry. None of my business.'

'You're quite right of course, they are.' She spoke evenly, still gazing out of the windscreen. He felt an immediate rush of affection and anxiety for her, and nearly missed a turning. Hang on, hang on, he thought, you saw this girl for the first time yesterday, you're making this up, you're just a thick copper to her.

'If you drop me on this corner, it's easy. Thank you very much for the lift.'

'Don't be cross.' He spoke involuntarily but managed to meet Francesca's startled stare squarely as he halted the car. They sat and looked at each other thoughtfully, Francesca observing the little dark-green flecks in the brown eyes.

'You sound like one of my brothers,' she observed conversationally.

'I didn't mean to do that.' He felt amazingly alive and excited without having the faintest idea what to do next. Ask her out? On an hour's acquaintance, and professional acquaintance at that? He sat looking at her, with years of experience offering him no guidance at all.

'Oh!' Francesca, sounding faintly stagey, broke the silence. 'There are the colleagues whom I am meeting, obviously on their way back. I ought to go.' She reached for the door handle and made a nonsense of trying to open it.

'Hang on,' McLeish said, recovering his voice. 'I'll let you out.' He marched round the car and released her, watching with appreciation as she emerged in a flurry of excellent long legs. Get your mouth open, idiot, he thought savagely. 'I'll give you a ring after I've spoken to Mr Byers,' he offered. 'Usually a word from the police is enough in these cases,' he added fatally, hearing himself sound like a caricature of the friendly neighbourhood policeman, a figure for whom he had no time at all.

'I should think a word would do, from you,' Francesca agreed. 'I just wish I could be a fly on the wall when you and that nice sergeant of yours march in to Gordon and John. The whole thing has been a revelation to me you know. I wonder which of those camp lads with perms is Sheena's husband — I just can't put a face to him.' McLeish beamed at her but noticed out of the corner of an eye that they were attracting considerable attention from her colleagues, lingering courteously at the door of the Department. Francesca saw them too.

'I must go. We have to see a delegation from a firm which is going bust, and we have to tell the Minister the two facts we actually know, before he sees them.' She looked up at him. 'I'd be very grateful to know how you get on. It would be nicer not to be threatened with unspeakable things.'

McLeish laughed with pleasure at this temperate view of the matter, and managed to ask her for a number at which he could call her. She gave him a neatly engraved business card, and scribbled her home number on the back, turning just perceptibly pink.

'I must run,' she stated, standing still.

'Yes. I'll ring you.' She nodded, and shot across the road, running easily on her high heels. He watched, silently, waiting for her to vanish through the door, but she turned and waved to him before she went in, swallowed up in the small group at the door of the building.

CHAPTER 6

'Very good of you to see us at such short notice, David.' Derrick Jamieson, MP, wrung the Minister for Industry's hand. 'May I introduce Sir James Blackett, the Chairman, and Mr Peter Hampton, the Managing Director of Britex Fabrics, and Mr William Blackett who is also on the Britex Board and a very old friend.'

'Good to see you.' David Llewellyn, Minister for Industry, a small dark-haired, faintly bow-legged Welshman, beamed kindly upon an evidently nervous Jamieson. 'May I, in my turn, introduce my colleagues, Mr Blackshaw, head of the Industrial Development Unit, Miss Wilson, another member of the Unit, and my Private Secretary David Jonas.'

Henry and Francesca shook hands courteously, and settled themselves on either side of the Minister. They had arrived fifteen minutes early, as requested, and had waited ten minutes in the private office while the Minister dealt with two phone calls. Henry had fidgeted, but Francesca had been unperturbed, observing reasonably that this always happened with last-minute meetings which had been wedged into a Minister's already appallingly overcrowded schedule; not to fret, the Minister could not be expected to be wholly with it.

She had competently used the time to make sure that Henry was introduced to the key people in the busy crowded room that constituted the Minister's private office, and had herself briefed David Jonas, the Private Secretary, an elegant, exhausted young man. He listened to Francesca and observed that it was clearly the usual shambles, the Minister had not had time to read anything, and that, as Francesca would know, Jamieson, the MP who had asked for this meeting, was a political friend and ally of the Minister's.

'Do you know that sort of thing?' Henry had asked *sotto voce* when the elegant young man turned away to sort out a problem.

'The use of the words "as you know" is a Civil Service code. It means as you ought to know.'

When they had finally got the Minister's attention, or as much of it as was likely to be available, Francesca had taken about ninety seconds to give an outline of the company's history, current situation and likely prospects, which the Minister had absorbed with equally impressive speed.

'It's been losing money hand over fist for three years, keeping going by selling off the good bits. Now the banks are closing in, there aren't any more good bits to sell, and there are 1400 jobs on the line? I don't know, Francesca, you haven't been here very long, but every time your smiling face comes round my door, my heart sinks. I know you bring tidings of some major industrial disaster, usually in a friend's constituency. I expect I shall soon feel the same about you, Mr Blackshaw.' Llewellyn had beamed upon them both with obvious good will, and they had both grinned back, enjoying the Welsh eloquence and careful use of language.

Henry returned his attention to the room where the Minister was now competently opening the meeting, saying how glad he was that he had been on the spot, that he and his Department had known something of the difficulties at Britex Fabrics, and that he was here to listen and to see what help the Department could give. It all sounded remarkably calm and orderly and concerned, and Henry had to remind himself that the man had never heard of Britex Fabrics ten minutes before this meeting. As the MP, Jamieson, equally competently expressed thanks and his intention of calling on Sir James to describe the situation, Henry observed that all three members of the Britex Board had been momentarily totally distracted by the fact that David Jonas was taking a note of the meeting while Francesca sat silent at the Minister's left, very clearly an adviser. Not what we're used to in Yorkshire, he thought with amusement, and was brought up short by the realization that as recently as yesterday he would not have expected women to do anything other than take a note of the meeting, either.

He looked with affection at this particular female professional, and was taken aback to see that she was watching the remarkably good-looking Britex Managing Director under her eyelashes.

'I too would like to thank you, Minister, for making yourself available today.' Sir James had recovered, and swung efficiently into his prepared speech. 'You must understand that this is a sad day for our company, which was founded over a hundred years ago and which has been the major employer in Towneley since the war. The company has always been profitable and even three years ago we were employing 2,500 people. It is the competition from low priced imports — priced, we believe, below the cost of production — that has cut savagely into our market. We have always taken the view that our responsibilities to our work people meant that we should try to keep our labour force together and to fight back, but over recent months we have had no choice but to declare substantial redundancies. We have taken losses of £6m in each of the last two years and shall do worse this year, rather than let our people down. But we have reached the stage where, unless Government can help us, as directors we can do no more and will have to call in the receiver.'

Yes, well, thought Henry in the respectful silence that succeeded this statement, not bad, though the detached observer might well conclude that the decision to keep on your labour force while making huge losses sprang less from altruism than the inability to grasp the fact that the world had fundamentally changed. It was indeed cheap imports that had undercut Britex Fabric's business, with every chain store now selling thermal underwear made up in Taiwan or Poland at half the cost of the Britex product — but how were you going to turn back that particular clock? He glanced sideways at Francesca who was printing carefully in block capitals the words 'NO, BECAUSE MULTIFIBRE ARRANGEMENTS AND/OR EEC RULES.' As he watched she edged the paper into the Minister's sightline.

'It's a question of what our international commitments allow us to do, isn't it?' David Llewellyn leaned forward, glancing at Francesca's piece of paper as he did so. 'As you know, we have recently renegotiated the multifibre arrangements which limit imports from countries outside the EEC. We are, of course, precluded from action against our Common Market partners, unless the industry can prove to us that imports are being sold below the cost of production. We do, however, have powers under the Industry Act to offer selective financial assistance to firms where there is a danger that jobs would be lost, but we have to be satisfied that, with assistance, a viable enterprise is being created.'

'So what can you do for us?' Peter Hampton spoke, abruptly breaking the flow of the meeting. Francesca looked up with interest, but said nothing. She had explained to Henry on the way to the Minister's office that officials did not speak when the Minister was seeing a delegation unless invited, or *in extremis,* to rescue the poor chap from some pit he was digging for his own feet.

'Ah.' David Llewellyn managed to sound as if Hampton had asked the only sensible question. 'That is why I have invited Mr Blackshaw to join us. As the head of the Industrial Development Unit he has the responsibility of assessing whether the company is viable or can be made so, and also for telling me what help we ought to be giving.'

William Blackett regarded him with hostility. 'Time is getting very short.'

'Oh we understand that, Mr Blackett,' the Minister assured him.

'We can move very quickly. That is the basis on which Mr Blackshaw's Unit is set up. David, how is my time?'

'Seven minutes, Minister.'

'Well, since I have to get there as well, I'm afraid we'd better go, hadn't we? I am sorry to have to leave you, but Mr Blackshaw and Miss Wilson will make arrangements with you to start the appraisal process as soon as possible.'

More courteous thanks, more handshakes, and David Llewellyn and the private secretary bustled out of the room, leaving the visitors with Francesca and Henry.

'Let's get a bit more comfortable, shall we?'

Francesca briskly shepherded the party towards the window, and offered tea which had arrived seconds after the Minister left. Henry noted that this commendable attempt to make the visitors feel at home was misfiring: all four men were failing to adjust to a woman taking charge of the meeting. He firmly elbowed Francesca to one side and approached, making civil enquiries about the train journey down and fishing for mutual acquaintances in the trade. By the time the party was seated and in possession of some lethal Departmental tea, Henry was in full charge of the meeting and the visitors had settled down and were producing papers. He gently led Sir James through the depressing history of the last three years, and the sombre list of decent profitable subsidiaries sold off. His sympathy was genuine; he knew enough of the pattern from his own experience, but without ever having had to face the prospect of receivership.

'The last straw, of course, was the failure of negotiations with America.' Sir James was in full flight and there seemed little prospect of Hampton getting a word in. 'We couldn't afford to develop a new spinning process ourselves — Hampton here was quite right — so we did it as a joint venture with a Wexel subsidiary. It looked like a winner, and that company could have been worth £10m or so. Turns out the process isn't reliable, and the Japs have something rather better, though a much less elegant piece of technology. So then we were down to looking at selling one of the two core businesses.'

'What a blow.' Francesca spoke with real sympathy, and Peter Hampton sat up sharply and considered her. 'You must have thought you were going to be OK,' she said to him, as if he was the only person in the room.

'Yes. Yes, I did. It's been a nightmare since.' He leaned forward to Francesca. 'Nothing goes right, you go along for a week or so, then there is another bill. Your people lose heart, and anyone who can gets another job.' He paused, and considered her, his blue eyes bright and warily amused. 'But you wouldn't have any experience of that sort of thing.'

'Everyone has experienced situations which get ineluctably worse and worse,' Francesca pointed out. 'But I agree with you, debts that you cannot pay are a particularly horrible refinement. Look,' she leaned forward, the warmth and directness of her personality lighting up the room, 'let us look at it, show us the worst. If there is a viable business in there and jobs are at risk, something can be done.'

Henry, firmly wresting the meeting back into his own hands, reminded the company that the Department was not in the business of rescuing banks or shareholders. If, in the end, the company turned out to be overburdened with debt, the Department might well recommend that it should go into receivership and assistance be given to those prepared to take over the assets from the receiver.

This unwelcome but necessary caveat was received calmly by Peter Hampton who observed that they would be no worse off than they already were on that basis, and with distaste but comprehension by Sir James.

'What do you do in this lot?' William Blackett made the question sound rude, but Francesca, unruffled, explained that she was the political wing, there to help Mr Blackshaw with general background and to advise him what assistance was available and to help with the advice to Ministers. 'I've thought of another worry, though,' she said, helpfully. 'You're a quoted company. We can come in disguised as the Regional Office making a courtesy visit, but will this leak? Ought you to make an announcement, or suspend your shares?'

Good question, thought Henry, though it would have been a great deal better if she had waited for him to ask it. Hampton and Sir James and William Blackett were looking both rattled and offended, and for the third time that afternoon he seized back the conduct of the meeting.

'I am sure this is a point to which you will be giving consideration,' he said firmly. 'If it will suit you, I could arrange to be with you the day after tomorrow. I suggest we might start with your London office, and we must at a later stage see the factory. I shall bring one of my people, a young accountant, with me.' He became aware of a thoughtful silence. 'Is the day not suitable?'

'No, no, it's not that.' Sir James was looking irritable. 'It has just occurred to all of us that we had not mentioned to you that one of our people — the purchasing manager — was murdered on Monday night on his way back to his hotel from our London office. We have had the police there all day, but I imagine they will have finished with us by the day after tomorrow.'

'How dreadful for you. What happened?' the irrepressible Francesca enquired.

'The police think it must have been a drug addict or something similar. His head was beaten in and his wallet and valuables taken. Quite near the hotel in Pindar Street.' William Blackett had reluctantly decided that Francesca might have some importance in the Department.

'Not all that far from where I live,' she observed. 'I am sorry, awful for you all, and of course, terribly disruptive at this point.'

'You can say that again,' Hampton observed with fervour. 'It's dreadful to sound so heartless, but it seemed to me that the gods were against us when I heard about poor Bill.

I'd just talked to him that afternoon. What do you want to see?'

'Everything,' Henry said briskly. 'More precisely, we need to see everything that an accountant writing a report for a bank would want to see. Has your bank asked for a report, by the way?'

'They made it clear that they would not consider any further extension of our overdraft without an accountant's report.'

'How are you going to manage short term for cash?' It was Francesca again. Henry cast her an exasperated look, since she had asked his next question but one, and she subsided. Peter Hampton grinned at him sympathetically, looking abruptly less tense. As Henry looked away, declining complicity, he just saw Hampton wink at Francesca.

'We'll need to talk to suppliers at some point,' Henry said, into the silence.

'Bugger that!' Peter Hampton sat up sharply. 'Sorry, but that really could put us into receivership. I'm in bother enough dodging flying writs. We don't have cash to pay bills, unless we can persuade the bank to let us have a bit more on the basis that you people are looking at us. Or, if you could have a word with the PAYE and VAT people not to press us, we could use that cash to stave off pressure.'

Henry thought about this perfectly logical request and realized that there were probably pitfalls which he had not seen. Beside him, Francesca shifted in her seat and he glanced at her enquiringly. She looked back at him, widened her eyes and pressed her lips together in a swift caricature of virtuous restraint. Peter Hampton had noticed the by-play and was openly grinning.

'Francesca, what is the form on these things?' Time enough to have a little chat with her afterwards, but for now an answer to the question was needed.

'Although formally the provisions of the Companies Acts do not bind the Crown, the Attorney General's best view is that we must all behave as if they did. So we can't give any comfort to creditors, unless and until we actually get Ministerial agreement to any assistance recommended. Similarly, the formal position is that we must hold out no hope of assistance to you or other directors of the company.'

The audience regarded her with some hostility, but after a minute Sir James conceded that this made sense, and Henry decided to conclude the meeting.

'Well, I'm afraid there is not a lot more I can do until we have had a look at the figures. If you can let us have anything tomorrow, or even later today, we will start straight away; otherwise we will be with you the day after tomorrow.'

The visitors rose to go, and Henry and Francesca went with them to the lifts. Henry, exchanging civil commonplaces with the Blacketts about mutual acquaintances in Yorkshire, could hear Francesca behind him exercising her charm on Peter Hampton. Rather uphill work, he thought; the chap was hardly responding, and had harked back to the point that he didn't want his suppliers approached at this stage.

He was deeply amused to hear Francesca, abandoning charm, tell him not to fuss, just as if he were a younger brother; the Department was not in the business of pushing people into receivership. They bade their visitors farewell in a final exchange of civilities.

'Francesca, could we have a word in my office?' She gave him a caricature hang-dog look, but he remained resolutely unamused. He asked for tea, firmly dismissed his secretary and explained to a much subdued Francesca that in any meeting at which he was senior officer present, he took the lead — just like a Minister, he volunteered, inspired. He reminded her that she had been dealing with anxious men from out of London, who had been deeply disconcerted at finding themselves explaining industrial problems to a snippet like her who added to the general sins of being young, a southerner, and a civil servant with an index-linked pension, the final, ineradicable sin of being a woman. 'The last time these chaps listened to a girl tell them the odds they were eight years old and at school,' he reminded her.

'Just use a bit of sensitivity and tact, ease them into the meeting, and shut up when someone senior is trying to get through a list of questions.'

Francesca, to his pleasure, neither wept nor sought to excuse herself, but, rather pink about the cheeks, apologized, drank her tea and left. He sat back to finish his tea, feeling pleased with himself and in control of his new environment. A fearsome crash from the corridor made him start, and he looked up to see Rajiv Sengupta at the door.

'May I come in? May one also enquire why Fran has just marched through my outer office, pausing only to kick two filing cabinets? We who have known her for some time conclude that something has vexed her.'

'Me,' said Henry promptly. 'I feared she might have gone off to weep.'

'Not Francesca. Er, Henry, what did you do?'

'Cursed her out for not allowing me to hold my own meeting.'

'How brave. I can see you are going to be a real asset to this Unit. I can't imagine why she didn't kick you rather than my filing cabinet. I actually came to discuss staffing. I hear from Francesca — between crashes, you understand — that we really have acquired another customer this afternoon. Which of the accountants do you want on it?'

They spent a peaceful and efficient forty minutes committing Martin Bailey's time fully to Britex and making consequent readjustments on other jobs. Henry found Rajiv shrewd as well as entertainingly malicious in his judgements of which of the secondees could effectively do which job. They were sitting back, pleased with each other, when Francesca put her head round the door.

'Draft note for the Minister of this afternoon's meeting herewith — I told David Jonas I would do it all, since he and the Minister were there for less than half of it. Would you look at it, please Henry, and then you can just tick it through.'

Henry, impressed, took the note which ran to a page and a half and summarized succinctly the main points. 'Very good,' he said, 'and very quick.'

'We have to be.'

Not forgiven yet, he thought, biting his lip to keep from grinning.

'What else are you doing?'

'I am holding a meeting on another case.' She picked up her note and left, stiff-backed. Both men watched her go, avoiding each other's eyes.

'"I kept my dignity",' Henry quoted, with affection when she was safely out of the room. '"Pig, says I, and swep' out."' He caught Rajiv's considering look. 'Don't worry about it — we'll get on. She'll learn. I'm now going home — I feel as if I have been here for months, and I'm worn out. See you tomorrow.'

CHAPTER 7

McLeish sat at his desk at Edgware Road the next morning and considered the papers on it dispiritedly. Statements from the hotelkeeper; and the typist who had found the body still to be read. No apparent motive other than the obvious one of robbery, and if that was right their chances of finding the murderer became slim, because there would be no connection between victim and murderer. Find him they must, however. Someone who could deliver two further blows with a hammer to make sure his victim was dead ought not to be walking the streets. Nor was he himself working well, he felt fidgety and stale. He looked up at Davidson working in his contained way on the other side of the room, and immediately remembered a suitable distraction.

'We ought to tell young Mr Wilson about our interview with his lady's husband.'

'Aye, we ought. I tried earlier this morning but I can't find him. The people he has at his house — I take it it's the housekeeper or some such — say he is rehearsing at the BBC and cannot be disturbed. Mrs Byers is somewhere modelling something, but the wee body on the telephone had no idea what or where. I've left messages. Shall I try to find Miss Wilson as well?'

The question was a little over-casual and McLeish looked up sharply.

'I tried myself this morning. I wondered whether to make an appointment or maybe just go up there when I've time around lunch and tell her about it.'

'That's an idea. I'm sure she would welcome personal handling of this matter.' Davidson's eyes were bright with interest, and McLeish gave him a sourly amused grin.

'Nice wee girl.' McLeish blinked at him. As a description of a young woman probably five foot eight in her socks it struck him as unusual.

'Ye were that busy giving her the eye, you missed all the detail. When we were round there, you know, she saw me looking at the food like a starving kitty, so she says she is hungry and feeds us bloody great plates of food, casual like. And I'm not her type, she just saw a body looking hungry and made sure he got fed. Shows a motherly nature which is aye a good thing in women.'

'All right, Bruce. You're the expert round here, women everywhere we look. How do I ask her out?' His sergeant gazed at him, eyebrows peaked into triangles of incredulity.

'Try a wee telephone call,' he suggested. 'Ask her if she'd like to come out for a drink tonight.'

'Won't she be rather surprised?'

'Why? She fancied you too, nae bother, couldn't take her eyes off you. I may have been starving but I saw that. Look, ring her up, you can lead in gently by telling her about our chat with Mr Byers. That'll amuse her — I mean, it gave me a laugh.'

'He wasn't expecting us, was he?' McLeish grinned at the memory.

He and his sergeant had descended on the premises of Gordon and John — green-and-white striped blind, green and white fittings in the shop, a chatty blonde seventeen-year-old on reception, who had been immediately enchanted by her first glimpse of Davidson. After the preliminaries they had asked for Mr Byers and the girl behind the desk, gazing rapturously at Davidson, had bent her mind to the question and after some thought had summoned Mr Franco to the front desk. Mr Franco, born Francis Byers, had irritably left a model-girl client and slouched elegantly over to the desk. He had, as Davidson observed with pleasure, nearly pissed himself when he came face to face, or rather face to collarbone, with McLeish. He had recovered fast, the nondescript face, rendered almost good looking by a stylish long blond mane of hair, hardening into older, tougher lines.

'You can't come 'ere.'

'Would you rather come to the station, then?' Davidson had enquired, and the manager, a lively Jew in his twenties with an incipient weight problem, had arrived from nowhere, sized the situation up with the speed of experience, and swept the whole party away to a crowded back office, returning himself to deal with Mr Franco's abandoned client. McLeish, looking particularly menacing in the tiny office, had explained the nature of the complaint and asked, pro forma, whether Mr Byers or any of his associates were involved, receiving the expected denial with scepticism. Mr Byers did, he assumed, understand that threatening behaviour was in itself an offence? And that the eyes of the CID in Hackney would be on his family and associates, twenty-four hours a day, if any further threats were received? Should any actual violence take place, of course, the whole Byers family and associates would receive the full attention of two separate police forces.

'She's my old lady. Why aren't you out catching murderers rather than helping a sod like 'im take Sheena away?' They had both been embarrassed to see that he had tears in his eyes.

'Whatever happens, you don't go uttering threats.' Davidson had swung into action. 'No more funny phone calls; you want to say something to her, you write it and send it through the post. You don't want the uniformed branch round here.'

That blow had gone home, McLeish had thought. His years as a policeman had left him confident that he knew the difference between a rational man who could be frightened into sensible behaviour, and the genuine hard man, often psychopathic, who would shrug off a police warning. This one wouldn't risk his livelihood; no need to consider a watch on either of the Wilson households. Pity, really; he wouldn't have minded a good excuse to keep a watch on one Wilson.

'You ring her up, I'll get some coffee,' volunteered Davidson now, seeing him still hesitant. McLeish, dithering, watched gloomily through the glass partition as Davidson wove his way to the machine, patting the prettiest of the WPCs gently on the bottom as he passed, clearly giving pleasure rather than offence. He seized the phone and resolutely dialled.

'Francesca Wilson's phone.' It was a pleasant, cultured male voice and McLeish blinked. Could it be that there were male secretaries in the Department of Industry? Did Francesca have one? He could hear a confused background noise and raised male voices, and realized that inviting Francesca out more or less in public was going to have its difficulties.

'Francesca Wilson.'

'Inspector McLeish here,' he said awkwardly, feeling the Friendly Neighbourhood Policeman personality threatening to envelop him. 'I thought you would be glad to know that we have interviewed Mr Byers.'

'Hang on, will you, Inspector? Gentlemen, could this meeting transfer itself next door. I am sorry, but I need quiet for this phone call . . . So, what happened?'

'We went to see him, and we told him that if the phone calls did not stop we would come and see him again.'

'Accompanied on any subsequent visit by several members of the uniformed branch, I take it?'

'That's right.' Quick with it, too, he thought, grinning into the receiver.

'You do have all the fun. I wish I had been there.'

'I was wondering whether you would like to come out for a drink some night?' McLeish plunged, deciding it was now or never. He held his breath through the slight pause that ensued.

'Yes, I should like to.' He let out the breath, carefully. 'What night had you in mind?'

'Tonight?'

'I can't.' The clear voice sounded genuinely regretful. 'I have a dinner for my old college. This particular festivity comes round once every five years.'

'Tomorrow any good?' McLeish, drawing confidence from the careful explanation, decided to push on.

'I have one thing to do, but I could meet you afterwards. Peregrine — you know, my brother — is recording an edition of "Sacred Music for a Sunday" or similar for the BBC. They rehearse all day, then record with a live audience at 6.30. It takes about an hour and a half, so I'll be through by eight. Actually you could come and be audience too, if it would amuse you. We have a spare ticket because another brother is also in the show as part of the Bach Choir.'

'I'd like that. Can I take you to supper afterwards?'

'That would be very nice.' Francesca sounded both pleased and mildly surprised, and McLeish found himself beaming at the telephone.

He listened with amusement as she attempted to instruct him about where to park, and observed with some firmness that the studio was in his manor and he would cope.

'All right, then. Come in a police motorcade, see if I'm embarrassed,' she said amicably. He was laughing as he said goodbye, and looked up to see his sergeant, balancing two cups of coffee, closing the door with an elbow.

'Got a date? Told you so, nae bother.'

'I have got a date, yes, but it seems to involve going with her mother and two of her brothers to hear two other brothers record a semi-religious song programme for the telly. I think we are having dinner by ourselves afterwards.'

'That's what all the girls do in Ayr,' Davidson observed, unsurprised.

'They take a brother or a cousin along on the first date. If everything's all right, the brother goes off with his mates, but at least the bloke's understood that the girl has family who mind on her.'

McLeish gazed at him, wondering whether the Wilson family could really be operating on the same conventions as appeared to govern the social behaviour of decent Scottish working-class families. 'Does the mother come too, on a first date?' he enquired.

'Aye, whiles. It depends. Where are you going to take the lass? I know a decent Italian place, he does a good meal and there'll be no embarrassment. No villains there, and not too many of the lads.'

'I don't want it complimentary.' McLeish spoke warningly, knowing his man.

'No, he won't offer unless he's asked,' Davidson said soothingly.

McLeish blenched, but decided to take the recommendation: it would be a good meal, and he knew nowhere else respectable round there.

* * *

Back at the Department of Trade and Industry, Henry Blackshaw was sitting, with the telephone cradled between his shoulder and his ear, doodling irritably as he listened to Britex's Managing Director.

'I thought it might be better not to start in London.' Peter Hampton was sounding weary. 'We still have the police here.'

Henry thought about this and decided it was nonsense. 'Mr Hampton, a police investigation on a murder case is likely to drag on a bit, isn't it? And the affairs of your company will not stand delay. I think the only way to proceed in this case is for my people to come in as arranged and get started. If we have to work round the police, we'll manage that too. In any case, we'll mostly want to collect papers on the first visit and take them away.'

Hampton did not receive this plan with any enthusiasm, but Henry gently overrode his objections. So worn out by the whole thing, poor bugger, that he just wanted to find a hole and pull it in after him. He dealt patiently with Hampton's last-ditch attempt to stall them, which involved the suggestion that Francesca might be too delicate and impressionable to work effectively in a situation where one of the staff had been brutally murdered. He decided as he put down the phone that the nerveless Francesca had better be warned that she was expected to show some maidenly delicacy and went, grinning to himself, down the passage to find her. Her office was, as usual, crowded, containing Rajiv as well as Martin Bailey, who was doing the main casework on Britex.

'Are you coming with us, Henry?' she asked disapprovingly. 'You are supposed to be running the place, not doing the casework yourself.'

'Fair point,' Henry acknowledged. 'But it's my field, textiles, and I want to do this one personally. Part of the learning process,' he added firmly, seeing Francesca still look doubtful.

'It's a big rescue,' Martin Bailey confirmed. 'Even off the published figures they need a £6m slug to keep the bank at bay.'

'It'll turn out much worse than that when we get in and have a look.' Henry spoke from long experience. 'So, I am leading this expedition; we are getting there at 8.30; and we'll visit the factory in Yorkshire next Monday — if that is all right with you, Francesca?'

'Sorry, Henry, purely personal preoccupation rather than disapproval,' she said, blushing. 'I'm dining at the American Embassy on Monday, and it is rather an upmarket bash, so I'd like time to change before dinner.'

'That'll be alright. I have a dinner in London myself.' Henry noticed Rajiv's gaze fixed thoughtfully on her, and wondered what he had missed.

'Francesca,' Rajiv said, 'Bill Westland would like a word with you. Could you drop by his office?'

'What about?'

'He did not honour me with his confidence. He is free now, I understand.'

'He'll have to wait till I've finished this,' Fran said dismissively and Rajiv, raising his eyes to heaven, collected Henry and went off down the corridor.

'She is remarkably cavalier about a summons from a Deputy Secretary, even if he does happen to be her godfather. Ah well, she'll learn.'

'What is it about this dinner at the Embassy?'

'Ah. Clever of you to notice. It is expected that she will meet there a very good friend of hers, the junior Senator from West Virginia, one Michael O'Brien. He is important in all sorts of complicated ways to our relationship with the Americans, and important to Fran in a quite specific way.'

'The chap she had an affair with?'

'Yes. I rather suspect that Bill Westland, put up to it by the Foreign Office, is going to ask her to put over a few messages about this and that at dinner.' He considered, the black eyes wide with speculative amusement. 'This would be ill-advised, since Fran was brought home early from Washington because their relationship was causing concern to the wetter of the Foreign Office policymakers.' He glanced at Henry who was slowly absorbing the implications. 'On the whole, Henry, it might be better if you could contrive to get the whole party marooned in Yorkshire. We should pray for snow.'

They had their sweet nerve, the policymakers, Henry thought, and enquired with interest of Rajiv what he thought Francesca would do. Rajiv pondered the question carefully and gave it as his view that the most likely outcome was that she would read Bill Westland, her godfather and a man thirty years her senior, a lecture on ethics, and refuse absolutely to cooperate.

'Her mother is a Scot,' he pointed out, 'and she comes by all this naturally. Ah, Bill, good evening.' He started to his feet, a little disconcerted, as Bill Westland swept in, looking furious.

'Have you got Francesca?'

'We thought you had, Bill.'

'Oh I had, blast the girl!' He glared at them both and sat down heavily. 'It's not altogether unreasonable of the FCO to hope that Fran would pass on a few tactful messages, particularly about New Jersey Steel. I mean she does work for HMG, we are all on the same side. Damned girl read me a lecture on ethics.' Rajiv's mouth quirked uncontrollably, and Henry hastily blew his nose. 'Told me to give the FCO the two-finger response, and then offered to do it herself if I found it too difficult from where I sat.' Rajiv and Henry made hasty, incoherent noises of sympathy. 'Trouble is, she can't do that. I'll have to invent some more flexible response for the FCO's benefit.'

'Why can't she?' Henry enquired, with interest. 'I thought no one could fire a civil servant.'

'No, that's right, she can't be fired. But it's a long life, we all know each other, we are all stuck with each other, rather like being in a religious order. If she offends the FCO at this stage, she'll somehow find herself blocked at some critical career point. She'll never know it happened, but she just won't get where she should. It doesn't take much, in a service where there is no shortage of excellent candidates for every good job. Protecting Francesca is, I must say, a difficult and thankless task but I had better try it. Send her to me when she surfaces, will you?'

He heaved himself out of the chair and went back down the corridor, leaving Rajiv and Henry trying not to meet each other's eyes.

Five minutes later Henry's door crashed open, and Francesca appeared, looking like a thundercloud. Rajiv rose smoothly, observing that he thought that was all that needed to be settled tonight Henry, and departed at speed. Henry wondered what he had done to be left to deal with Francesca in this mood, but was not intimidated.

'As the Minister said yesterday, Francesca, every time I see your smiling face come round my door I know there is trouble.'

'It's not you I'm cross with.'

'It's my wastepaper basket you're kicking, lass. What's the matter? Have a drink and tell me. Or don't, but stop circling about, I'm getting dizzy.'

She hesitated, then accepted a hefty double whisky and sat down.

He went on working, a drink at his elbow, waiting for her to settle.

'I've heard a bit about all this from Rajiv,' he volunteered into the silence, not looking at her as he worked.

'You've probably heard it all, knowing Rajiv.' She took a huge swallow of her drink and sighed. 'I think it is unreasonable of the Foreign Office to try and have it both ways, but I mind about steel as well, so I'll do what the bastards want and have a word with Michael.' She brooded, gazing out of the window. 'Don't ask how, is all I have to say.'

'What would your dad have told you to do?'

'I guess to do what they ask with good grace or refuse utterly. Or that's what people tell me he was like. He died when I was twelve, you see and was ill a lot before that, so I don't really know. I have to work it out for myself.'

'Or take it from me as a chap nearly old enough to be your dad.'

Henry spoke through a stab of appalling pity. 'You've a cool head, when you let yourself think. If you think you have to do it, then stop being angry and do it well.'

He thought for a moment he had been too blunt, but she smiled at him, sadly. 'They do miss the point, don't they? It's going to be quite difficult enough seeing Michael again without having to pass messages about steel financing.'

'A classic problem,' Henry observed, seeing her near tears. 'When do you start this conversation?'

'After the soup, surely?'

'And before the coffee.'

She smiled at him, blinking back tears. 'I can't believe you've only been here three days.'

'No more can I.'

'I expect life in the textile industry was much better regulated.'

'That's right girl. I thought I was going to be bored rigid in the Civil Service. I reckoned without you.' They looked at each other for a long moment, and Henry reminded himself that he was of an age with her dead father.

'Thanks, Henry. I'll go and make peace with Bill.'

He waved her out of the office, and decided he had better take himself out to dinner, smartly.

CHAPTER 8

It was a frankly miserable group that assembled next day at Britex's offices in Paddington. Henry had slept badly, Martin had been to the Annual Dinner of the London Chartered Accountants, and Francesca had been to a college reunion and made do with five hours' sleep, since she had got up at 6 a.m. to reread the Britex papers. Sartorially they were a pretty mixed bag, too. It was a cold, raw day and, huddled into a sheepskin coat, Henry felt like a bookie. Martin was wearing a suit with a heavy anorak over it, while Francesca had come as a Sloane Ranger in an expensive camel-hair coat which robbed her skin of all colour, long boots and a Gucci headscarf which did nothing for her classic long face.

Matters hardly improved as they arrived at the Managing Director's office to be met by an apologetic secretary who explained that Mr Hampton was down at Edgware Road police station signing a statement about poor Mr Fireman and would be delayed for at least an hour. She offered them an office, some coffee, and the Chief Accountant, then, flustered, had to withdraw item three when it transpired that Mr Hampton had left instructions that no one, but no one, was to talk to the visitors unless he was present. Henry, who perfectly understood the reasoning, accepted the office and the coffee, and decided to take the risk of being overheard and to use the time to educate his troops. He got Martin to outline the company's financial problems, then raised an eyebrow at Francesca, curious to see how much she had understood.

'They can't pay their interest, they are under pressure from creditors, but if they can sell the household-textile business, which is a real bummer, then they can pay off a few bills, lighten the load at the bank, and we can give them some money to reorganize the thermal-undie side.'

'Good as far as it goes,' Henry observed cautiously.

'As I understand it, we do have to decide whether the thermal-underwear side is viable, whether it can generate enough profit and enough cash to keep itself going. In my view it can't.' Martin Bailey spoke bluntly. 'No point at all in assisting a business if you have to do it every six months.'

'I couldn't agree more,' Francesca said promptly. 'But it is profitable, isn't it? Or did I read the papers upside-down?'

Both men shook their heads.

'Look Fran,' Martin said earnestly, 'Turnover of £20m in that business, and they made £250,000 trading profit, which is just over 1 per cent. For a start they probably didn't make that — it all depends on how good they are at valuing their stock, and I don't think either Henry or I would be amazed to find something very wrong with that. We'll find out when we visit the factory in Yorkshire.' He glanced apologetically at Henry, suddenly shy. Henry nodded, reflecting that the young man had the makings of a really good accountant, and pointed out that even if the stock were properly valued and they were making that profit, the business was fragile. It was a tiny profit given the turnover, and Britex just was not making enough gross margin, probably because the margin was not there to be made, textiles being severely depressed and under threat from imports. And of course, it could not fund interest off that slender profit.

'Surely this a function of volume? It is a high-fixed-cost business, is it not, and a small increase in volume increases profit very sharply.'

Francesca was sitting huddled in her chair, hands wrapped round her coffee cup.

'That is undoubtedly what will be argued,' Henry agreed. 'We have to decide how many more thermal vests the market can absorb, and whether they are going to buy them from Britex or from someone else. In this industry — which, as you will remember Francesca, is where I come from — there are certain hard facts. There is substantial over-capacity, which means you have to keep your prices down and work bloody hard to sell. I've had a look at their prices against their competitors. They are selling at about 10 per cent below the Marks and Spencer suppliers, and they'll have to go on doing that to be in with a chance.'

He fell silent, reckoning that Francesca had enough to digest. She was concentrating so hard that the coffee, the room, himself and Martin might as well not have existed.

She emerged from her trance to observe, 'So it has to be a two-pronged rescue plan. No, don't look like that, Henry, let me witter on. For me — that is to say, for the Minister — there are 1,400 jobs at risk in a black spot and Ministers are not going to see them go without testing all the theories to destruction.' She hunched forward, eyes slightly crossed. 'So Britex needs to get costs down and the sales up — why are you both laughing like that?'

'No, no, Fran, that's absolutely right, it's just that you sound like the Secretary of State.'

'There is no need to be rude. So it hasn't done these two simple things — bear with me, Martin — either because they ain't so simple, or because they are simple but you need cash and they don't got none.'

'Or both,' Henry agreed, amicably. 'When you see a well-managed business, you see a virtuous circle; sales go up, generating cash, some of which you can apply to devices for keeping costs down, some of which you apply to methods of generating more sales, like hiring extra salesmen, or opening shops, or whatever. This business here is in a vicious circle. I do not need to talk to the MD to know that about three months ago they cut the sales force, and that they buy materials in an expensive way because they do not have the cash to place their orders well ahead.'

'You've been reading the management accounts,' Martin said reproachfully. 'The sales force was reduced by 27 per cent four months ago, and gross margins are down to 18 per cent. And their material costs are 2 or 3 per cent higher than Allied's, for example.'

'Are they now? That's a little more than I would have expected.'

Henry sounded thoughtful, but discussion was cut off by the entrance of the Managing Director, Peter Hampton, full of apologies, but a good deal less stressed and more cheerful than when they had seen him at the Department two days before. On his own ground, of course, Henry thought, but was relieved to find him in a more receptive mood.

Hampton brightened visibly when he saw Francesca, and held her hand longer than necessary as he greeted her.

'Was the chap who was murdered a friend?' Francesca with her customary directness had cut through the apologies, and Peter Hampton looked momentarily disconcerted.

'Well, not really. But he had been forty years with the company and was very important to the purchasing function. As I told the police.'

'What do they think happened?' Henry enquired courteously.

'They tell me it's most likely to have been a drug addict prepared to take anything he could get.' Peter Hampton sounded unconcerned and Francesca looked disapproving. He caught her eye. 'I don't mean to sound callous, I'm sorry, but the truth is that my first thought was, how were we going to manage the purchasing function? I have to go up tonight and see his family, and it will hit me then.' He looked steadily at Francesca who was openly thinking about him. 'That's stress for you, I suppose; all humanity lost.'

'What police did you see? It's my local nick, I live round the corner.'

'Very competent chap called McLeish.' Francesca, slightly pink, explained that she had met him with her pop-star brother who had contributed to the load on an over-worked police force in the area.

Henry called the meeting to order and worked carefully through his list of questions and documents needed, the two juniors both taking notes. He looked up at the clock, and was surprised to find that it was 12.30. Hampton followed his glance, and promptly offered lunch.

'Breakfast was a long time ago,' he observed.

'And you've been answering questions ever since,' Francesca said, grinning.

'Yes. And the police were much easier than you lot.' Hampton laughed back at her, plainly charmed, and Henry noticed again that this was an attractive man and that Francesca liked the look of him.

'I'd love some lunch,' she said, hopefully. 'I'm starving.'

'Well, in that case we have to eat, I see that.' Peter Hampton smiled at her. 'There's a good pub round the corner if that's all right?'

It was indeed a good pub and all four of them felt much better for a square meal. 'Extraordinary, isn't it?' Francesca observed, cleaning her plate with a piece of bread. 'Look at us. Life and energy has returned with a meal.'

'Or two meals,' Henry agreed, watching fascinated as Francesca ate the rest of Martin's chips and eyed Peter Hampton's plate hopefully.

'Do you want another dinner, then, Francesca?' Hampton had caught the look.

'No,' she said, considering the point. 'But I will eat your chips rather than have them go to waste.' Peter Hampton, plainly delighted, offered to go halves and they shared the rest.

'Where did you come from Peter? Before Britex, I mean.' Francesca finished her drink.

'I did an MBA at Manchester, then trained as an accountant with Peat's in Birmingham, worked there for three years, then went to Droitplex as Finance Director. I always wanted to be an MD, so when I was offered Britex three years ago I jumped at it. I didn't realize quite what a mess the business was in.'

'Over-extended, I take it?' Henry asked.

'Yes, and not much management — the ones we've kept are all right, but not that much calibre; the Finance Director was a disaster, and it took me too long to get rid of him.' He was ostensibly addressing Henry but his attention was focused on Francesca.

'Not an easy trade, either,' she said, politely.

'Bit of a disaster all round,' he agreed. 'But maybe we can bring it round with some help?' Francesca, caught unawares, fumbled for an answer while he watched her.

'Do you have a family, Peter?' Henry came swiftly to the rescue, annoyed by this attempt to put pressure on his staff.

'Two sons, who live with my wife.'

'How old are they?' Francesca, poise restored, asked with interest.

'Nine and seven. I see them once a month. You married, Francesca?'

'Divorced, but no children.' They looked at each other steadily, and Henry felt the hairs at the back of his neck prickle.

'Unless you want anything else to eat, Fran, like a second pudding or cheese, we ought to get back,' he said briskly, and called for the bill. Peter Hampton fetched Francesca's coat and helped her on with it, leaving Henry and Martin to extract theirs from an overloaded coat rack.

'I'd like to invite you out for a drink,' he said to her, glancing to make sure that Henry and Martin were out of earshot. 'I expect it is against the rules.'

'It is, at this stage. But thank you for the thought. Perhaps when all this is over?' She smiled at him, and Henry, emerging from the Gents, saw the smile and realized, abruptly, that this girl mattered to him, and he a happily married man with teenage children. He returned to collect her, noting with relief that Peter Hampton was openly disappointed with whatever she had said to him. They emerged, all slightly flushed, into the cold November day.

'We should pray for snow,' Francesca observed, dancing down the street.

'Oh yes,' Peter Hampton agreed fervently. 'Any amount of it. It would do our sales more good than a price cut.'

They said goodbye to each other on the pavement, the three civil servants leaning slightly sideways against the weight of their briefcases. 'I'm not nursing any great hopes, you know,' Hampton said directly to Francesca. 'I know the business is in a hell of a mess, and the industry prospects are poor. It's the work force I mind about.'

'That's what Ministers are going to mind about, too,' Francesca pointed out. 'Don't let's jump to conclusions. My good colleagues here can struggle with the numbers and let's see where we get to. We'll be with you in Yorkshire next week.' She caught Henry's eye, obviously remembered who was supposed to be in charge of the party and said hastily that she understood at least that these were the arrangements that had been made. Everybody shook hands, Hampton holding on to Francesca's while he said his goodbyes, and the civil servants hailed a passing taxi.

'Martin, we need those numbers crunched, quickly. Will you please work out exactly the percentage difference in material costs between this lot and what Allied is paying. I may be able to help there, but I need to understand what it is and how it comes about. I want you also to think about cash control — I have an impression it is not as good as it ought to be. What are they doing with the seconds? Do they go to market stalls; who looks after the cash there?'

'Right.' Martin was writing notes to himself, slowly, in immaculately neat handwriting.

'I have to report to the Minister in a preliminary note,' Francesca volunteered helpfully. 'I will put it through you Henry, so you can comment.'

Henry thanked her gravely, and she fell silent while he went back to brooding about the company. 'What did you think of Hampton?' he demanded, generally. 'I thought him much less resistant and difficult today.'

'Well, he had finished with the police, hadn't he?' Francesca observed, reasonably. 'And he was obviously cheered by the fact that the police saw no connection between the murder and the company. I mean, the poor chap wasn't killed on duty, or as a result of an industrial accident for which managers must blame themselves.'

'I suppose that's it,' Henry acknowledged. 'All the same, I was only quite impressed, so I will ask around in the trade to get a cross-bearing.'

'He was cheered up by having Francesca around, too,' Martin said, grudgingly, and she eyed him thoughtfully.

'I don't suppose he meets many women running a factory in Yorkshire. Or not many women who don't work for him. Makes a change.' She spoke entirely dispassionately and without false modesty, and Henry considered her with respect.

'Any road,' he said, 'I don't suppose I need say it but it would be unwise to mix socially in this situation because it could compromise us.'

'If you mean me, I know that,' Francesca said, amused. 'It's just the same as leading them on to believe we are going to rescue them if we aren't.'

'We'll have to think very carefully about this lot,' Henry confirmed. 'I'm going to drop you two at the Department and go on and try to talk to an old mate at Allied, see if I can clear my mind. I'll be back later.'

CHAPTER 9

John McLeish was a conspicuous figure in any surroundings, but standing in the entrance hall at Lime Grove he was something else, Francesca thought, pausing at the door. He was not watching the door but someone in the crowd of performers, editors, technicians and their friends. She admired his absolute concentration for a moment, then went over to him and touched his sleeve. He smiled down at her, coming out of his trance.

'Someone over there you know?' she asked.

'Yes. I'll worry about him later. How are you?'

'Just fine, thank you,' Francesca replied demurely, basking in his obvious admiration. She had found time to bath and to wash her hair which was indeed still damp behind her ears. Her calf-length black coat with its high stand-up collar was smart without being oppressively so, and she was justifiably confident about the long-sleeved blue silk dress underneath as well. He was still looking down at her, and she felt a sharp thump of excitement.

'Have you found the others?' she asked. 'No, how could you, you haven't met the rest of us.'

'That has to be your family over there, doesn't it?'

She followed his nod, and indeed there they were, Charlie, his dark blond hair falling into his eyes as usual because he was worried that his hairline at the front was receding, and Jeremy, dark and olive-skinned like Peregrine but a bit taller, both flanking her mother who was looking very prosperous in a fur coat.

'Come on, then.' They threaded their way through the crowd, and Fran's family greeted her with kisses and McLeish with obviously habitual friendliness. McLeish, who had been watching Francesca's mother with particular interest, looked down into Francesca's blue eyes set in a plump, square face, totally unlike Francesca's and Perry's Norman bones. He exchanged courtesies, distracted by Francesca who was stroking her mother's coat and teasing her about it, as her mother confessed that Perry had bought it for her.

'I suppose you have the television and a bungalow already,' she observed sardonically. 'Did you go to the Probation Officers' Committee in it? They'll know what to think, won't they?'

Mrs Wilson rose magisterially above this, and said easily to McLeish that she rather thought she had seen him at Edgware Road, could that be? She was the probation officer for the Halligan boys and thought that she had seen him on that case. McLeish agreed that the Halligan boys were also customers of his. A dreadful pair, he thought silently, considering this pleasant middle-aged lady; how did she cope?

'Almost the definition of incorrigible.' An amused voice, pitched higher than Francesca's.

'All of that. And dangerous.' McLeish spoke soberly, and noticed the three Wilson children prick up their ears.

'Darlings,' Mrs Wilson had noticed them too, 'they visit me at an office next door to the police station. If anything happened to me they would be the first suspects. And anyway, they think I am a harmless old fool.' She beamed at her children, the blue eyes alight with amused malice, and they considered her with something between pride and exasperation.

'Oh well, useless to argue, but do remember we five would be orphans if you were taken.' Francesca turned away momentarily to talk to Jeremy, leaving McLeish to observe that Mrs Wilson was the source of Francesca's elegant legs though otherwise none of the children looked like her. It must have been the late Mr Wilson who had the long nose and the high cheekbones and the high rounded arch above the brows. And presumably he had treated his wife with just the same gently amused and patronizing affection which the children used to her. In which, he thought, they were wholly mistaken, but for reasons of her own Mrs Wilson was playing it that way.

'Hello, Sheena.' Jeremy was beaming as Sheena Roberts, spectacular in red silk, came towards them, turning every head in the hall. Jeremy was openly adoring, and McLeish could feel Francesca bristle. Charlie's admiration was obviously sincere, but McLeish noticed that he was not in fact attracted to her at all.

'Where's Perry?'

All the Wilsons looked at her blankly, but Mrs Wilson recovered first. 'He has to sit down and think about what he is going to do when he sings. He needs at least half an hour to himself before he performs. I'm so sorry you've just missed him.'

The explanation plainly struck Sheena as unsatisfactory but she accepted it. 'Who's 'is backing group tonight, then?' she enquired.

'The Bach Choir,' said Francesca, unsmiling and with each syllable perfectly placed. McLeish kept his face straight with a horrendous effort but Charlie had to blow his nose. Jeremy gave his sister a look of deep reproach, and proceeded to bore Sheena with an explanation of the origin and make-up of the Bach Choir. Mercifully the bell rang to summon them to their places in the hall.

'Have you been to a recording like this before?' Francesca asked McLeish, who shook his head, reflecting that while a five-act play in Urdu would be fine with him, providing Francesca was beside him, the scene was intrinsically interesting. The small audience — probably not more than 400 people — was seated on a steeply sloping tier of seats looking down on a large, brightly lit stage, occupied mostly by the Bach Choir, also arranged in tiers. In front of them, and also brightly lit, was a smaller area containing a piano, two chairs and a flight of steps. To the left of the stage a small orchestra was assembled, whose personnel were mostly engaged in tuning up. The lights over the audience went down, and a comfortable, bearded man walked purposefully on the stage, introduced himself as the floor manager, and welcomed them all to 'Songs for a Sunday', offering a brisk outline of the programme's history and a description of tonight's guests.

'We may have to stop at any point to get a retake of some small part of the programme, but we try not to do that too much. We do ask you to save your applause till the end of each song, or piece of music, but then we'd like you to applaud so everyone at home can hear. And now, I would like to introduce you to the youngest of the performers tonight, Perry Wilson, who has shot to fame with his recording of "Wrong Road" which has just earned him a Golden Disc.'

He extended a hand and Perry walked from behind a flat at the side of the stage, moving neatly to avoid a coil of cable. He was dressed in a plain grey suit, very much like a school suit but with an elegance of cut that no school suit in the world could have achieved. He wore a pale blue shirt — McLeish remembered that white photographs badly on television — and a mid-blue, plain tie, and looked like the middle-aged housewife's dream young man, serious but sexy. He was greeted, unexpectedly, by shrieks of 'Perry, Perry' from the right-hand side of the audience, and Francesca leaned forward, scowling, to look.

McLeish had already noticed a row of peacock hairstyles towards the front of the audience, and it was towards this row that two large men were purposefully moving. Perry wisely ignored the demonstration altogether and directed his sudden dazzling smile to the row where his family and Sheena were sitting. He accepted the microphone, welcomed the audience again, and spoke briefly about the two songs he would be singing. The audience blatantly adored him, and there was a collective sigh as he left.

'They ought not to ask singers to talk to audiences first,' Francesca observed irritably. 'You can't do that if you are going to sing.'

McLeish courteously expressed interest, hoping he was not sounding sardonic. He realized however that Francesca's whole attention was concentrated on the stage where the rest of the cast was being introduced, ending with the hostess, Mary Sheen, a fading blonde in her fifties possessed of an astonishingly powerful soprano voice, who was received with real warmth by the audience.

More lights flickered out, the Bach Choir fell silent and still, as did the small orchestra, and powerful spotlights directed themselves on to the small area containing the chairs and the piano. Mary Sheen sat down in one of the chairs, a make-up girl hastily powdered her forehead, and she nodded to the floor manager. Cameras turned and swooped towards her, each one apparently in the custody of at least four men. The floor manager, behind the nearest of the cameras, held up his arm, and swept it down definitely, and Mary Sheen began to speak, addressing the camera as easily as if it were an old friend.

She was introducing Perry, describing his early career as a treble and his recent successes, and as she stretched out a hand in welcome, McLeish felt rather than saw the teenagers sit up as one woman. But under the severe survey of the BBC's security guards they managed to avoid any demonstration other than an instantly suppressed squeal of excitement.

Perry, acknowledging the introduction, was positioning himself by the piano, and unostentatiously sucking air into his diaphragm.

McLeish felt Francesca next to him breathe in sympathy. As the orchestra started up, she relaxed suddenly, and when he glanced at her he saw her intent on the stage, waiting in confident expectation.

As well she might, he realized about a minute later. Perry was singing *'Comfort ye, comfort ye my people'* from Handel's *Messiah,* and singing magnificently. It was a true, powerful, high tenor, superbly used. A musician, McLeish thought, listening to the beautiful, clean phrasing, who sang with real passion and the unmistakable urgent need to communicate the sense of what he sang. The audience was listening in a frozen, intent silence, hearing the command to take comfort, to believe, to understand that salvation would come, as a personal message.

'Every valley shall be exalted,' Perry sang, and the world brightened and the sun shone, and for McLeish the hall and the audience vanished as he returned to a childhood holiday on a cousin's farm in the Borders, and smelt again the grass in the sun, and felt the wind blowing cold on the tops. He was just conscious of Francesca beside him, unmoving, watching Perry as the golden voice, effortless and clear, sang on. *'And the rough places plain.'* He finished in a shower of grace notes, each separate and distinct. The orchestra played the final four bars and there was a full ten-second pause before ragged applause started and swelled to a crescendo as the audience woke from its trance.

'Fantastic,' McLeish said quietly to Francesca under cover of the applause.

'He's always like that.' She blew her nose and he saw that there were tears in her eyes. 'I never believe he is going to do it, but he does every time. In all other respects he is barely intelligent.' She spoke with an elder sister's resentful but total love.

On stage Mary Sheen was speaking warmly of Perry's talent, throwing in a graceful tribute to Handel in passing. Since they had been rehearsing all day, McLeish reflected that she was probably less amazed than the audience, but she was, endearingly, obviously moved by the performance.

The audience sat courteously through the Bach Choir and the ageing contralto singing hymns, and Mary Sheen singing 'Bless this House' with a slight but perceptible stretch on the top note at the end, but when Perry was once more announced they sat up and bristled with anticipation. What, McLeish wondered, in the words of the old tag, was he going to do as an encore after his stunning first solo? The pianist with some relish broke into the massed chords that constitute the introduction to Sir Arthur Sullivan's deeply felt piece of Victorian sentimentality, 'The Lost Chord', and Perry's golden voice came in quietly, every word perfectly articulated and distinct, the Bach Choir behind him, quietly 'aahing' in harmony. McLeish, less involved with the singing this time, reflected that actually Sheena had it right; the mighty Bach Choir was indeed acting as Perry's backing group on this occasion. Perry was enjoying himself, he thought, telling the audience the old fable of the composer who had once found a harmony so complete and so magical that it had seemed to encompass everything, but had lost it and had in the end concluded he would not find it again in this life. As they approached the last quatrain, the Bach Choir 'aahed' more loudly, working towards a crescendo; Perry's head went back as he sucked in air, and a truly astonishing amount of sound came out, as if an invisible volume control had been turned up. The clear high tenor rose effortlessly above the Bach Choir's best efforts, unforced and unstrained, every word audible.

'It may be that Death's bright angel Will speak in that chord again,
It may be that only in heaven I shall hear that grand amen.'

Perry concluded, and for a minute everyone in the audience felt the presence of the bright angel, so clearly did Perry see him. The applause cracked out more easily this time, but it could not be stopped. Mary Sheen gestured, helpless but smiling, to the director who signalled to the cameras to stop, and McLeish sat back, watching Francesca and remembering her singing with the tape of her brother's voice when he and Davidson had first met her, incredibly only four days ago. She felt him watching her, and grinned at him, indicating the floor manager, who had his right elbow crooked and hand held close to his face so he could see his watch in the half darkness while his left arm circled in a signal to unseen beings.

'Overtime coming up,' she murmured in his ear. 'If everyone doesn't get off the stage fast they'll be in trouble. All the lights will go out in about thirty seconds. I have been privileged, on a similar occasion, to witness the plug being pulled, leaving half the LSO and their instruments stranded centre stage in pitch darkness.'

McLeish saw that indeed the cast was leaving as rapidly as possible, Perry escorting Mary Sheen with that courteous undergraduate air. It must be the suit McLeish thought, darkly, remembering the dazzling creature in leather casuals and all the trimmings of the pop star whom he had first encountered. The Wilsons stood up, groping for coats and bags. Francesca looked past him at her mother and he saw them smile at each other with the dazzled pride of two parents. Of course, he thought, she must have taken her father's place.

'I wish I could sing like that,' blond Charlie observed amicably. 'He is extraordinary, isn't he?' His sister nodded, smiling, but McLeish noted that Jeremy was treating the whole occasion with some reserve.

'Jeremy and Tristram are also tenors,' his mother observed, drily.

'Charlie is a baritone, Francesca and I are altos.'

'Where are we having supper, darling?' Jeremy had obviously decided to change the subject. McLeish decided he had better assert himself quickly and said that he and Francesca had a table booked for 8.30, on the assumption that they would just have time to congratulate Perry. He observed that both the boys and Mrs Wilson looked disappointed, but decided to stand his ground. He glanced cautiously at Francesca to see if she was going to sabotage the plan, but she was beaming across the hall at Perry who was surrounded by teenagers for whom he was good-temperedly signing autographs. He grinned back at his sister, and then turned to kiss Sheena who had appeared from nowhere and was clinging prettily to his arm. Francesca scowled.

McLeish touched her arm in reproach and she looked at him, surprised.

He looked back at her, suddenly unable to speak or look away. How extraordinary, he thought, this is the girl I'm going to marry, this is how people feel and it's how they get married, and there she is. She looked back at him, seriously, frowning slightly.

'I must see Perry, then we can go,' she said, tentatively.

'Of course.' McLeish recovered, and the natural force of his personality reasserted itself. 'Follow me, lady.'

'Yes, well,' Perry observed as they arrived at his side, 'there must be advantages in being a foot taller than anyone else. How are you, Inspector?'

Every head in the crowd surrounding Perry turned to observe McLeish, who said imperturbably that he was well, and offered his congratulations. Francesca kissed her brother. 'Lovely,' she said, adding courteously, 'Didn't you think so, Sheena?' Sheena replied that she thought Perry had sung wonderful but that he was tired and needed to go home. Both Perry and Francesca looked surprised.

'But you're having dinner with Mum, aren't you? She is just over there with Charlie and Jeremy.'

'Perry.' Sheena pressed herself close to him. 'Can't we have an evening to ourselves? Can't the boys take your mum to dinner?' Perry glanced swiftly at Francesca who was looking grim, and then hopefully at McLeish who decided it was not for him to get Perry off the hook on which he had impaled himself.

'Mum.' Perry kissed his parent who had arrived, beaming with pleasure. 'How nice to see you. Would it be all right if we ate rather quickly, it's my fifth late night in succession.' Mrs Wilson's gaze swept comprehensively over the group and rested on Sheena.

'But of course, Perry. Why don't you just join us for a drink, and then you can go home and have a sandwich?'

So his mother lets him off hooks, McLeish noted. He touched Francesca's arm warningly, she was tense and obviously seething.

She nodded to him, then reached up and kissed Charlie, saying something quietly in his ear.

‘I’ve got plenty,’ he said indignantly. ‘It must be five years since I ran out of cash in a restaurant. What a bossy you are.’ He looked at McLeish who was trying very hard not to laugh. ‘Does she boss you around?’

‘Not yet,’ McLeish said demurely, and on that line removed Francesca firmly from the group amid a flurry of kisses and plans for lunch from her family.

‘What a bitch,’ she exploded, as they reached the carpark. ‘Mum was looking forward to going out to a glossy restaurant with her brilliant son.’

‘Your mother is a sensible woman not to compete for him.’ He opened the car door for her as she worked her way through this thought.

‘I suppose it’s sex,’ she observed, in the tones of one reluctantly recognizing cholera or schizophrenia. ‘It’s extraordinary, you know. Perry loves both Mum and me, but what he goes round with — well, none of them have as much as an O-level in needlework or knitting.’

McLeish considered her. ‘For a man, you see,’ he said cautiously, ‘it’s a question of what turns him on.’ For a moment he thought he had caused lasting offence but her face cleared, and she started to laugh.

‘Sorry. Boring for you. I must be hungry.’

Reads my mind and all, he thought with an alarmed sense of exhilaration, and drove sedately to the place Davidson had recommended. He was received with exactly the right balance of familiarity and deference, and was additionally cheered by the admiring attention that Francesca was attracting.

From a mixed beginning the evening turned to pure gold for him.

Francesca had resolutely decided to forget her brother’s behaviour and her mother’s disappointment and was enjoying herself. She was extraordinarily easy to talk to; it was such a quick, impatient mind, wholly unimpressed by received theory, rather like a first-class barrister’s. They had reached the pudding by now, and Francesca was working her way through a large fruit salad. McLeish considered the last ten years of his life, his eye registering almost unconsciously the presence of a noted villain several tables away. He sighed, and decided he had to start somewhere.

'Well, I did a year walking a beat — you've seen people do that, but it is where it all starts, where you learn to observe and see little things out of place, people doing odd things, wrong cars, all that. Then I moved into the CID where I had meant to go all along, and did two years in Tottenham. Then I did my Sergeant's exams, and I was sent to Bramshill for a year. Then the Flying Squad.' He looked at her hopefully, and she agreed that everyone had watched *The Sweeney*.

'But presumably it isn't quite as exciting as on the telly?'

McLeish thought about it, and opined that actually it was quite as exciting as portrayed, merely different, and that truth was a good deal stranger than anything that got on to the box. 'But it isn't policy or desk work — or rather, there is a lot of desk work, but it is entirely directed to solving today's problem and getting another villain put away. And you're fighting a war, which not everyone understands. No question of the people you're dealing with being on the same side, except when it suits them and then only for a day or two.'

'What happened to the idea of the friendly neighbourhood police force?'

'Not my field. The uniformed branch do that. I catch villains.'

He was leaning forward, looking much too big for the table, in the attempt to communicate and Francesca looked at him squarely, trying to consider him as a policeman as well as a highly fanciable man. It was easy to imagine him rushing from a car to catch a villain in the authentic television style. For all his height he moved quickly and easily, and the huge hands were in no way clumsy.

'What is the reward structure? I mean, what do you get good marks for in your trade?' She saw he was momentarily puzzled. 'I mean, in my trade, your seniors write reports on you every year, and they have to report on specific qualities, on a scale. Like, for example, "Willingness to accept responsibility" or "Numeracy". So we all, roughly speaking, understand what you get points for, and indeed what questions you have to attempt.'

McLeish considered her with great interest. 'It's a bit simpler than that in my field. It's all down to how many convictions you get. The best you can say of someone you work with is that he is a good thief-taker.'

Francesca reflected that this covered quite a lot of the qualities considered worthy of assessment by the Administrative Civil Service and said so. 'At least you know where you've been at the end of the day.'

'I'm not sure about that at all. My mum always says that housework isn't really satisfying because you only have to do it all again. You can feel like that when you're catching villains — there's always more where those came from.'

'As fast as you tidy one lot away, somebody gets a lot more out?'

'That sort of thing.' He smiled at her peacefully, thinking what a bright, talented creature she was, and it occurred to him to ask her what she had read at Cambridge.

'Law.'

'I expect you were good at it.' She did not comment and the implications suddenly occurred to him. 'Did you get a First?'

'No, no, a 2:1, but it didn't take any work,' she said, briskly spooning up the last of the juice, making a thorough job of it. He sat, dismayed, thinking about his own lame Second from Reading, for which he had sweated.

'It was a swindle. I have a photographic memory, so it was money for old rope.'

'Do you really?' McLeish was distracted from the horrendous implications of being involved with a girl who seemed to be more able than he was, by simple interest. 'Can you reproduce the pudding menu here, for instance?'

'No, because I didn't really look at it, and I have to do that. I mean, I have to focus. But if I do, for about forty-eight hours I can call up the relevant page, and read it. Absolutely invaluable for exams. Both Part 1 and Part 2 Law were feats of memory if you understood the subject.'

'I read Engineering and slogged for a Second.'

'Wrong subject for you, surely? I would have placed you in something more philosophical or more imaginative — history, I suppose.' Francesca spoke completely without coquetry, offering this view as a matter of professional judgement, and he sat, stunned, with new vistas opening before him.

'We didn't have anyone who thought like that at Reading,' he said when he got his breath back.

'Did you not? Cambridge was stuffed with people who thought like that, but I don't believe anyone would have bothered to tell me if I had not asked. I had a Classics scholarship — another subject where a photographic memory helps — but I didn't want to go on, so I asked what else I could do. The Principal suggested Law. With what result you see.'

McLeish found himself wondering at the close of this admirable history how the independent Francesca had ever come to seek advice.

Or brought herself to accept it, having sought it. The answer occurred to him. 'The Principal was a woman?'

'Well, yes, at Newnham.' She looked suspiciously at him, and he smiled innocently back. She might be academically as smart as paint but there was an awful lot she didn't know. He glanced up at the clock and was frankly staggered to see that it was 11.30, and that they had been there for nearly three hours. Francesca followed his gaze.

'I've got an 8.30 meeting,' she said, in amused horror. 'I'll never make it.'

'I'll get you home quickly,' he promised and did just that, depositing her at the door ten minutes later. She thanked him gravely for dinner and he thanked her, equally seriously, for taking him to hear Perry sing. He escorted her punctiliously to her door, and hesitated, trying to decide whether a social kiss on the cheek would be correct. She settled the question by reaching up and kissing him lightly, steadying herself with a hand on his shoulder. It affected them both like an electric shock, and as she stood back he saw that the blue eyes looked enormous, and the amusement had gone from her face.

'Will you come out at the weekend?' he asked, breathing out carefully.

'I'm here for the weekend, but I've got a dinner on Monday,' she said, and he noticed the slight reservation surrounding Monday.

Another bloke, he thought, his senses sharpened.

'Saturday?'

'That would be lovely.' But another bloke she isn't quite sure about, or who isn't available, he thought.

'Let yourself in, Francesca. I want to see you over the doorstep in this district.' She laughed at him, but did as she was asked, stopping to give him a tiny wave before she closed the door.

CHAPTER 10

McLeish was at his desk by 8.30 the next morning, still feeling a warm glow from the night before. He beamed at Davidson who walked in at 9.30 looking tired, but observing him carefully. Davidson grinned back.

'Had a good time did you? When are you seeing her again?'

'At the weekend — dunno after that. She's got a date on Monday.' He shook himself out of his preoccupation. 'Let's have another look at the Fireman file. I don't know what it is, but I don't think it is an ordinary mugging.'

Davidson sniffed. 'There are unkind coppers who might suggest you feel that because it involves a company where the lassie you have your eye on is also involved. There's nae sign of anything out of the way.'

McLeish was riffling through papers, hunting. 'His watch was taken, and his briefcase and his wallet, and none of them have turned up. The ordinary mugger would have ditched the empty wallet and the case, and pawned the watch. You couldn't sell it, it was initialled, rolled gold, and came for forty years' service with the one firm. We tried the pawnshops, I take it? Nothing? Doesn't that seem odd to you?'

Davidson thought. 'Not really. Even a stupid pawnshop owner might well remember that watch and who popped it.

I reckon the chappie threw it into the river along with the empty wallet and the case. Or he just put it in a bin.' Both men silently contemplated the unlikelihood of a gold watch's surviving the attentions of London's derelicts, or London's dustmen come to that.

McLeish tried again. 'Look, an ordinary thief doesn't kill a bloke except accidentally, and there was nothing accidental about this. This villain killed his man, taking some pains about it. Now either he is out of his head with drugs, in which case he'll turn a gold watch into cash quite quickly, or he is someone who knows that victim and meant to kill him, for some reason we haven't fathomed, in which case he will be afraid to get rid of the watch for fear the disposal points to him. And the watch hasn't turned up.'

'Guv'nor, he threw it in the river. All right, I know, you've got a feeling, haven't you?'

'Yes, I have. From the moment I saw the body.'

Davidson nodded resignedly. He had worked with McLeish for three years and knew that beneath that rugger-player exterior he was a highly imaginative and sensitive policeman, qualities which normally he suppressed rigidly since he was clear that most police work was best achieved by careful attention to detail and to routine; and he knew, as all policeman do, that most murders are committed by the obvious suspect. Typically there was absolutely no mystery about either the identity of the murderer or his motivation.

'Humour me, Bruce. Who could want to murder Fireman? He's a widower, three children, two grandchildren, all of them grief-stricken according to the Yorkshire end.'

'Ah. He had a wee girlfriend whom he was refusing to marry, and her brother topped him?' offered Davidson obligingly.

'He lived next door to his mother, aged eighty-eight, and went in every day,' McLeish reported gloomily, finding the relevant paragraph.

'Played bowls, churchgoer, sidesman indeed. No other hobbies.'

‘Not much space for a wee girlfriend in that,’ Davidson agreed. ‘But you never know. Will the Yorkshire force do much more for you?’

‘Very much within limits. They are sure it was a mugger — London being entirely populated with them, as all in Yorkshire know — and in any case they have their hands full. They have the Moors Rapist on the loose still, and it is coming up to the full moon.’

‘Who inherits Fireman’s cash?’

‘His children, equally. There is only really a house, and £5,000 in savings. £50,000 all in, perhaps. Yorkshire report both sons in good jobs and the daughter well married.’

Davidson fell silent, feeling that he had done his bit for creative thinking, and not liking to reiterate his own strongly held view that the wretched Fireman had met a thief crazed by drink or drugs with consequences as certain as running into a three-ton truck.

‘I’ll maybe go up there.’ McLeish sounded dogged. ‘I may get a better feel for the case than I can here. I ought to go to the funeral — that’s Wednesday.’

‘They rang from Yorkshire?’ Davidson had been asked to establish the day of the funeral but had not had time that day.

‘No, no. Francesca — Miss Wilson — mentioned it in passing. She and her colleagues had wanted to visit the factory on the Wednesday, but had had to change to Monday to avoid the funeral.’ McLeish kept his head down, but Davidson could see he had turned pink. He was beginning to worry that McLeish, having plainly fallen like a ton of bricks for the girl, was letting his judgement be dangerously distorted.

But attending the victim’s funeral was a step conventional enough to go unnoticed, and McLeish’s lasting belief in routine meant that he was at the same time working his way through all the registered addicts and other customers with a record of violence in the district, at the same time as he was engaging in flights of speculation. They worked steadily through the rest of the caseload, fighting the losing battle to keep up with the paper which is the key to all good police work. Davidson, working separately, arrived at the Byers case, and lifted his head.

'Anything else on Byers?'

'I managed a word with Peregrine — Mr Wilson — at the concert last night, and with Mrs Byers. No worry, all funny phone calls stopped.'

Davidson nodded. No further trouble to be expected either, he thought; it shouldn't take that family of well-informed villains long to grasp that the whole Wilson family was under the personal protection of a detective inspector at one of the toughest stations in London.

Secure in this conviction, he marked the file to go into the central system, so that he could clear a space in his crammed filing cabinets.

He listened with half an ear as McLeish made the phone calls necessary to get himself to Yorkshire for the funeral and to chat with the local force, and with rather more attention as McLeish cleared Saturday night — the young Miss Wilson being available, he remembered — and volunteered himself to work late on Monday — Miss Wilson being at a dinner.

'I need the whole weekend off though, guv'nor,' he reminded McLeish when he paused for breath. 'My lassie is here for Saturday and Sunday.'

'That's fine — I had remembered. When had you planned to join us again?'

'Monday, if that's all right? You know where I am.'

In the event it was not until just before midnight on Monday that they met again, McLeish having been distracted in the interim by a robbery with violence that had left an Indian sub-postmaster in hospital with two bullets in his spine, and Davidson by a rape case. Davidson and he ate in a McDonald's hastily, Davidson treating his exhausted superior with some care.

'No connection with the Fireman case?' he asked cautiously. 'Just round the corner, wasn't it?'

'No, I mean, yes it was just round the corner but no connection. This one was a professional, wore a mask and used a shooter. Same as the Notting Hill Gate job last month. Poor bloody sub-postmaster, taking his duties seriously, wouldn't show him how to open the safe so he shot him in front of his wife and made her open it. Real villain, no frenzy there; just the sort I want tucked away for a good long stretch.'

Davidson offered to drive back to the station, and McLeish had just closed his eyes thankfully in the passenger seat when the radio summoned them urgently. Davidson snatched the receiver in an attempt to prevent McLeish being woken, and all but drove the car off the road at the message.

'Mrs Byers hurt? What happened? No, nae bother, we're on our way.'

Cursing, he flung the car round the next corner, oversteering, so that McLeish as he struggled awake again was thrown hard against his seat belt.

'What happened? No need to take the lamp post with you.'

'Sorry. Attack on Mrs Byers outside young Wilson's house.'

'Never!' McLeish sounded appalled. 'It's an insult.'

'Yes,' Davidson agreed, and glanced at his superior who was sitting bolt upright, bristling, the dark hair standing up. Not a sight you would wish to meet on a dark night. 'The ambulance is behind us, by the way.'

McLeish turned slightly in his seat, shading his eyes against the headlights, and Davidson swung the car out of the way, pulling out immediately to follow the ambulance. The small convoy reached Perry Wilson's house three minutes later, blue lights flashing, reflecting off the walls as curious faces appeared at every window.

Davidson slid the car's nearside wheels on to the pavement, clear of the ambulance so as not to restrict its exit, and he and McLeish piled out to join three ambulancemen bent over a huddled figure lying almost underneath the open door of the brown Rolls. Long dark hair lay like a fan across the pavement and McLeish drew breath sharply as he saw that she lay in a pool of blood, with more blood pouring from the side of her head just underneath the hairline.

'No sign of spinal damage. We're moving her.' The senior ambulanceman spoke without deference.

'Yes, carry on.' McLeish had a notebook out, and was drawing swiftly, marking the position of the body and the car, while Davidson drew a chalk line around the recumbent Sheena, both of them so concentrated that they only belatedly noticed Peregrine weeping with distress as he clung to Sheena's outstretched hand. Davidson efficiently shifted him to get some space for the ambulancemen, who had clapped a pad to Sheena's head and were manoeuvring her on to a stretcher. The whole process took astonishingly little time, and Perry, galvanized, had only just time to scramble into the ambulance with her.

'Going to St Mary's,' the driver called to McLeish, as he pulled out.

McLeish nodded, and stood for a moment working out what to do next.

'Anyone see the attack?' he enquired generally of Perry's motley retinue who were arranged variously around the car and on the steps of the house.

'No.' The pony-tailed driver-cum-bodyguard was white with shock and rage. 'I can't think why Sheena went outside — we'd told her not to, and I'd have gone for whatever she wanted. She can't drive. All I heard was a scream and a thud, and I didn't think it had anything to do with us anyway. I did go and look straightaway though,' he added, catching McLeish's cold eye. 'But it took a minute to work out what I'd heard, know what I mean?'

McLeish established that he was talking to one Michael Howden, commonly known as Biff. 'Why did Mrs Byers go outside?'

'You mean Sheena? I dunno. She was sitting there, then she said, shit, she'd forgotten something, and went out the room. She never came back and we heard this scream.'

'She was getting something from the car, wasn't she?' volunteered another member of the entourage. McLeish nodded and walked round to look at the car. Just inside the passenger door, on the ample floor, lay a briefcase, with the familiar EIIR device showing clearly in the streetlights. He squinted round to look at the label without touching the case. *'F. M. Wilson, Department of Trade and Industry'*: of course — Francesca's case. Who else in that group would carry a Government-issue briefcase?

'Francesca,' he said to Davidson, assailed by a cold panic.

'Thought of that,' Davidson said. 'We can be wrong all the way after all. No answer from the phone, so I've asked the uniformed boys to go round and ring the bell. And camp on her doorstep, if need be.'

'Look.' It was the pony-tailed Biff, intelligence taking over from rage. 'He was after Sheena, wasn't he? He can't have got round to Francesca as well in the time. She's at the American Embassy, I took her there — you could ring them up.'

McLeish looked under his eyelashes at Davidson, who nodded slightly, meaning that was in hand.

'Why didn't Sheena ask me to get the flaming briefcase?'

'Did she forget to do it earlier, and not feel like asking you?' McLeish asked thoughtfully, and Biff nodded.

'That'll be it,' he said, with conviction. 'That's what she did, she remembered, and she felt badly, so she went to get it herself, forgetting we'd told her not to go out on her own.'

Yes, well, thought McLeish as he drove off to St Mary's, that was all straightforward enough, but where was Francesca? Did Embassy dinners really go on until 12.30, or had she run into trouble on the way home? Well, the uniformed branch were looking for her and he had a job to do, and he drove through the night trying to suppress the inward vision of Francesca, huddled as Sheena had been, in a pool of blood.

Two hours later the position was wholly unimproved. None of Perry's retinue, nor Perry himself had seen either the attack or the attacker.

Mr Byers had been dragged protesting from his bed at around 2 a.m., and, having no alibi and plenty of time in which to have got home after any assault, was residing in the cells at Edgware Road, refusing to answer any questions whatsoever without the presence of his solicitor. Sheena, deeply unconscious, was in intensive care.

Francesca had apparently vanished into thin air, the dinner at the Embassy having decorously concluded towards midnight. It was now two and a half hours after that time, but she had not returned home, nor, as McLeish grimly supposed must be some consolation, been found lying in a pool of blood anywhere. He put his head down on the table and fell instantly asleep, an ability which most policemen acquire early as an alternative to leaving the force.

* * *

An hour later McLeish forced himself to the surface, with Davidson's voice in his ear.

'The good news is that we've found her, and she's perfectly safe. She spent the evening since leaving the Embassy under the eyes of six of the Special Branch's finest, and she is on the way home now with one of their drivers.'

McLeish rubbed his eyes, feeling tears of tiredness and relief not far below the surface. Then he remembered Davidson's preamble.

'And the bad news?'

'Ah.' Davidson, uninvited, sat down on the opposite side of the desk, swinging his legs, half turned to the door. 'The Special Branch were not, of course, laid on to look after Miss Wilson, but to ensure the safety of Senator Michael O'Brien — ye mind who he is? Yes, well he is apparently an old friend of Miss Wilson's and they went on for a wee dram at the Dorchester where he and his people are staying.'

Addressing the door rather than McLeish, he added that the Special Branch laddie, sensing some personal interest, had volunteered that it had been arranged well in advance that

Miss Wilson would join the party, and that a driver had been on standby to take her home in the early hours of the morning. The Special Branch laddie had no doubt felt himself to be helpful in volunteering this entirely gratuitous information.

'No doubt.' McLeish sourly digested this unwelcome piece of news.

He had been experienced enough to realize that there was another man currently in his Francesca's life, but that adult realization did not save him from a pang of misery when the other man materialized quite so specifically.

'Coffee?' Davidson suggested helpfully, as a way of getting himself momentarily out of the room. By the time he returned he was relieved to see that his boss was looking no worse than grim.

'He should have driven her home himself,' he observed to the returning Davidson.

'She likely told him not to be so silly, the driver could perfectly well take her, do you not think?'

One forgot, McLeish thought, considering his sergeant with respect, the extent of his experience with women. 'Did she know we were checking up on her?'

'There was no way of avoiding asking her where she had been. She shouldn't know that the laddie from Special Branch gave out her programme for the rest of the evening.'

'I suspect she'll have guessed,' McLeish acknowledged reluctantly.

'She's used to a bureaucracy all gossiping to each other. She'll assume we know exactly what time she went home, and where from.'

Davidson grinned at the vision of the Department of Trade and Industry implied by McLeish's views, but had to agree that he was probably right. An interesting social problem *that* would involve for McLeish when he next met Francesca. He could see his boss thinking the same.

'Have you spoken to her?'

'Aye, I did. Special Branch have phones in all their cars. She intends to get up at 8 a.m. and go to work, so I persuaded her to stay home and call the hospital rather than to go there and hold her brother's hand.'

McLeish reflected respectfully that Francesca must be both tough and conscientious. Most girls, and indeed quite a few men, would be late in to work after getting home at three in the morning, particularly in circumstances which he found himself unwilling to consider too closely.

'I take it our man is in place now? Both she and her brother ought to be guarded, even if we are locking the stable door after the horse has bolted.'

'We have the horse under guard, ye remember. And he has no alibi at all.'

'That's very odd.' McLeish spoke slowly, and Davidson sank back on to the desk.

'You're right. I must be tired. If he were going to do it he'd have arranged for all his family and every associate not currently inside to have been with him at the material time. Probably celebrating the birthday of his wee grey-haired mother.'

Both men sat and considered the other possibilities. 'He hired it done?' Davidson suggested tentatively.

'Perhaps, but I would have expected him to do the wife himself, and hire someone to do the other bloke, wouldn't you?'

Davidson gave him a sidelong look. 'In similar circumstances I should have felt it my duty to do them both myself,' he said, primly, restoring McLeish to good humour.

'I do apologize, Bruce. It's the low moral standards of the decadent South that are beginning to undermine me.'

'Ah well, ye've been here all your life, it can't be helped. Ye need to find a nice Scots lass to marry.'

'I'm trying to, even if she is only a half Scot.' McLeish spoke evenly, and Davidson's eyebrows shot up. He watched his boss, momentarily gravelled for words, but McLeish was reading the case report with such concentration that Davidson knew he might as well not have been in the room. He cleared his throat.

'Ye went out with her on Saturday?'

McLeish stopped reading. 'Yes, I did. We went to the cinema, where she held my hand in the frightening bits, and I kissed her goodnight on the doorstep.' He returned forbiddingly to the papers.

'Whoever-it-was hit Mrs Byers over the head as she was bending to fetch something from the car, they reckon. That will have been Francesca's briefcase. She must have left it in the car by accident. Biff Howden had been sent to pick Francesca up from her train and get her to the party. She changed at the Embassy. Now why was she particularly concerned? What was she carrying?'

Davidson riffled through his own notes. 'Confidential information on the company she had been visiting in Yorkshire — Britex Fabrics. She was particularly concerned, she said, because it was not just commercially confidential material but the company is quoted on the Stock Market and it would have been particularly damaging to have information leak out ahead of the Annual Report.' He looked hopefully at McLeish to see if any of that helped, and saw his boss freeze in thought, all the personality concentrated on chasing an idea, the wide shoulders hunched over the desk which always looked too small for him, hazel eyes narrowed in concentration.

'Is it possible that someone was looking for that material? I know you think I have an obsession with the Fireman case, but it is wrong as it stands. If someone at Britex is involved, then they were after Francesca's briefcase rather than Mrs Byers. Will she be asleep?'

McLeish had his hand on the phone, as Davidson struggled to think.

'I'll try anyway.' He hesitated. 'No I won't, I'll go and get her at 8 a.m.'

The phone rang sharply and his eyebrows went up as he listened to the message. 'Yes, put her on. It's Francesca,' he observed to Davidson, who rose to creep out of the room, only to be told impatiently to sit down again, he needed to hear this.

'John McLeish here.' Davidson watched his chief with admiration as he ploughed firmly on into the conversation.

'Yes, we do have a guard on Peregrine and there is one outside your door, too. Look, Mrs Byers was attacked while hunting for your briefcase. What was in it?'

He moved the phone sharply away from his ear to avoid being deafened by the wail of misery from the other end.

'I cannot bear it. I was truly grateful to that tiresome girl for being both civil and understanding about the nonsense I had made, and for trotting off kindly to look for my case. I went back to drink my coffee with my mind at rest, and she went out and was as near murdered as makes no difference. I've just talked to Perry — the doctors are warning him about brain damage. It was bad enough if I had been the cause of her running into an irate and murderous husband when she might otherwise have been safe, but if she was hurt because of something in my case, it is too awful. What will Perry do?'

'Francesca!' McLeish, miserable for her, still recognized incipient hysteria when he heard it. 'Will you calm down and concentrate? Shall I come and fetch you and we can talk down here?' He listened patiently while Francesca got herself under control.

'Sorry,' she said, after a bit. 'It's been a long evening.'

McLeish heard the attempt at bravado and his mouth quirked, but he resisted the temptation to comment.

'But I expect you know that?' The bravado was now very marked. 'I do think someone might have got a message to me — I'd have come straight to the hospital to keep Perry company at least.'

'We had a little difficulty finding you,' McLeish observed drily, realizing as he spoke that she would have abandoned a lover without a backward glance if she had thought that her brother needed her.

'Why don't you go to bed now and we'll send a driver up for you in the morning?'

'You are kind,' she said, in tones suggesting the exact opposite. 'I must sleep now because I am working in a few hours. I will gladly come to the station, rather than talk on the phone about the company. You may not believe it from this evening's performance but I am normally — we all are — very careful about chatting casually about quoted companies. Yes, please, a driver would be quicker, there never are any taxis round here.'

'Eight o'clock, then.' McLeish rang off, and his sergeant volunteered hastily to go and fetch her.

'No, I'll do it. May as well sort this out quickly.' He looked enquiringly at Davidson who was looking uneasy. 'I'm not going to ask her about the other bloke, I just think I ought to see her again soon before she gets jumpy.'

He collected papers and strode out of the office, leaving Davidson feeling, as he often did, that a high wind had whistled past his head. He wondered how Francesca was going to receive McLeish in this masterful and uncompromising mood. Poorly, he rather thought, being herself accustomed to command.

He walked heavily out of the office, to find McLeish hunched over an early edition of the *Daily Mail,* according it his usual obliterating concentration. He glanced over McLeish's shoulder at the front page to be met by an excellent photograph of Francesca laughing up at the junior Senator from West Virginia. They made an absolute contrast in type, the Senator with the square-cut Irish features running to fat round the jowls, an easy-going man who sat light to his responsibilities, and Francesca's austere Norman face which even in laughter looked serious and conscientious. Too serious, he thought, and much improved by the company of what was all too clearly not a serious man. He became aware at this point in his reflections that McLeish was speaking and recovered himself.

'Very good photo,' he pointed out. McLeish ignored this offering completely and, speaking slowly and carefully, told him to call the hospital again to find out if there was any change in Sheena Byers's condition. 'If that isn't too much trouble?'

Davidson, who thought on the whole he had deserved it, accepted this treatment with equanimity, ignoring sympathetic looks from the desk sergeant. 'See you later in the day, sir,' he called after the retreating McLeish.

CHAPTER 11

McLeish, greeting Francesca at 8 a.m. on the dot, thought she looked ill and tired, not at all like a girl who had spent half the night in the arms of a lover. She greeted him warily, reminding him painfully of a child who is not quite sure how cross her parents are going to be. He decided to treat her very carefully indeed, and guided her to the car, chatting about the weather. In this spirit he helped her into her seat and switched on the car radio, with Francesca watching him as if he were a time bomb. The radio promptly undid his plans.

'Senator Michael O'Brien leaves for Hamburg from Heathrow today,' the announcer recorded. 'He is to visit five European capitals in an effort to solve the problems being caused for the steel industry in the USA by recent Common Market action.'

McLeish froze in his seat, not daring to look sideways.

'I see you have the James Miles Brett tape.' Francesca, sounding as cool and as distant as a visiting duchess, waved the cassette. 'Might I put it on?'

'Sure. Yes. Of course.' He took it from her left-handed, still not daring to look at her, slammed it into the deck, cutting the announcer off in mid-recital of Michael O'Brien's political history and future prospects. The pure rounded treble filled the car.

'It is a staggering voice,' he volunteered cautiously after a few minutes.

'Like a lark.' Receiving no answer, he cautiously slewed his eyes towards his passenger who was gazing out of her window. Something in the rigidity of her shoulders told him she was weeping, and his throat tightened with pity for her and pain for himself and his half-formed hopes.

'Francesca,' he said, all plans abandoned, 'don't cry. He'll be back some time, won't he?'

'I haven't got a handkerchief.' He fished out a box of Kleenex and thrust it anxiously at her, passing the station as quickly as possible and starting another circuit. She blew her nose thoroughly, and scrubbed at her face.

'Could we just stop for a minute?' McLeish halted abruptly and reached to turn off the tape, but she stopped him, and turned it down only so that they spoke against the background of the marvellous voice singing a Bach cantata. He was relieved to see that she was no longer weeping.

'That affair is over, but anyone who I — that is, anyone who is going to be a friend, needs to understand about Michael and me. He virtually saved my life, or at least my self-esteem, when my marriage foundered. He's a good friend and a sensible man.' She sniffed. 'I suppose he taught me to take life a bit more easily, that people, particularly men, were not irreplaceable.'

'Like buses.'

'What? Oh yes, I see, there'll always be another one coming along.'

She grinned, recovering fast, he noticed, even the dark hair looking less flattened. 'Did you invite me here to assist you with your enquiries, and if so, hadn't we better get on with it?'

McLeish nodded, 'I'm making for the station. We need a full statement from you. I believe this attack on Mrs Byers links to the murder we had last Monday.'

'I haven't been able to think of anything else all night. I called the hospital this morning and spoke to Perry. Sheena is a little better, not conscious or anything, but giving less anxiety. Perry spent the hours of darkness summoning top surgeons from America. I imagine he is wildly popular at St Mary's by now.'

She blew her nose again and turned the driver's mirror to examine her eyes. McLeish patiently rescued it from her, noticing again that she seemed to lack practical sense, for all the brains. He let her out of the car after watching her engage in her usual fight with the door handle, and they marched in soberly side by side to greet Bruce Davidson, also red-eyed and tired. She smiled at him and gave him the better news of Sheena.

The two men settled down with her in their office while she explained exactly what had been in her briefcase. McLeish sat back, puzzled, after ten minutes. 'Who could use all that material? What would they do with it?'

'Well, you couldn't do anything with it except conclude that the company is bust. But that is common ground between us and them. I was only in such a fuss because the company is still trading and I might have been responsible for pushing it into its grave before we had really decided that the only thing we could give it was a decent burial. The interim results are overdue — they are held up in order to embody some statement about banking facilities — but they won't amaze anyone. My boss at the Department says they are already fully discounted in the market.' Momentarily she considered McLeish under her eyelashes. 'Is it possible that there is no connection? Could it not have been Mr Byers acting out of simple jealousy?'

'Both Davidson and I are made very unhappy by the fact that he has no alibi at all.' Francesca looked blank, then recovered.

'Of course. It would have been silly, wouldn't it? Unless he was carried away by passion.' She contrived to make it sound like chickenpox.

A big man, a couple of stone overweight, with long blond hair showing dark at the roots, put his head round the door. 'John? I saw Byers drinking in the Queens at 10.30 last night. Understand you might be interested. Was that in his statement?'

'No, it bloody wasn't. Why could you not say so before?'

'I've only just got here, I was off duty. I came as soon as I had read the logbook.'

McLeish grunted, but did not apologize and found himself receiving a minatory look from Francesca. He scowled at her as the big man withdrew.

'Now look what you've done.' Francesca was unmoved by the scowl.

'Personally I think it was Mr Byers, or possibly his grandmother, and that you've managed to involve yourself with a completely different case. Like reading the paper too quickly so you read across two headlines.'

'You're an ungrateful lassie, you are,' observed Davidson sharply, taking them both completely by surprise. 'It was your wee briefcase he was worrying over, and your safety.' His audience gazed at him dumbfounded.

'I'll arrange to talk to Byers.' McLeish lunged masterfully to his feet and fled from the office leaving Francesca to cope, which she promptly proceeded to do.

'I would have thought your boss was big enough to look after himself.'

Davidson compressed his lips. 'I never like to hear lasses getting at a man when he is doing his best to look after them.'

Francesca was drawing breath to denounce comprehensively any suggestion that she could not look after herself or any six similar when McLeish's head came round the door. 'You're supposed to be in a meeting, are you not?' he said distantly to Francesca. 'Come on then, I'll take you.'

They both marched out to the car, neither speaking until they were well away from the station.

'Francesca.' She turned to him enquiringly, and he kissed her cheek.

She smelt of lily of the valley, he thought, distracted.

'John.' She was rather flushed but still in control. 'Where does all this leave you? Do you really think it has to do with Britex rather than Sheena and her cohorts?'

'I don't know. At the very least I have to find out where the relevant Britex people were last night.'

She looked at him, her eyes widening as she worked out the implications. 'But you'll have to tell them I made a nonsense with my briefcase.'

McLeish who had seen this one coming for several hours said steadily that he was sorry, but yes, this was inevitable. She considered him carefully, then stared bleakly out of the windscreen, biting her lip, plainly visualizing, in detail, a series of difficult interviews. 'You aren't in real trouble. I mean, the case was in your brother's car, and you knew where it was. It's not as if you'd dropped it by a canal.'

She considered him, with simple interest.

'If I had not been mildly careless, but had done something really idiotic such as would have got me into serious trouble, I take it you would still drop me in it?'

'Yes. I'm a policeman.' He took a deep breath. 'Am I seeing you tomorrow?'

'Yes,' she said, thoughtfully, still watching him. 'I haven't told you that James is staying with me?'

'James?' He wondered dizzily if this was yet another rival for her affections.

'James Miles Brett. The boy on your tape. He is the St Joseph's treble at the moment, as Perry was twelve years ago. He lives out of London, but he is doing two concerts, one here and one in Edinburgh with Perry. James and his mum are staying with me, Perry's household being, as you perceive, unsuitable. Just till Friday. So you'll probably meet him.'

McLeish expressed temperate pleasure, and drove off reflecting that she must be leading one of the busiest lives in London, encompassing, as it appeared to, a full-time job, four brothers, at least one lover and probably others he did not know about, and now a child prodigy and its mum. A good deal of determination was going to be required to insert himself into this scenario.

He arrived at the station to find that he and Davidson were seeing Peter Hampton at 9.30. 'He was in London, last night, guv'nor, staying at the Glengarry — you know, that big hotel near King's Cross. He's coming here, said all he needed was more police at the office.'

McLeish drank coffee and read his notes until Hampton arrived looking distinctly ruffled, the blond hair flattened and in need of a wash, and the skin sallow with tiredness. McLeish stolidly recited the facts of the attack on Sheena and the possible involvement with Britex, going out of his way to emphasize that Francesca's briefcase had not left the car.

'Probably safer there than in the American Embassy,' Hampton observed, gulping down a second coffee, his colour coming back. 'I may smack her bottom for her next time I see her, but she's a good girl. I came down with her on the train from Towneley yesterday. You were going to ask where I was, weren't you? Fair enough.'

'You came down by train, not by car?' McLeish, bristling, was aware he was sounding wooden.

'Yes. I usually drive but I thought I'd come down with Fran — the Department of Industry people that is. I was picked up at King's Cross by the chap I'd come down to see. I spent the evening with him at his house in Tottenham and he drove me back to the hotel around 11 p.m., although I didn't particularly notice the time.' The man had relaxed, McLeish noted, this interview was evidently causing him no trouble.

'We may want to interview the man you spent the evening with.'

'If you must. He wants me to come into his firm — it's a nice little business making security equipment — and he needs an MD. He's in his fifties and he wants to ease up a bit. Your man said the attack was around midnight? I'd left him by then and was back at the hotel.'

'Would the night clerk remember you?'

'He might, but I'd not put money on it. I was in bed — alone as it happens — by midnight.' He grinned at McLeish who had just been wondering what he was going to be offered as an alibi. 'In any case, Inspector, everything Fran had in that briefcase, I gave her. Not much sense my stealing it back.'

McLeish silently agreed with him, and said as much to Davidson when he had seen Hampton out.

'Unless he gave her something he'd not meant to. Bit pleased with himself, isn't he?'

'Yes. Yes, he is. Good-looking bloke, though; I noticed before.' He glanced across at Davidson to catch a very sidelong look.

'He fancies his chances with the Wilson lassie.'

McLeish grunted, and observed that Hampton probably fancied his chances with a lot of women, and on that note William Blackett was ushered in.

'I don't know what we pay these civil servants for,' he observed sourly. 'Stupid girl can't even keep our papers safe.' He listened discontentedly as McLeish pointed out that Francesca had not really lost the papers, but appeared totally unconvinced. Nor was he disposed to be helpful about his whereabouts, but finally disclosed that he had gone on from a trade dinner to a late drink with a friend.

'I take it the friend will be prepared to confirm this?' McLeish was feeling the strain of two virtually sleepless nights and sounded crisper than he had meant to. Blackett reddened.

'If you have to ask them.'

'Where were you having a drink?'

'At a club.'

'Which club?' McLeish asked after a discouraging pause.

'The Star and Garter. Beauchamp Street.'

Behind Blackett, Davidson stirred and scraped his chair back, in signal that he knew something of the subject matter and that McLeish should persist.

'You arrived at what time?'

'About 11.30.'

'And left when?' Blackett fidgeted uncomfortably, and said he didn't really know. McLeish, tired, and bored by the effort of extracting information piece by piece, let the silence go on until Blackett felt pressured into speech.

'I was with a girl. An air hostess. Swedish.' This with an unsuccessful attempt at a man-to-man approach.

'Where can we contact her?' McLeish strove to keep his voice level, and after several false starts, Blackett managed to tell them that he had the girl's number. He produced a card which told two experienced policemen at a glance that the girl was a prostitute, no more Swedish than either of them, and could be found when they needed her.

'I hope you can manage without me for a couple of days, Inspector?'

Blackett had recovered himself a little. 'I'm going to Verbier to check on the family chalet because we're letting it this season, or rather my father is.'

'Verbier in Switzerland?'

'Yes.' Blackett confirmed, just indicating his surprise that McLeish knew where it was, and they let him go, having taken his address.

Davidson went straight off to check on the girl, while McLeish considered the interview. An expensive evening, it sounded like.

Whatever Britex's problems, Blackett seemed to have a bob or so to spare.

'£100 to £150 a go with that lass,' Davidson confirmed, arriving back.

'She gave you a price?'

'No, no. I know another girl in the field, nae bother. Couldn't find the lassie herself, but the story will check, won't it?'

'Oh yes,' McLeish agreed. 'Do you think he does that often?'

'Often enough, I'd say. He wasn't particularly embarrassed.'

McLeish sighed in agreement, and, deciding he could not yet decently ring the Department of Trade and Industry, plunged back into the paperwork.

Francesca arrived at the sanctuary of her office resisting a strong desire to weep out of sheer tension and tiredness. She distracted herself by making a list, as she did every single day and assigning priorities to the items on her list, none of which related in any way to her emotional life. Soothed by this activity and the momentary illusion of control it gave her, she rang up Bill Westland's office, since that appeared first on her list, and booked a time to see him. She was just working out how to tackle the next priority, which was to see Henry Blackshaw, when he arrived in her office. Adhering to another of her self-taught principles, that of confessing straightaway to any disasters, she told him all, including the attack on Sheena, adding that the result, netted down, was that she had not recovered her briefcase until 8 a.m. Henry, who knew enough of the background to provide a sub-text, was unworried by any potential complaints but appalled for her.

'Go home, girl. Get some sleep. You'll not be much use until you do.'

She looked at him, surprised. 'I've much too much to do. I'm used to working like this — good heavens, where would we all be if I couldn't function after a late night? I have to see Bill Westland, anyway.'

Henry decided not to allow himself to be sidetracked or embarrassed.

'So see him quickly, and go home. I take it you managed to do what he wanted?'

She looked at him, stone-faced, blue shadows under her eyes very clear against her general pallor, and for a moment he feared he had offended her. She suddenly relaxed, and grinned at him, maliciously amused and pleased with herself in an entirely feminine way. 'Yes, I did. I had a brilliant idea — no, don't ask, I couldn't possibly tell you — and moreover one which will by-pass that useless egocentric twit in our Embassy in Washington. He'll have to agree, and he'll know it comes from me. It'll all happen about lunchtime when they get up over there.'

'Not a forgiving nature, Fran?'

'Absolutely not. Forgiving simply encourages people to commit further atrocities. As it is, that particular ornament of the FCO will think twice about trying to cross me up again.'

Henry contemplated with interest this new vision of a Civil Service red in tooth and claw, and thought that Francesca was in this, as in many other ways, wholly unfeminine. Most women in his experience preferred to believe that the world was just and the people in it well intentioned. Francesca, on the other hand, had an eye like a knife for equivocation or deception. He offered her this view, and she smiled on him kindly.

'You can't have four brothers without knowing that men function on getting one up on the next chap. Also, I am the eldest child of a widow, and you learn a good deal about being dumped on.' She made this point without any discernible trace of self-pity, merely as a comment. 'So you see, I try to get my retaliation in first, as the rugger players say.'

She returned, definitively, to her list, as Henry, father of three indulged young, sat opposite, appalled by this bleak vision of the world, but understanding that he had no experience that would enable him to contradict it. It explained, he thought sadly, both her success and the difficulties she made for herself. He was wondering how to communicate something of this when the phone rang, and he listened as she agreed to a meeting at lunchtime.

'The Aquarius Choir — what is it, a Civil Service choir?' he said, incredulously. 'Come on, Fran, you need not do that today.'

'Yes, I do have to. We've got a problem.'

He waited, but she showed no sign of being willing to expand.

'Is it a good choir?'

'It is quite a small choir, and it contains many older people who have sung with it for many years.'

Henry, who sang in the excellent choir of his local church in Huddersfield, had no difficulty with this succinct description.

'Then why are you in it?'

'Because there was some feeling that not enough interest was being taken by the Department's fast stream. I mean, in its heyday Deputy Secretaries and the like used to sing in it. So I volunteered. It's no trouble for me, I've sung in a *Messiah* every Christmas and Easter since I was about ten.'

'Were you head girl of your school by any chance?'

'Yes. Why?' She looked at him suspiciously, and he laughed.

'Francesca, will you please go home? Or I'll buy you a proper lunch.'

'I can't,' she said, driven to the wall. 'The thing is, there is a fuss. Perry is due to be the tenor soloist, and some of the older and sillier ladies — of both sexes — have got in a state about the publicity. Perry is only doing it for me and will duck out in a flash if he can. I know exactly how to cope, but I have to be there or it will all be a shambles.'

She was near to tears, and Henry yielded promptly, bidding her come to his office and tell him about Britex when she had dealt with Bill Westland.

Twenty minutes later he had Rajiv, Martin Bailey and Francesca all drinking coffee in his office.

'I've had a phone call from my American friends,' he began briskly.

'The offer to buy Britex's household-textiles business is not going to go forward.'

'Oh, Lord. Did they get cold feet again?'

'No, Rajiv, I did. Look, think about it. What they wanted to do was to buy the business and move the manufacturing to that factory of theirs in Birmingham. Now that would dig Britex out of a financial hole in the short term, but they'd then be left with a factory two-thirds empty and nowhere to lay off the overheads. They'd have to make another load of people redundant, and in a year's time they'll be in a hole again because the overheads are too high.'

'So you suggested that your Americans close their Birmingham factory and move that business into Britex's factory instead?'

'Well done, girl. But then what happens? How do they and Britex manage to run production lines side by side?'

'There are two buildings — I mean, Britex could keep one?'

'I thought I had a better idea. My American friends could buy the whole company, with a slug of assistance from HMG. They would be a much better bet in the long term than the people running the company right now.'

'But isn't Peter Hampton quite good?' Francesca was looking worried and distressed.

'Well, lass, who has presided over the company's decline? They told me when I came here that we were in the job-preservation business, and that didn't mean management jobs if management had effed it up.'

Martin Bailey observed that the Americans would surely not be prepared to buy the company, they'd only want to buy the assets, and that meant a receivership. Henry nodded, in confirmation of a point that seemed obvious to him, but Francesca and Rajiv looked at each other. Henry swept on, ignoring them. 'So the Americans are flying over later today, we meet the Britex directors tomorrow in Yorkshire — they are all there for the funeral of that poor chap who got mugged — and we stay the night and go round the factory with the Americans in the morning.'

'Ministers!' said Rajiv and Francesca, in unison. 'Henry, we have to consult.'

Rajiv as senior man got his breath back first. 'Henry, we do have procedures. We ought to go to the committee, and ask them to consider this as a proposal before we go rushing off.'

'It isn't a proposal before the Americans have decided whether they are interested.' Henry pointed out. 'What can we go to the committee with? I'm not prepared to recommend any rescue package for Britex with its present debts and its present management, so what is the committee going to do? Tell me I'm wrong?'

'We couldn't, could we?' Francesca observed, coolly. 'Rajiv, I have to say it would not be helpful to ask the committee. Much better, surely, to let Henry, as the hard-nosed commercial adviser, sell that one to Ministers rather than have them feel that the civil servants were being obstructive, as per usual.' She grinned at him. 'May Martin and I come too? I wouldn't want to miss this.'

Rajiv considered her carefully. 'Yes,' he said pleasantly. 'You may. I am not feeling quite disagreeable enough to send you and Henry by yourselves, but I see no reason why you — and Martin if he wants — should not come and watch Henry telling a Minister of the Crown that the only rescue package he would support, in a political mate's constituency, involves handing the company to some dodgy Americans.'

'There is nothing dodgy about these Americans,' Henry protested.

'It's a huge, well-respected textile company.'

Rajiv sighed and said that Henry should nonetheless understand that to this administration all foreigners were, by definition, dodgy.

Particularly American foreigners. The meeting dispersed, gloomily, but Francesca lingered.

'Henry,' she said coaxingly. 'Your secretary told me that you are singing in the *Messiah* just before Christmas in Huddersfield. You wouldn't like to do the same for the Aquarius Choir, would you? You needn't rehearse, only we are very short of men and a decent bass would do wonders for us.'

'How do you know I am a decent bass?'

'Well, you must be a bass. And I know your choir. The chap who taught Perry at St Joe's came from there.'

Henry tidied his desk as he thought about this efficient piece of staffwork. He decided he would rather enjoy singing the *Messiah* twice and let Francesca lead him to the rehearsal room and introduce him to the choirmaster, tactfully expressing his sense of obligation to the choir for being prepared to consider letting him in this late in their preparations. Francesca cast him just the sort of approving glance, he felt, with which she would have recognized a piece of mannerly behaviour from one of her brothers, and waited to listen to him sing part of one of the bass recitatives, and to sight-read an unfamiliar Brahms anthem.

'Thank you very much, Mr Blackshaw,' the choirmaster, a slight man in his forties with glasses, said briskly. 'You are rehearsing in Huddersfield as well? I am sure you will be able to catch up here.' He glanced sardonically across the room, and rose to his feet from behind the piano, eyes fixed speculatively on a small group of middle-aged ladies gathered round a tall, harassed, balding man.

'Ah, Sandy,' the tall man hailed him in a relieved shout, but paused punctiliously to be introduced to Henry. 'Just before we start to sing, we have a small matter to discuss.'

Henry watched with interest while he made no fewer than three attempts at the next sentence. Francesca, who had been sitting waiting with courteous patience, stirred after his third shot, and said generally that Michael had already told her that some anxiety was being expressed about undesirable publicity that might be attracted to the choir by the presence of her brother, Peregrine Wilson, as the tenor soloist. It was clearly right that this anxiety should be aired. Henry, enjoying himself hugely, waited for someone to air any anxiety that might be being felt, and a thin, nervous middle-aged lady obliged him by making a disjointed statement which touched at some length on the traditions of the Choir, and the difficulties of controlling access to St Mary's, both apparently assuming equal importance in her mind.

'Of course,' she concluded, with a waspish glance at Francesca, 'I appreciate that some members who are used to singing with larger choirs may feel differently, and it would not be for me to push my views in these circumstances.'

'I hope, Helen, that it is for all of us, as fellow members of the Aquarius Choir, to speak our minds on this issue,' Francesca said formidably, giving Henry a sudden vision of her in twenty years' time.

'Perhaps I could help the discussion a bit? When Sandy Laing, as choirmaster, and Michael Snowden, as Chairman of the Choir Association, invited Peregrine nine months ago to be the tenor soloist at this performance of the *Messiah,* I believe they hoped to be getting a high-quality young choral tenor, who would be particularly happy to sing with us because of a family connection.' She paused, and Henry mentally saluted the negotiating competence which had reminded all present just who had selected her brother, and that he was a higher-quality article than they could have hoped to secure in the open market.

She glanced at Sandy Laing and went on. 'None of us bargained for the fact that in the nine months intervening Peregrine would also become an internationally known popular recording star whose very presence at a concert might draw an undesirable audience. Peregrine understands this very well, and I am quite sure that, rather than cause us any difficulty or embarrassment, he would wish to withdraw from this engagement.'

Sandy Laing came in as smoothly as if he had been rehearsed. 'I recognize members' anxieties, but I believe we would have the most serious difficulty in finding a replacement for Peregrine, at this stage and given the time of year.' He flicked a glance at Michael Snowden who managed this time not to drop the baton.

'For myself, I have to confess that I am tempted by the vision of St Mary's actually full, though perhaps not with quite the audience we had envisaged. I should like to feel that for once the hard work of everyone here would be rewarded and that we should be enabled to make a major contribution to the funds of the Civil Service Sanatorium, and the Post Office Rest Home.' Francesca's bleak eye alone kept Henry from choking. 'I wonder how difficult it would in practice be to control an audience when Peregrine performs. Francesca? Do you have much experience of this?'

'I cannot believe that Peregrine's appearance in what his more flamboyant supporters must view as a long boring piece of religious music is going to cause undue excitement. I would like to think, moreover, that any of his fan club who did attend would benefit thereby.'

The choir considered this right and left judiciously.

'Indeed,' Sandy Laing agreed cordially. 'But, Helen, what do you feel? How do you see the balance between taking an undoubted risk on Peregrine, or ending up with a less well-rehearsed tenor soloist, less of an audience, and less of a contribution to the Sanatorium?'

The unfortunate Helen, plainly uncomfortable at finding herself singled out and conscious that her support was ebbing away, produced a series of disjunctive statements which amounted to a total, if ungraceful, capitulation, while Francesca watched unblinkingly, her face set in an expression of courteous concern. Sandy Laing was also watching in catlike silence, but Michael Snowden was making helpful, assenting noises in counterpoint to Helen's grudging acquiescences.

'Splendid,' he cried, coming strategically up to full volume as she faltered. 'I am glad that we have aired this concern, and very glad that we have decided as we did. We had better now start to rehearse if we are to be ready for our large audience.' He nodded winsomely to Francesca, confirming Henry's observation that she had orchestrated the whole performance. She avoided his eye as they assembled to sing, and the rehearsal passed off without further incident. At the end she collected the conductor and the three of them walked off together to get a sandwich.

'We do still need more men,' he said, gloomily accepting a sandwich.

'Can we co-opt more Wilsons, Francesca?'

'When Helen has simmered down a bit, I don't see why we shouldn't co-opt Charles and Jeremy. That'll make another bass, and a tenor. Can't have Tristram because the Bach Choir is doing carols that night. Shall I go and try the idea on Michael?'

Sandy Laing nodded and she skipped off, still chewing a sandwich.

'Dear Francesca. I can safely leave that in her hands and we'll have some reinforcements for the day as well as yourself. You know that all four boys are old boys of the choir school where I teach. No? Do you know the story of how this came about?' He was obviously longing to tell it, and Henry was equally willing to listen, urging him on by observing that he had not realized all four boys had been at the same school.

'Well, that was partly my doing. We do the voice tests in March every year, when the boys are eight. It's a dreadful occasion, endless little boys and their anxious mothers and a lot of musical dross to be got through to find any speck of gold. The year Perry came, I was in my first year teaching at the school; it was getting to the end of the morning and I was getting tired.' He smiled reminiscently. 'The school secretary came through in a fuss because there was one boy who didn't have a mother, just a not much older sister, and was that all right? So I said we might as well hear the child, and in came Perry and Francesca, both of them skinny little things. Francesca was about twelve and everything was too short and too tight, and she was obviously very anxious. So I treated her as if she was a mother, and shook hands with her, and said of course she could play the piano for Perry. He wasn't nervous at all. He sang the test piece, which I had only heard about fifty times — just opened his mouth and this wonderful sound came out, astonishing amount of volume, too.'

He smiled again, in memory. 'Of course I knew immediately we must have him, but I did all the tests just in case he was a musical idiot, but he has perfect pitch as well, and I was just putting up a little prayer of thankfulness, when Francesca said that he could sight-read. Well — at eight years old they mostly can't, you know, but I gave him the Burdon "Nunc Dimittis" which I had on the piano.'

'That's the difficult one, more or less plainsong?'

'That's right. Well, the headmaster had arrived by then, summoned by bush telegraph, but Perry just glanced at the Burdon and said he had heard it sung so it would not be a fair test of sight-reading. I asked him to go ahead anyway. The Headmaster and I were both nearly in tears at the end of it, and totally agreed, you know, that we must get him before any other school nobbled him. So we advanced on Francesca, who was clearly in charge.'

'That I can imagine.' Henry spoke seriously.

'She said, like someone fifteen years her senior, that she would have to consult her parents, because St Joseph's was her idea rather than theirs. She added that if the test was over she thought she had better go home, because she had three other younger brothers in the waiting-room since the twins had been too little to leave behind and her mother had gone with her father to hospital that morning. I don't think Peter — who was Headmaster then — and I even looked at each other but we asked, more or less in chorus, whether any of them sung and she replied that they all did but Perry was the best; quite matter of factly, you know.'

'I do indeed.' Henry was both fascinated and appalled. 'What happened then?'

'We forgot about lunch, and lured all five of them into a rehearsal room and got them to do their party pieces, including Francesca. We offered Charlie a bursary on the spot because we had just lost a ten-year-old to another school, and we invented a procedure whereby we guaranteed entry to the twins for two years on. They were only six then, of course. So all the boys came to us, but as Francesca said, Perry was the best, though Tristram ran him close as a treble. One of the best days' work I ever did for the school.'

Henry, an only child who had barely been responsible for a goldfish until he had joined Allied Textiles at twenty-eight, contemplated this story, and wondered whether, had circumstances been different, he would have had the attack and the character to transport four younger brothers to an unfamiliar part of London on a day when his father had been taken seriously ill into hospital.

'We finally remembered about lunch when one of the twins could contain himself no longer.' Sandy Laing was laughing. 'But it must have been a huge strain on Francesca. The father died later that year — I never knew him. Francesca used to come to school occasions when her mother was working — I am afraid we all fell into the habit of treating her as if she were a parent, but she is only two years older than Charles.'

Yes indeed, thought Henry and it all went some way to explaining why she was both ferociously capable and utterly unwilling to put herself in a position where she might have to carry that sort of responsibility again.

CHAPTER 12

John McLeish sat on the half empty train to Doncaster on Wednesday morning, guiltily hoping he wasn't wasting police time. He was on his way to attend the funeral of William Fireman, which was legitimate police work, but he was spending the night in Doncaster afterwards almost entirely because Francesca would be there. She had rung him apologetically to explain that she could not keep their date for Wednesday because she had to accompany her boss to Doncaster to meet the Britex Board, most of whom would be there to attend the funeral. McLeish had promptly reinstated their date for the Thursday, and decided to spend Wednesday night in Doncaster too. He did, of course, need time to talk to the Doncaster CID — but he was also resolved to spin out the talks so that he could catch the same train home as Francesca. He needed to get closer to the Department of Industry team, true — but he also wanted to carry Francesca off for supper with him before her family or other concerns could overwhelm her. Also, he might manage to get her to himself for a bit tonight, since she had been sure the meeting would not go on late.

He was met by a detective inspector whom he instantly recognized as a fellow rugby-player.

'Brady. How are you? Very good of you to come yourself.'

'I heard it was you, so I decided to take an interest.' Brady, a stocky chap perhaps a couple of years older than McLeish, was a walking illustration of the dangers of abandoning a competitive sport too abruptly. He was a good three stone heavier than when he had been a fly-half for the London Scottish, and had lost a good deal of hair as well. He was, endearingly, beaming with pleasure at seeing McLeish.

'I'll take you to the pub for lunch and we can talk.' If you are unwilling to become a Freemason, McLeish reflected, being a near international class rugby-player was almost as useful in the Force. They took drinks over to a corner table from which they could survey the room, and ordered a solid lunch.

'I've come up for the funeral and to get the local gossip.'

'And you've come to the right man. My wife's a local girl, you know. Related to half the town, and that's why I am here. Julie never could settle in London, so I left the Met and came here when I got the chance; better for the kids, too. I miss London, though.' He contemplated his beer sadly. 'Sorry, where was I? Well, everyone says Britex is in trouble, not paying its bills, that's for a start. Hang on, though, John — why do you think it isn't just a mugging anyway?'

McLeish explained about the possible link with the attack on Sheena Byers, but it did sound increasingly thin, even to him, as he expounded his theory. Rather to his surprise, Brady was interested and commented that there were really dangerous tensions in firms where the business was going badly, which might easily lead to violence; his own brother-in-law, normally the mildest of men and wholly under the thumb of Brady's sister, had threatened his business partner with a knife at a stage when the business was drifting towards receivership. Mercifully Brady himself had been present or there was no knowing where the affair might have ended. McLeish considered this, but said sadly that nothing about Fireman suggested he would present that sort of challenge.

'Someone got their hand in the till, and he found them at it?' Brady offered.

'I'm looking for something like that, and that is why I want to talk to the Department of Industry people who are in there now — *that* you keep to yourself by the way, it isn't public.'

'Ah, that's where the girl comes in?' McLeish jumped involuntarily. 'The girl with the briefcase, I mean.' Brady looked entirely innocent but McLeish, who remembered him as a very tricky fly-half indeed, was on guard.

Brady smiled at him disarmingly. 'Well, I'll tell you what else I know. It's an old firm, about a hundred years old, originally run by the Blackett great-grandfather. The current Sir James is the Chairman — you interviewed him? He's all right, good name in the district. The son, William, was Sales Director, but when the old MD left, no one thought William should be Managing Director, so they brought in this Peter Hampton. William took offence, and went off to a supplier firm. He's on the Board of Britex, of course, because he's a Blackett.'

'Or because he has a lot of shares?'

'Not him. That all went some time ago. Julie's second cousin on her mother's side is a partner in the local firm that does the audit, and he told me William B. sold the lot out two years ago.'

'Not a bad idea if the firm is going bust now.'

'Yeh, but that's not why he did it, not according to Julie's cousin. He needed the cash. He's got a bloody great house over to Keighley, four kids all at boarding-school, skiing holidays, dances in London, all that. He's strapped for cash now, according to the local Barclays man, but all he loses if Britex goes belly-up is a non-executive director's salary. His main salary is from Alutex, though I do hear they're in bother too. But that doesn't help you, does it? I mean, Fireman didn't work at Alutex.'

'No, I can't see where that fits in. What about Hampton?'

Brady's mouth compressed momentarily, and he signalled for coffee.

'Bit of a wide boy. Thinks he's God's gift, always women around him. Split up with his wife a couple of years ago, moved into his own flat. Plenty of cash to flash about.' Brady was sounding distinctly sour, and McLeish enquired whether Hampton had got up the collective police nose in the area.

'No, I just don't like the bloke — nothing known against him, except for a drunk-driving two years ago. The rest of the Board are local lads. The Sales Director and the production chap are executive — I mean they work full time — and the biggest of the local solicitors and another Blackett cousin are on as non-executives. I dunno what either of them does for the money.'

He looked at his watch, and signalled for the bill. 'We'd better get on — I'm coming to the funeral anyway because the wife is second cousin to the daughter-in-law. I'll take you to the station, then to the Grand after. The Department of Industry people are staying there, as I expect you know?'

McLeish decided resignedly that Davidson had been talking, but confirmed that he had indeed known, adding quellingly that he had hoped he would have a chance to talk to the senior man in charge of the investigation. Brady confirmed his worst fears by suppressing a grin, as he opined that this was a sound and well-conceived plan.

They drove sedately to the small church where William Fireman, son, father and grandfather, was to be buried.

* * *

In the course of his ten years as a policeman, McLeish had attended a lot of funerals, but he found himself most painfully affected by this one. It was a dull heavy day, more like December than November. The congregation was subdued and shocked, and in the front pews the dead man's daughter and sister wept steadily. His mother, a tiny shrunken creature with flying white hair, huddled into a thick blue coat now much too large for her, was totally disoriented, either as a result of extreme old age or shock. She kept asking fretfully and anxiously for

Bill, and being reminded in embarrassed undertones that he was gone, granny, after which she would relapse into worried mutterings. It was both heart-breaking and deeply unnerving, and McLeish could only sympathize when the daughter, out of tension and misery, slapped one of the children a little too hard, and the child's wails were added to the general turmoil.

He looked, unconsciously, for some distraction and his eye lit on Peter Hampton sitting just behind the family pews, pale and sombre in a well-cut dark grey suit and black tie. He leaned forward just at that moment with an easy all-in-one movement to put a comforting hand on the old woman's shoulder, and McLeish considered him carefully. He had been in London the night that Fireman died. In fact, the only reason he had not been sought to identify the body was that Fireman's business card had carried only the Yorkshire address, not the London office. Looking round the congregation carefully, he noted William Blackett with a long-nosed, bad-tempered blonde in a mink coat, presumably his wife, and decided that Blackett probably needed the odd Scandinavian tart, even if she did come from Stoke-on-Trent. Sir James sat in the pew beside her, accompanied by the Rolls Royce version of Mrs Blackett, older, taller, thinner, more elegant, in a beautifully cut black cloth coat. Michael Currie and his wife were in the pew behind with a small grey man who was presumably the solicitor Board member, and the Finlays. He caught the eye of Barry Richards, the personnel man who had identified the body, and nodded to him. He wondered dispassionately, remembering the savagely disfigured head, whether he was on a complete wild-goose chase while somewhere in London a psychotic thief or a drug addict went free, and decided in a sudden access of energy that he must do some proper work on this case, and either lay his vague uneasiness or turn it into a real suspicion. Nothing else would do justice to a man of whom the vicar was now speaking with a regret whose genuineness echoed round the church. No one but he thought there was any doubt about the way Fireman had died, so he would get no more than grudging help, given the overload of work that is the lot of every policeman in the Met; but he would do this one single-handed if he had to.

The whole congregation followed the coffin to the grave, while McLeish stood quietly right at the back. Brady and his wife were up by the grave, as family, with Peter Hampton close to them. The final, painful words were said, and Fireman's mother, huddled in her wheelchair and now weeping, was wheeled away by a solid grandson, trailed by his wife and small daughter. Brady and his wife, she mopping away tears, joined him, then Peter Hampton came over. McLeish, emotions on edge from the funeral, felt Brady's wife start slightly, and just caught the long, considering, oddly hostile exchange of looks between her and Hampton. He glanced at Brady, who was studiously gazing into the middle distance, and considered Hampton again, realizing that he had missed a trick. There was something between him and Brady's wife which Brady was hoping very hard not to have to challenge.

'Hello Julie.' Brady's wife and McLeish turned towards the speaker who bent to kiss her.

'Simon. Didn't know you'd be here. John, this is Simon Ketterick, he's another cousin of mine, and that makes him a cousin of Jennifer's too.'

'Not just here because I'm family, though. I dealt with old Bill every day, they don't come like that anymore. I work for Alutex who are a supplier, you see. Cotton thread,' he explained to McLeish.

'You remember I was telling you, John? Simon, John McLeish here has come from the Met because Bill was killed down there.'

'You're a policeman too?' Ketterick took a step back involuntarily, and converted it into a joke by throwing up both hands in mock horror, but he had, McLeish noted, been momentarily totally taken aback. He considered the man with interest as he remembered that he too had been in London, meeting with William Blackett, on the day of the murder.

'I thought Bill was mugged,' William Blackett, who had appeared from nowhere, boomed at him, and several people looked round.

McLeish agreed that that seemed the most likely solution, but that he was completing his enquiries in Yorkshire. He was watching Ketterick as he spoke, and intercepted an obviously warning look from William Blackett, which alerted all his policeman's instincts.

'Any suspects yet?' Ketterick asked, feeling McLeish's attention on him.

'Early days still. I think the family are waiting for us to go.'

The group made its way slowly past the family, McLeish fading into the background while Ketterick and William Blackett stopped to speak to the dead man's sister, a carelessly dressed plump woman, volubly chatty, and Julie Brady stopped to greet a young woman of her own age, obviously a daughter-in-law to the late William Fireman. At the gate, just beyond the family, Simon Ketterick paused to look back, caught McLeish's eye and looked away hastily. As he watched stolidly, Peter Hampton emerged from the group and stopped to speak to Julie Brady, the blond head bent close to hers, then touched her shoulder for a second in farewell — a gesture so easy and yet so intimate that he might as well have kissed her. McLeish found he was holding his breath, and he looked round cautiously for Brady who was firmly turning his back on the whole scene, rocking slightly on his heels as he talked to William Blackett.

Two hours later, as the car drew up in front of the Grand, McLeish's new vision of Peter Hampton was brought sharply into focus when he saw him with Francesca. She had her back to the road and was facing Hampton, urgently explaining something to him, hands flying and dark hair standing up in spikes. He was looking down at her, amused and concentrated, and the spark between them caught other eyes than McLeish's own.

'I'd watch that one,' Brady said sourly, pulling the handbrake on.

'An eye for the women — they do say that's why his wife left. Look at him chatting up that girl.'

'That girl is Francesca Wilson, one of the Department of Industry team. It could be business.'

'He's still giving it the personal touch, isn't he?' Brady observed, unanswerably.

McLeish decided to move away from a subject that was difficult for them both. 'I need a bit of help with this case, Mike. For want of any of the other obvious motives, I'm looking at money. Can you get to see a few bank statements for me? I know it takes time, which you haven't got any more than I have, but I'd be obliged.'

'You're right we're short of time. But for you, John, I'll do it. Give me a list.'

'Thanks,' McLeish said gratefully. 'It'll be a short one I hope, but as you know it's the long lists that sometimes get the results.'

They talked on for a bit in the hotel bar, sharing gossip, and McLeish noticed how much Brady cheered up in the company of an old acquaintance. He refused a second beer, and said abruptly that it was time he went back to taking some exercise, he felt rotten now he no longer played rugby and Julie was complaining he was getting fat.

McLeish, who had remained exactly the same shape as in the days when he was playing in international trials, sympathized and recommended running.

'Yup, I'll try that. Must get home, or she'll complain about keeping supper.' He hesitated. 'Difficult being a detective's wife. She doesn't really understand it; she thinks I could organize myself better, or hire some more people to help.' He looked helplessly at McLeish, who started to laugh, leaving Brady with nothing to do but join in.

'Did me good,' he observed, when they had both stopped being amused by the vision of a police force where you could hire extra help when things got busy. 'Ah well, it'll pass. Good to have seen you, John — my sergeant will take you round tomorrow, but you let me know anything else you want and I'll get it.'

McLeish thanked him, and invited him and his wife to come and stay a weekend in London in his flat. His view of Brady's troubles was reinforced by his obvious pleasure at the invitation, and his prompt acceptance. 'That's kind of you, John. She loves going to London, but the hotels are so pricey I can't swing it. Look forward to it. I'll be off, then.' Brady was looking past him as he spoke. 'Your young lady is on her way over.'

He took himself off with a quick, knowing grin just before Francesca and Peter Hampton arrived, and paused by McLeish.

'I know you have a meeting,' McLeish said to her, finding himself childishly needing to indicate to Hampton the terms on which he stood with Francesca.

'And I have a Board meeting after that,' Hampton agreed amicably, taking the statement as addressed to both of them. 'Can we have a drink afterwards?' he asked Francesca as if McLeish were not there at all, and she blushed.

'Give you lunch tomorrow, then, if tonight is difficult,' he said easily.

'Will we be seeing you again, Inspector, or were you just here for the funeral?' It was a neat attempt to relegate McLeish to the ranks of licensed plodder, and he felt pretty wooden as he replied that he had a few more enquiries to complete. Mercifully Francesca appeared to be too preoccupied with some inward anxiety to notice this by-play.

'Well, Frannie,' Hampton said, annoying McLeish mightily with his use of a diminutive which he had only heard her brothers use.

'Time we went. Don't look so anxious, girl — we all know the Department isn't here in force to bring us news we want to hear.'

He put a hand on her arm with the easy physical confidence of the man who has always had success with women, and she smiled at him, visibly relaxing. McLeish, the sudden temper which had been both an asset and a major liability on the rugby field momentarily overcoming him, heard himself reminding her that he hoped to see her after the meeting. Hampton's eyes widened, and he had the satisfactory certainty of realizing he had startled the man.

'You a suspect too, Frannie?'

'I don't think so. I know Inspector McLeish from another case.'

Ouch, McLeish thought, flattened by this minimal acknowledgement, but she caught his expression and smiled apologetically. Unfeminine in this as in many other respects, he observed, and rattled rather than pleased by two men squabbling over her. He watched them go, and went off himself to ring Davidson in London and see how he was doing with the sub-postmaster shooting case. It was an hour and a half before he appeared in the bar again, since he did not want Francesca or Hampton to think he had been patiently waiting for them. To his relief he found Francesca, with her Departmental colleagues, in a state of over-excitement, rather flushed and in the middle of her second drink. She greeted him with such open pleasure that he nearly kissed her, but thought better of it.

'Goodness, that was a difficult meeting,' she said in explanation.

'You've met Henry Blackshaw and Martin Bailey briefly, I understand? I'm going to organize dinner. Have you eaten, John?'

'Not yet.' He caught a very considering look from Henry Blackshaw who dispatched Francesca and Martin Bailey to negotiate a table, and McLeish seized his chance. 'You know that we are interesting ourselves in the affairs of Britex inasmuch as they might have a bearing on the murder of William Fireman?'

Henry, refusing to be hurried, ordered another drink for them both, admiring the patience with which the policeman simply sat without fidgeting or talking, waiting for him to respond. 'I'm in a difficult position, lad,' he said, at last. 'We have to respect a confidence. I understand one of my predecessors found a very clever tax fraud in one company where assistance was being considered, but he was told that nothing could be said to the Inland Revenue.'

'This is a murder investigation.'

'I understand that.'

Both men fell silent, working out where their respective loyalties and duties lay, and at this complicated moment Francesca returned with Martin announcing triumphantly the availability of a table if they came now. McLeish, with only a fractional hesitation, said he would settle for a sandwich at the bar, but Francesca's quick ear had caught the pause.

'Why aren't you joining us, John?'

'He's investigating the Britex people, Francesca. It will not do for him to be seen too much with us, or people will think we are breaking confidences.'

'But Henry . . . I mean, even in present circumstances?'

Henry grunted, sat down again on a bar stool and gazed at the carpet, quite unselfconsciously thinking out his answer. Francesca, impatient and anxious, made to speak but a glance from Henry decided her not to.

'All right,' Henry said, emerging from his thoughts. 'Go away, Francesca and Martin, and start ordering — I'll have steak medium rare and no foreign muck with it. I want another word with the Inspector here, but he still isn't going to eat with us in a public place. Get on, girl.'

'Chips and ketchup with the steak? Prawn cocktail first?' she asked cheekily.

'That's right, lass. All t' trimmings,' Henry confirmed, much to McLeish's admiration. He took McLeish out to the car-park, where they sat in Henry's old but beautifully looked-after Jaguar, and he explained that the Department had already resolved not to recommend assistance to Britex as it presently stood but instead to consider assisting a buy-out from a Receiver.

'What that means is that we won't be doing any more investigation into the business as it stands. We'll be looking at a new plan, and a new set of assumptions put up to us by new people, and much of what has happened to this business in the past will be irrelevant.'

McLeish, who had understood the point instantly, nodded in acceptance, reflecting that it should, however, make it easier for him to get close to Francesca if she were not inhibited by their jobs causing a conflict of interest. Among her other outstanding qualities in his eyes was that she took her work as seriously as he did his.

'What are you looking for?' asked Henry.

'Motive. In my trade you try money or sex first. Sex isn't obviously likely in this case, so I'm thinking about money.'

'We've not found anything dodgy. The accounts are reasonably up to date, the last audit certificate which is nine months ago is clean — that is, there are no qualifications to it — and management accounts are up to date. There may be nasties hidden, but they are not obvious. Mind you, we've only had three or four days with their books and one visit to the factory.'

McLeish decided that the expert advice he needed was probably sitting with him in the car, and asked Henry to recommend the best way for an individual to steal money from a company. He realized that it might be thought an odd question to put to a distinguished accountant, but Blackshaw took the question entirely matter of factly, and settled down to bend the accumulated knowledge of a long career as an auditor and a finance director to the question.

'The only fiddles worth doing are the ones that leave you with usable cash. You can take actual cash, but there usually isn't much about in a manufacturing business. Or you can run an accounting fraud — you open an account for a fictitious supplier, and when there is enough of the firm's money in that account you put it somewhere safe, and you run. Or, of course, you just make a deal with a supplier whereby he gets the order and you get a backhander in used fivers. That's the simple one, if only because lots of suppliers actually offer backhanders, and they make it easy for you to take them. I'd go for that.'

'How does that work, exactly?'

'Ah. Someone at the supplier end — call him Tom — suggests to someone at the customer end — call him Dick — that he should place an order with Tom's firm rather than another, in return for which Tom will give him, personally, some cash in his hand. Dick should reply indignantly that he would take his business to another supplier, but in fact he takes the cash.'

McLeish thought about it. 'So Tom doesn't get any cash, he just gets the order for his firm?'

'Depends. Tom and Dick may make a deal whereby they *both* get cash, so they are both stealing from their respective firms. You may well have Harry from the supplier company in the fiddle, too, because you need someone to authorize the cash.'

'Who are all these people, come to think of it? I mean, how senior would they have to be?'

'Well, Dick is probably the head of purchasing. Tom, at the supplier end, has to be more senior because he has to get the cash put through the supplier company's accounts somewhere.' Henry paused, thoughtfully. 'No, I think Tom has to be a director, or if he isn't, he needs Harry who is a director to cover him. Harry may or may not be taking some of the cash for himself.'

'The head of purchasing at Britex was the late William Fireman, and there is nothing about his life to suggest he would be party to this sort of deal. I'll get his bank account checked, of course.'

Henry considered him with some sympathy, and suggested a quick hunt through both companies' management accounts might yield a useful result. McLeish considered this gloomily. Without access to Britex's books, and given the general accounting expertise readily available to him, he could not see how to tackle it quickly. He decided to try for the other end.

'How do people hide a lot of cash?'

'Set up an account anywhere where they believe money is more important than the administration of justice.

Switzerland, the Cayman Islands, lots of places. On consideration, I'd plump for Switzerland.'

McLeish sighed. 'So we would probably not find anything in any UK bank accounts?'

'You shouldn't, but people do the stupidest things. One I caught, as an auditor, had all the money in a deposit account. Told the manager it was a legacy. But on the whole, no.' He thought for a bit. 'I did my training in the Inland Revenue. If you have a dodgy customer, you make him account for all expenditure and all income, and look at the gap. If I were you, I'd start from there, and look for someone living beyond his income.'

'That I can do, but what about having a look at the suppliers? Take a guess that someone chose that option, and go round them?'

Henry opined that he would not bother with the really big suppliers, such as the Allied subsidiary which supplied the yarn, but recommended serious attention to the smaller suppliers. 'Look for someone trying to break in, and concentrate on the last two years,' he suggested.

'You'll be missing your dinner,' McLeish reminded him and they got out of the car and made for the dining-room.

'I'll tell you another thing, though,' Henry volunteered as they strolled through the carpark. 'If there is a fiddle anywhere, it'll be documented — I mean the method and the amounts will be written down. Think on, lad. There's no honour among thieves, so there will always be a record of who gets what. In fact, the accounting will probably be of a higher standard than you find in the rest of the business.'

McLeish considered this with interest. 'You mean the second set of books will be better than the first?'

'Something like that,' Henry agreed approvingly. 'It is a bit easier for me to talk to you now that we, and the company, know we are not recommending assistance.' He hesitated. 'However, given that Francesca is not that experienced, I have made it clear to her that she is not to discuss the company with you, and that still goes.'

'She has only answered the most basic questions.' McLeish spoke hastily. 'Very professional.'

'Known her long?' Henry asked innocently.

'No, no, I only met her — what? — last week.' He paused, amazed at this thought and Henry, vastly amused, waited patiently. 'It seems longer,' he said helplessly.

'Like that, is it?' He smiled at McLeish, enviously. 'She's a good girl. I thought Hampton — the Britex MD — was a bit struck too, but I warned her off him.'

'Does the warning-off still apply now that you aren't going to recommend assistance and he won't be a customer of the Department's?'

'Oh yes. There's all sorts of reasons why I don't want her socializing with Hampton.'

McLeish was prevented from asking him to elucidate by Francesca's indicating by gesture that Henry's dinner had arrived.

'See you later in the bar, lad,' Henry said comfortingly.

They met in the bar an hour later, and Peter Hampton joined them.

He was looking, McLeish thought sourly, remarkably cheerful for a man whose company had foundered. He stood chatting to Francesca and McLeish looked away from them for a minute, but his attention was recalled by a smart dig in the ribs from Henry.

'Hey up. They've gone to the disco. I'm going to chaperone.'

Suppressing the thought that Francesca was hardly going to welcome this, McLeish followed him, and blinked into the wildly gyrating lights of the hotel disco. Francesca and Hampton were very easy to see. She had taken off the over-severe jacket of her Jaeger suit and was dancing in a white, straight-cut, high-necked blouse which she had untucked from the neat flared skirt, while Hampton had removed his jacket and rolled up the sleeves of his pale blue shirt. They both looked very tall, elegant and assured, among the variously dressed young.

The floor was not crowded and the other half-dozen couples on it were dancing hugged closely together, while Hampton and Francesca were dancing at a little distance from each other, but in perfect unison, watching each other seriously as they each mirrored the other's movements. The music changed noisily, to the accompaniment of unintelligible bellowed comment from the slight blond youth who was in charge of the entertainment, to a fast rock beat and the two he was watching stopped for a minute to consider, then, moving as one person, slid into the rhythm. Hampton, very concentrated, the long body perfectly balanced, swung Francesca towards him and spun her round, sliding forward to catch her again as she came out of a neat double spin, skirt flying to reveal most of her excellent legs. They both spun again, coming out to face each other, touch hands, spin, come back and catch each other's hands. They paused for a second, holding hands, Francesca leaning back slightly against Hampton's balancing weight; his lips moved inaudibly and her serious face lit in a huge grin. She leant back further, and making nothing of it, did a back bend so her hair just touched the ground behind her, Hampton supporting her at the full stretch of both their arms with no apparent effort. She came up neatly in one movement, let go of his hands, then touched them lightly in acknowledgement. They spun away from each other, and spun back, perfectly in time, Hampton again steadying her as they met in the middle. They touched hands, and Hampton without breaking step moved a little back from her and clapped his hands sharply, and the whole room warmed to Francesca's wide smile as she reached for his waiting hands, and slid through his legs in a flurry of long legs and flying skirt to come up the other side, perfectly in time to the beat.

Scattered applause broke out, which Hampton acknowledged with a dip of the head, but which Francesca patently did not even hear.

Without looking at each other they broke into a series of intricate turns and twists, Hampton controlling the movement and supporting her, making it look easy. She stumbled very slightly on one spin, and he checked her, holding her from behind with his arms crossed round her and said something, his lips very close to her ear, as he pulled her lightly against his chest. Her head turned in surprise, as clear as if she had spoken, then she smiled in acknowledgement of a message and they started again.

'Told her not to lead,' Henry observed, watching intently. 'And she listened, by heck.' He cursed himself for tactlessness the minute the words were out of his mouth, but McLeish had grimly assessed the situation for himself. They were moving together as if they had been doing it all their lives, and, as he knew, that perfect understanding was well-nigh irresistible when you found it, in any physical activity.

Watching them he remembered the exact feel of the ball smacking into his hands from a perfect pass from the fly-half, and the wild pleasure of racing down the field knowing exactly where the next forward was if you needed him. It was painful to have had to witness Hampton exerting effortlessly a very masculine authority. It was worse to watch them dance.

The music finally clashed to a halt, and solid applause broke out from what was by now a substantial watching crowd. McLeish turned hastily away as Hampton came off the floor with his arm lightly but proprietarily round Francesca who was breathless and shining with pleasure.

'I didn't know you could do that, lass.' Henry shouldered the conversational burden.

'I didn't know I still could, either.' Francesca, bright pink with exertion and joy was tucking her shirt in like a tidy child. 'Perry and I, as teenagers, used to be very good.'

'I had a misspent youth in dance halls,' Hampton said smugly.

Francesca smiled on him and demanded a glass of orange juice which got them all back to the bar. McLeish got her her orange juice, and joined civilly in the general chat, wondering if it would not be more dignified and more realistic to give up and go to bed. Hampton was standing very close to Francesca, and she put a hand on his arm to support herself as she examined the heel of a shoe.

'I'll miss this part of the world,' Hampton observed suddenly, and Henry and Francesca exchanged startled looks. 'No need to be embarrassed, beautiful — the Inspector here knows all about the company, and we all know I'll get the push if we are to have new owners.'

McLeish, resenting bitterly the caress in his voice as he spoke to Francesca, nonetheless admired the man's style.

'What will you do, Peter?' Francesca asked.

'I've got a mate in North London running a small burglar-alarm business. He's been wanting me to come in with him for some time. This shambles here is probably what I've been needing to get me to do that.' He smiled at Francesca. 'Don't look so worried, lovely.' She looked back at him, her eyebrows peaking in surprise, then smiled at him ravishingly while McLeish gritted his teeth.

'Well, any sector with a bit of growth in it has to be better than textiles, doesn't it?' she offered.

Henry Blackshaw started to laugh, and said in explanation that it was entirely typical of Francesca to have grasped, first off, that burglary was a major growth sector; and while they were all laughing, Sir James Blackett, rather red about the cheeks, arrived, and said heavily that he would be glad if he could remove Hampton here for a little conference. McLeish would willingly have embraced him, but Francesca looked disappointed. Hampton hesitated, but said goodnight punctiliously to Henry and McLeish, leaving Francesca till last.

He took both her hands and kissed her formally, on the cheek, a little too close to her mouth. 'We have to dance again when all this is over,' he said to her, as if the other two were not in the room, and she looked back at him, amused and challenged.

'We'll see you tomorrow, Peter,' she said demurely, neatly avoiding the issue, and watching him for a minute as he walked off after his Chairman.

'Time I went to bed, too,' Henry observed into a difficult silence, finishing his drink. 'I've got past these late hours.' He ignored Francesca's raised eyebrows, said firmly that ten o'clock was quite late enough for him, and took himself off, leaving McLeish not quite knowing what to do now that he had Francesca to himself. The situation was resolved for him, as the night manager came over and in confidential tones audible all over the bar established that he was indeed Detective Inspector McLeish and explained that Detective Sergeant Davidson had rung and wished him urgently to ring back.

Torn between relief and frustration, he excused himself to Francesca, who said that since he was occupied she too would go to bed. She leaned over to him and kissed him lightly, and said she would see him tomorrow evening, if not before, so that he went off to make his phone call a little heartened.

Francesca caught up with Henry at the reception desk where he was patiently waiting behind an American visitor trying to order the *Herald-Tribune* for the morning.

'What have you done with young McLeish?' Henry demanded. 'I took off to give him a chance with you.'

'Nothing could have been more conspicuous,' she agreed, with affection. 'The Edgware Road nick rang up for him, and it was obviously all going to take hours, so I gave up. He's quite big enough to look after himself, you know. So am I.'

'Bollocks. If ever I saw a girl in need of care and attention, and a decent serious man, it's you. Not a Jack-the-Lad like Hampton who, as you ought to be able to see for yourself, sits too light to the saddle. He's left one wife and his children already, and he's out of a job. What's wrong with a devoted policeman?'

'I don't necessarily want a devoted man. What a dull idea.'

'You're showing off, and you don't fool me.' Henry glared at her. 'Might it not actually be more fun to have a bloke you could rely on a bit, instead of one who is married to someone else or generally footloose? Someone who would look after you a bit?' He looked into the set face, level with his own. 'Oh, what's the use — I'm probably spoiling the poor bloke's chances with every word, I say.' He looked at her more carefully. 'Frannie, don't cry.' He fished out a clean handkerchief and thrust it anxiously at her, and she buried her face in it while he patted her shoulder. 'If I hadn't been married for twenty-five years come January, I'd offer myself,' he said seriously, and she smiled at him.

'Oh Henry. I just don't find men very dependable and I don't want to get into the habit of depending on one again.'

'Give the poor bloke a chance, eh?'

'Well, I was going to anyway, because I fancy him.' She bent a hard-case scowl on both the fascinated night porter and Henry, who said equably that if she could manage to fancy a reliable bloke that was a good start, and sent her off to bed.

CHAPTER 13

The morning of Thursday dawned bright and clear, which McLeish thought, was just as well. He had slept badly, made miserable by not getting any time with Francesca and had finally sunk into a heavy sleep at around 5 a.m. At 7 a.m. the phone shrilled in his ear and he fought his way out of the blankets, and grunted into it by way of answer.

'John, it's Bruce. I'm sorry to rouse you, but I've waited a bit. Sheena Byers is showing real signs of improvement today, and I thought you'd like to know. Not conscious, but they think she will recover consciousness. The wee boy is with her.'

It took McLeish a minute to work out that Davidson meant that Peregrine Wilson was at her side. 'Ah,' he said, his mind starting to function. 'I'll tell Francesca. You still have a policeman at the hospital, I hope?'

Davidson confirmed that the chap was still there, and McLeish got himself groggily out of bed and stood under the shower until he felt better. He shaved and dressed, and he decided he could ring Francesca with the hope of being first with the good news. He woke her up but she received his news with all the enthusiasm he could have wished.

'Have breakfast with me?' he suggested when he could get a word in.

'Oh yes. Give me ten minutes.'

McLeish went sedately downstairs and ordered breakfast for two.

He was gratefully drinking coffee when Francesca burst into the dining-room.

'How marvellous!' she said, breathlessly, pulling up a chair and dazzling the solitary waiter with her smile. 'Yes please, I'm starving, I'll have one of everything.' The waiter withdrew, smiling benevolently, having obviously received a totally erroneous message, as McLeish could not resist pointing out.

'Nonsense,' Francesca said briefly, through a mouthful of his toast.

'People in the situation you suggest come down at different times for breakfast and pretend not to know each other if they should accidentally find themselves in the same room. I should know.' She paused and gave him a glinting look. 'Please pass the marmalade.'

McLeish passed it obediently, wondering how much of this he would have to put up with if he ever did become her lover.

'So, what are you doing today?' she asked, having finished an enormous meal and looking hungrily at the last piece of toast on his plate.

'Collecting background,' he said, firmly buttering the toast for himself. 'What are you?'

'Either escorting strange Americans round the Britex factory, or not, as the case might be. Anyway, duty calls. Good luck, and I'll see you tonight.' She smiled at him so warmly that he touched her cheek in farewell as he passed and had the ineffable satisfaction of seeing Peter Hampton come into the dining-room just at that moment. If that delivers a totally erroneous message then let it, he thought with primitive pleasure, greeting Hampton civilly on his way out.

He decided to go back to his room to apply himself to the telephone, from where, ten minutes later, he had an excellent view of Francesca, Henry and Martin getting into a taxi. Francesca had her coat half on and was carrying her briefcase with the strap undone, chatting to Martin while she tried to do up the strap and instruct a taxi driver simultaneously. Henry and Martin, working as a team, put her into her coat, strapped up her briefcase and thrust her into the car, patiently catching her as she tripped over the kerb. For a girl who could execute a complex dance routine from scratch with a man she had never danced with before, she was surprisingly clumsy in everyday things, but he understood suddenly that the clumsiness came from trying to do too many things at once. He decided he must explain that to her one day, if he got the chance.

* * *

The Department of Industry contingent meanwhile was engaged in internal argument about how to handle the day. Two directors of Connecticut Cottons were flying up for a meeting at 10.30 with the Directors of Britex, and it had been agreed that they would then have a meeting with the Department of Industry team and tour the factory, following which everyone would retire and think, as Francesca put it. The question was how much the Department should do: should they stay discreetly in the background, having offered assurances of support, or should they make their presence felt and the assurances more concrete by touring the factory with the Americans?

Henry Blackshaw was listening to Martin and Francesca argue it out again.

'Americans are dreadfully polite,' Francesca was saying earnestly. 'They'll feel they have to talk to us if we come with them and they'll miss all sorts of things about the factory.'

'It'd be all right if it was just Henry and I,' Martin observed. 'It's you they'll want to be polite to. And they'll be distracted by wanting to chat you up.'

'I don't think it has anything to do with sex. It's just too many people. I vote we sit in an office doing the notes and looking supportive. Meeting, then lunch, then the 3.30 home.'

'It's like running a cadet corps having you around, Fran; you always have to think where the next meal is coming from.'

'Shut up, Martin, I know you mind quite as much about your meals, it's just that I'm prepared to organize.'

Henry broke into their scrap with his considered decision that he would personally accompany the tour since he knew these Americans and they would feel no need to be civil to him. Francesca and Martin could spend some time sorting out with the Britex people lists of suppliers and principal customers, this being almost the first piece of paper a prospective buyer would want. Yes, he knew they had most of it; could they please check it and make sure it was in a readily digestible state?

'You actually want us out of the way, but ostensibly doing something useful, Henry,' Francesca pointed out. 'I don't mind,' she added hastily, 'I'm just getting clear what I'm doing.'

'It comes of giving them the vote,' Martin said into the silence.

'Aye, that was a mistake,' Henry agreed heavily. 'Right, lass, we'll drop you and Martin at Britex and I'll go on to the airport. I want those lists. Get them typed, too.'

'Sir,' both his subordinates said together, and fell about while Henry reflected comfortably that this giggling pair would have produced, by lunch-time, a first-class analysis of customers and suppliers.

He collected the Connecticut directors, Hal Guadareschi and Ed Patello whom he had known for many years, two amiable, apparently relaxed Americans in their mid-fifties, both born of Italian immigrant parents, but changed by the USA so that only the most fleeting trace of the Milanese peasantry from whence they sprang showed beneath the careful, amicable surface of the prosperous American businessman.

He briefed them in the car and took them straight to Peter Hampton's office when he arrived, catching a reassuring glance of Martin and Francesca seated at a paper-covered table, heads bent in concentration.

In his long career as an auditor, he had several times walked a factory accompanying a prospective purchaser and the existing management, and that situation was always fraught with social pitfalls.

Himself, by no means an insensitive man, had learned just to keep his mind on the job and ignore all the emotions, but as a connoisseur of these parties he decided that Hal, Ed and Peter Hampton were making a particularly graceful occasion of it. Hal and Ed started off by commenting knowledgeably and favourably on what there was of quality in the factory, while taking it in turns to elucidate, quietly, the extent of the problems. Hampton had warned the shop floor of their visit, describing them as American technical experts come to consider what improvements could be made to the lines. Henry was not sure to what extent his cover story deceived a shop floor alert for trouble, but the Americans' soft-spoken command of their subject and the ease with which they dealt with the workforce, stopping to ask a quiet question here and there, or to watch with undeviating concentration the way a particular machine was working, were in themselves impressive.

At one point Hal fell behind and was found watching one of the big looms, standing silent amid the thought-shattering banging of the looms. He finally turned and walked slowly back to the group, took the foreman a little away and said something to him, the broad, clumsy-seeming hands moving with precision. The foreman looked startled, nodded, signalled a fitter who was lounging on the top of the row, and disappeared purposefully. Peter Hampton raised an eyebrow enquiringly as Hal returned.

'Bar on the shuttle — five, no six — out of alignment,' he said apologetically.

'Where's your wrench, Hal?' his fellow director asked teasingly, and Hal, with his easy smile, said that there were perfectly good mechanics about who could fix it up without his interfering further in someone else's business.

'Missed that,' Peter Hampton said easily. 'Thank you,' and he led the group on, with Henry at the rear thinking about him. He was behaving impressively today despite the difficulties and Henry wondered whether he had been fair in his initial judgement of Hampton's quality. In the end, the only way you could judge a managing director was by his results, and by that test Hampton was a failure; his business was in worse shape now than it had been when he took it over. But he knew his business and was obviously a hard worker.

He had perhaps been unlucky in finding himself in the eye of the hurricane that had hit the European textile Industry, and in finding himself in charge of a company with substantial borrowings which was, like an over-canvased sailing-ship, thereby less equipped to ride out the storm. He watched Hampton swapping jokes with Ed, apparently without a care in the world, and decided that both were true: he was a flawed character, but also an intelligent manager who had been unlucky.

He caught up with Ed, who was suggesting that they might have lunch after the tour, and after lunch they might perhaps be allowed to see a list of the firm's principal customers and suppliers. 'I imagine they'll include some mutual friends?' he said easily to Hampton.

'That list is being prepared now,' Hampton said drily, sliding a look at Henry. 'We had lists of course, but Henry's people are organizing them in a different way.' Henry smiled at him blandly. 'Are we allowing them to join us for lunch, Henry?'

'Oh yes, I think so,' Henry said placidly, and explained who he had with him.

'Francesca, eh?' Ed smiled, amused. 'My sister's name. She Italian by origin?'

'I shouldn't think so,' Hampton said. 'Pure Norman, I would have thought — you know, long nose, absolutely regular features. Straight off a tapestry.'

Henry contemplated reflectively a notice adjuring employees to wear ear protection at all times or risk premature deafness. So Hampton too had thought of the Bayeux tapestry; it made him more imaginative than the usual run of MDs in a production industry, and also indicated a real and intelligent interest in Francesca.

'The Normans colonized Italy too,' Hal Guadareschi pointed out, surprising Henry again. 'Have to have a look at her.'

Henry with some firmness said they could postpone this pleasure while he had a preliminary chat before lunch, and asked Peter Hampton if he would mind going to round up Martin and Francesca and the product of their morning's work. He settled into the boardroom with Ed and Hal, waiting patiently for them to gather their thoughts together.

* * *

Francesca and Martin had meanwhile finished the first draft of the lists, and Francesca, who was easily bored, had prowled restlessly out into the corridor, leaving the patient and audit-trained Martin to double-check and cross-add his lists.

'Fran. Ask someone for the Alutex, Allied Yarns and Browns ledgers, will you?' he called after her, not lifting his head from the lists. She pushed through a door labelled 'Purchasing' and found herself in a small, overcrowded office looking at the backs of two men who were hunting through a filing cabinet, papers spread out all around them.

One of them dropped a file, knocked his elbow on the edge of a filing drawer and swore as she wished them good morning.

'Sorry to make you jump, Mr Blackett.' She smiled nervously at William Blackett as he stared up at her, clasping his elbow, livid patches on the cheeks particularly bright against his general pallor.

'Ah. Miss Wilson. You again. Didn't realize you were here. Just doing some tidying up.' All three of them blinked at the chaos on the floor.

'Do you know Simon Ketterick? One of my salesmen at Alutex. We are just trying to help Peter Hampton get our records straight.'

Francesca gazed at him, wondering what the records had looked like before they started tidying, but was distracted by Ketterick reaching across the table to shake hands. His hand was so cold and damp that she started very slightly, and looked at him carefully. Only a little taller than her, but probably a stone and a half lighter, skeletally thin. She wondered if he had been ill.

'Sorry again to disturb you. Have you by any chance the Alutex ledger for the last year?'

'Why do you need that?' Blackett sounded both alarmed and aggressive, and she decided to play dumb.

'I haven't the slightest idea. My colleague Martin is an accountant, as you know, and he seemed to think it would be useful.'

Blackett, still looking doubtful and ruffled, stared helplessly down at the mess, but Ketterick produced the ledger and handed it over, dropping a piece of A4 as he did so, which Francesca neatly caught.

'Don't know if I need this,' she said, considering it carefully, 'but it is to do with a supplier, so perhaps I'd better take it.'

Ketterick moved round to her side to look at the paper, and she tried not to flinch away from a particularly foul-smelling breath. 'No, no, but that is one of the things we need,' he said, firmly and took it from her, brushing her hand; again she noticed how pale and cold his skin was. He showed the paper quickly to Blackett, and the man's jaw dropped down momentarily, but he recovered himself.

'If there is nothing else, Miss Wilson, perhaps I can take you back to where you are working.'

Francesca, embarrassed, started to apologize and back out, but the door banged open and she had to move swiftly sideways to avoid a clout in the back as Peter Hampton came briskly through the door, and stopped, gazing at the mess.

'Martin sent me to look for some ledgers, and I found Mr Blackett here so I asked him.' Francesca, realizing immediately that he was furious, tried to get her version of the story in first, and edged round him towards the door, but he stopped her.

'Francesca, would you please ask only Michael Currie or Jim Finlay for anything you want, and stay where you are put? We cannot have visitors wandering around.'

'I'm sorry. I should have waited.'

'I'll take you back, if you now have everything you need.' Francesca, unnerved, said she was sure she did and she could find her own way back, sorry, but Hampton was tight-lipped and silent as he walked her to the room where Martin was adding up columns of figures, opened the door, and stood aside to let her through.

Francesca's heart sank as she realized that further trouble was at hand. Martin, his back to them, was patiently working his way through a wall cupboard, stacking papers and boxes on the table next to him.

He turned to greet them, two heavily discoloured silver cups in his hands, sweeping another box and some outsize paperclips from the untidy shelves as he did so. Then he saw Peter Hampton's expression, and closed his mouth on the explanation he had been about to offer.

'Could we just agree that you two ask me for anything you happen to want?' Peter Hampton said, grittily. 'No, for God's sake, don't put everything back in the cupboard — just leave it alone, will you?' He watched, stony-faced, as the two civil servants slunk back to their chairs, apologetically, and bent over their papers, then walked out, shutting the door over-emphatically.

* * *

Back in the boardroom, Ed and Hal had worked round to the meat of the discussion.

'The kit's not bad, Henry, and the factory's well laid out.' Ed Patello looked at his hands. 'That's the good news. The quality on household textiles is shit-awful; the trouble with an integrated factory is that your mistakes live with you.

A bad piece of spinning is still there as a flaw in the finished sheet. That is, unless you pick it up at an early stage and scrap it. Their standards are just not high enough.'

'We can fix that,' Hal pointed out, 'but it'll take a long time and I'd guess we'd have to bring our own people over. You can get a lot more use out of this lot than these guys here are managing. Their maintenance is poor, no proper schedules.'

Henry sighed. 'Of course, our people don't adjust their own machines because of the unions.'

'We'd have to have a special deal if we were to take over here, Henry. I hope your people understand that.'

Henry confirmed, unblushingly, that the Government well understood that many restrictive practices embodied in union agreements were wholly untenable in any industrial structure, but warned that they were unlikely to say so publicly. The Americans nodded and fell silent, while Henry, out of long experience, waited out the silence. Hal finally broke.

'I don't know how to say this, Henry,' he observed, showing no signs of diffidence whatsoever, 'but Ed and I are in agreement that there is no way Connecticut Cottons would get involved with this factory unless we could be offered substantial assurances by your government of financial and business support on a major scale.'

Henry, who had been waiting for some version of this speech, confirmed that this too was understood.

'As to management, Henry, I guess we'd have to rely on our own people supplemented by some local recruitment. I don't like to take on a management that has already failed, and I would have to say that I would not be sure that the chief executive, to be specific, is as involved with the detail as we would like to see. I believe, Henry, that a manager that we had trained would have noticed that misaligned shuttle. Equally, I would not like to feel that one of our people would be allowing so many flaws through to the final article.'

Henry noted with interest that Ed's was exactly the same verdict as his own initial reaction — Hampton sat a little too light in the saddle and did not really control all the business. That might not matter in the boom times, but it was all important when the markets turned sour.

'Maybe we ought to break now?' Hal suggested. 'It's been some time since breakfast. Shall we find the others?'

'The arrangement was that they would find us — here they come.'

The door opened to admit Martin and Francesca, both looking crushed, and Hampton scowling.

'One list is still being typed, Henry, and will be finished after lunch,' Francesca said briskly and turned to greet Ed and Hal who were regarding her with interest. Amid civilities they all went out and waited while cars were fielded to go to the nearest hotel. Francesca was standing by Henry's elbow, uncharacteristically silent.

'Trouble?' he said to her quietly under cover of the negotiations as to who went in which car.

'Yes, a bit. Peter is cross with us. Tell you later. Not serious, don't worry.'

Nonetheless he did. She stuck by his side so that they and Ed travelled in one car, with Hampton, Hal and Martin in the other, and at lunch she was careful and rather quiet, and sat herself firmly between Ed and Hal. He was amused to notice that the Americans were respectful of her, rather than charmed.

As the party broke up at the end of the meal, he saw Hampton make a beeline for her and say something obviously apologetic. She smiled back, equally obviously relieved. He edged closer to where they stood, Hampton very close to her, looking down, saying, 'I'm sorry I can't come with you to the station, but I must go and talk to these chaps.'

'Of course you must.'

'I'll ring you when I'm coming down, OK? And sorry to snap this morning. Stress or something.'

'No, it was my fault. I didn't think.'

Henry collected her and Martin with a look and the group broke up, the Departmental team going to the station and the others back to Britex. They caught the train with none too much time to spare.

Francesca looked round for John McLeish and was disappointed to find he was obviously not on the train anywhere. She took her coat off and found Henry watching her.

'What was the difficulty, Francesca?'

'I went down the passage to look for something Martin wanted, and ran into William Blackett and one of his salesmen sorting out a filing cabinet. They were pissed off because I picked up a piece of paper they didn't want me to see, and Peter was furious because he didn't want me wandering around upsetting people.'

'As you seem to have done. Bit tactless, lass.'

'Martin didn't do any better. They are touchy today.'

'What happened, Martin?'

'Fran was getting hungry, so I looked in a cupboard for a biscuit, and got the freezing treatment from Hampton. He didn't creep up and apologize to me afterwards, either, but then he doesn't fancy me.'

'Imagine how distressed you would be if he did,' Francesca pointed out, coldly. 'No actually, Martin, I thought it was kind and tactful not to say you'd only been in that cupboard because of me. I always knew there must be something in the public-school system.'

'What was in the cupboard — papers?'

'A load of old rubbish.' Martin assured him. 'Two cups for some long-gone swimming gala, draft accounts for three years ago, and a couple of boxes.'

Henry sighed. 'Try and be a bit careful when people are on edge, though. All right, Frannie, tell me about the bit of paper; what was it?'

'I read it quite carefully. Hold on while I try and think.' She propped both elbows on the table in front of her and closed her eyes. 'The heading is ALUTEX and it's a handwritten schedule of figures, in four columns. One script, three figures. Let me just try and get the column headings. The headings are — ah — it's date, then the next one is order number, then it's val — that's value presumably, then the next one is com. What's com?'

'Commission.' Both men spoke at once and Henry asked cautiously what she was doing.

Her eyes opened in surprise. 'I have a photographic memory. I thought you knew. If no one worries me, I may be able to reproduce the rest of it.' She closed her eyes again and Henry and Martin exchanged looks.

'Make a bloody useful auditor,' Henry murmured to Martin.

'There are four sub-headings under the com column, just letters, P, S, W, and Total. The left-hand column goes June 6, July 10, August 12, Sept 4, something, can't see further. The next column goes two nought nought three.' She ran off the next four numbers and said fretfully that that was as far as she could go, then moved to the next column. 'Starts with pounds three four six seven five nought.'

'Can you do the com column?' Martin was producing a table to her dictation.

'Under P. it says pounds 2080; pounds 1040 under S.; and pounds 2080 under W. Total pounds 5200.'

'One and a half per cent,' Henry said promptly, and Martin nodded.

Francesca opened her eyes again and Martin passed her the table he had drawn up. She read down the figures, closing her eyes every now and then to consult the picture in her head. Henry thought he had rarely seen anything more disconcerting than the matter-of-fact way she treated this unnerving ability.

'It looks like an ordinary salesman's record,' Martin observed, puzzled.

'Why did they get uptight? Is 1½ per cent high for the trade, Henry?'

'About average. Was there a salesman's name on it?'

Francesca closed her eyes. 'No.'

Henry shrugged. 'There may be some hanky-panky with some salesmen on a higher rate than others. That's always embarrassing. I'll warn Hal, but he'll be looking for all that. OK, let's look at these schedules so we can talk sense about the market when Hal and Ed come and ask for money.'

'They were interested, then?' Martin asked.

'Oh yes. They were on the hook, but on a receivership basis not as a going concern. Barclays is going to go down on this one. Connecticut won't want to pay anything like enough to get Barclays' debenture paid off, and we shouldn't be assisting them if they were prepared to. We ought to be able to control the situation, though, so Britex can go into receivership, but have a deal set up so all the customers and suppliers know that Connecticut will take it over.'

They discussed the schedule exhaustively and then Francesca removed herself to another table, closed her eyes and was asleep within minutes.

'Active social life, that one,' Henry observed drily and Martin Bailey, who was newly married, said wistfully that he remembered those days well. Just before Kings Cross they woke her up, but she was obviously still tired and as the train pulled in, Henry told her he would take her home. She was protesting feebly that it was out of his way when Henry saw John McLeish on the platform.

'The boyfriend's come to meet you, Fran. Must have got the earlier train.'

'To whom are you referring?' she asked cautiously.

'Your policeman,' Martin confirmed. 'The large one.'

'Well, that's very nice.' She reached for her briefcase and brought it crashing down on herself, together with a mackintosh belonging to another passenger. Henry pushed down the window and waved to McLeish.

'We've got her, lad, she's busy vandalizing the train,' he called cheerfully, adding a further ingredient to Francesca's embarrassment.

'You're tired,' McLeish said in greeting, taking her briefcase from her. 'Come on, we're going straight to eat.'

'See you tomorrow,' Francesca called, waving to them as McLeish efficiently took her away. Henry watched them go, trying not to feel envious.

CHAPTER 14

McLeish groaned to himself as he started his run round Holland Park. He had been feeling heavy and tired and unfit, and had decided that he must start to do a long run on his off-duty days. He was due to pick up Francesca at noon, to take her to Newmarket for the racing, but had decided to finish up some tiresome paperwork and had thought he might as well have a run on his way in, and change at the station.

He distracted himself from the pain of getting going by thinking about Francesca. After he had met her from the train on Thursday and given her dinner, he had considered fleetingly whether it would be worth trying to sweep her out of the restaurant and into his bed, but she was still looking exhausted. So he had taken her sedately home at 8.30 and met James Miles Brett and his mother, and watched with interest and respect while Francesca had shown James how to do his Latin translation and accompanied him on the piano through a difficult Bach cantata. At least James and his mother had now gone, so he would not have to share Francesca with the maths prep or the clarinet practice or whatever else young James could have devised.

He grinned to himself as he remembered the instantly suppressed look of disappointment with which Francesca had bade him goodnight when he left at 10 p.m.

He swung round his final circuit, breathing more easily even though he was now running uphill, and steadily overhauled another runner who was making heavy weather of the hill. A jogger, not a runner, he thought professionally, not moving from the hip, and obviously labouring. A girl, he observed further as he got closer and pulled out to overtake, running evenly. The girl turned her head as he came level, checking him in mid-stride because it was Francesca, scarlet and struggling for breath. She stopped, astonished, and he blinked at the vision she presented, with her elegant length obscured by a dingy grey tracksuit much too big on the top and too long in the leg.

'I didn't know you ran,' he said, watching with fascination the slogan *CM Wilson, Locke's* rising and falling as she fought for breath.

'The word "ran" hardly meets the case,' she pointed out between gasps. 'It really isn't my thing, but I just felt I must have some exercise and it was too cold to go swimming, which I am good at. I wish I'd stayed in bed.'

McLeish closed his eyes, momentarily dizzied by the vision of Francesca staying in bed. She considered him, still breathing hard.

'Do you want to come back and have coffee? Or have you got too much to do?'

McLeish promptly consigned all the morning's chores and the rest of his run to the scrap heap, and drove back behind her car to the now-familiar little terrace house.

She let them into the house and busied herself in the kitchen making coffee. She was extremely conscious of McLeish, and sneaked a glance at him as he leant against the kitchen divider watching her fill the kettle, seeming even larger than usual in the bright blue tracksuit with the London Scottish flash on it. He felt her eyes on him and looked steadily back at her, the hazel eyes very bright. In a blessed moment of sanity she saw him clear, a good and loving man, sensitive and unsure of his welcome in the light of some confusing signals she had been giving. She put the kettle down and drew a deep breath.

'John. Good morning.'

His whole face lifted into a grin and he padded over to her and put his arms round her.

'And good morning to you,' he said softly, and kissed her gently on the cheek. She turned her head, so that he was kissing her lips and put her arms around his neck. He kissed her till she was breathless and shaking as she leant against him.

'Darling Fran. I haven't even shaved.'

'Oh dear.' She moved her cheek against his and stroked the thick dark hair at the back of his head. 'I could rise above this problem.'

She settled back on her heels to look into his eyes, and then, as she was always to remember, he simply picked her up and carried her up to her bed with no apparent strain or self-consciousness. He was also impressively unbothered by having to separate her from her running shoes, whose laces had become hopelessly knotted as she tried to take them off in a hurry. He then took the rest of her clothes off for her, without in any way losing impetus.

Both of them fell asleep afterwards. It was McLeish who woke first, and gently roused her as she lay with her cheek tucked in between his neck and collarbone.

'You lured me here with promises of coffee,' he pointed out smugly. 'No darling, don't move, I'll get it.'

'No, no, I read somewhere that gentlemen are exhausted afterwards.'

Francesca, barely awake, rolled out of bed on to her feet, and pulled blindly at her dressing-gown which came off the hook with the sound of rending fabric. 'Blast.'

McLeish propped himself up on a pillow and observed her with love as she tried to force an arm down an inside out sleeve. He reached out and disentangled her. 'It's just as well I'm neat-handed,' he observed. 'I'd have had to make love to you with your running shoes on otherwise. Do you always wind the laces round the shoes and finish up with a double bow?'

'They are an old pair of Charlie's and they are a bit big. I'm sorry it was all so difficult.'

'The tracksuit is Charlie's too, I take it?' McLeish pulled her down beside him and kissed her, wondering if he would be allowed to give her a new one for Christmas.

She found the belt of her dressing-gown and tied it round her with dignity. 'Are we going to the races? Or shall I put my shoes on again, so you can take them off? I'm only asking.'

McLeish lay back and considered the options. 'I'd like to stay here all day, but I said we'd meet Mike and Jenny and I think they will have started out already. They won't mind too much if we don't turn up.'

'Of course we go.' Francesca sounded shocked. 'You can't mess your friends round like that. We've got all weekend.' She caught his eye. 'That is, unless you are doing something else tomorrow?'

He assured her gravely that while he had not been so bold as to hope to spend the night with her, he had hoped to see her on Sunday, so he had kept it free.

'Would you have sought to seduce me if I had not offered?' Francesca had her back to him and was sorting through clothes as he put his tracksuit back on, preparatory to collecting his clothes from the car.

'Yes I would.' He swung her round indignantly to face him. 'I fancied you from the first time I ever saw you. I wasn't quite sure what you wanted, mind, so it might have taken me a little longer.' He pushed her fringe back from her eyes. 'It's not good for you taking all the decisions,' he said seriously. 'You don't have to; let me do a few of them. Wear that blue dress — I like it.' She grinned at him, amused but unconvinced, he observed.

* * *

He drove like a dervish to Newmarket and they arrived just before the first race, finding his friends exactly where they had agreed. Mike was a chartered accountant in a crack city firm, who had played rugby with McLeish and remained fascinated by the police and police work. His wife Jenny had worked as a secretary before settling down to produce three small children in as many years, and McLeish noticed a shade of reserve in her greeting of Francesca. All reserve was dispelled, however, when the whole party backed an outsider on Mike's recommendation at 10 to 1, and a shocked Francesca repudiated his suggestion that they should put the lot on the next race.

'I put a fiver on,' she pointed out to Mike, 'so I've got fifty whole pounds, which is one-fifth of a washing-machine. I'm not going to put all that on a horse!' This totally illogical sentiment so plainly reflected Jenny's feelings that she instantly warmed to Francesca, while Mike was simply amused. The two women went off, chatting amicably, to put the fiver on the next race.

'You've got a star there, John.' Mike, as broad as McLeish but three inches shorter, nodded at Francesca's retreating back. 'One of our lads is seconded to the Department and he marked my card. Very much one of their high-flyers I hear. Got them all under control.'

McLeish, thinking of the morning, beamed at him wordlessly and Mike's eyebrows went up.

'All except you, then. Lucky sod. Ah, those were the days — you just wait until you have three under four and they all cry in the night. Nice-looking girl too.'

'I'm afraid she has me under control, too.' He watched placidly as she hurried back to him and smiled down at her with pleasure. She was so quick and such a good-looker, and after this he would be going home with her, and they would go to bed and he would find out what she really liked. She looked beyond him, the bright face suddenly strained and anxious.

'My ex-husband is here.'

'So smile, don't look so worried. Where?'

'Coming over to us.' She smiled up at him, ravishingly but artificially. 'I'll just wave.'

McLeish, feeling fully as self-conscious as Francesca, turned to greet a man of his own age, very nearly as tall but slightly built, blond and quite extraordinarily good looking, provided you ignored the tense, bad-tempered line of the mouth in repose.

'Francis Lewendon, John McLeish,' Francesca said in bright, social tones.

'How nice to see you, darling.' Francis Lewendon bent to kiss her, disconcerting her and making her blush. McLeish watched unmoving, recognizing a private fight in which assistance would be unwelcome, and was rewarded by seeing Francesca, unhampered, get her blush under control and greet, with careful kindness, Francis Lewendon's second wife, a tall plain girl, also slight and blonde, who was plainly terrified of her. He spared an ear from dealing with Lewendon's courteous pleasantries to listen to Francesca silkily enquiring whether Miranda was doing anything with herself, or (with a pitying inflection) whether looking after Francis constituted a full-time job?

'I'm a policeman,' he said firmly, in answer to a direct question, watching Francis Lewendon very slightly grit his teeth in response to Francesca's skilled point-scoring. The well-set blue eyes widened.

'CID presumably? A Chief Inspector?'

'Not yet, but it's the next step.'

'I had a great friend at school who joined the police and is now doing rather well. William Forrester.'

McLeish reflected with resignation that he might have known that this polished specimen and the Lancia-driving Hon. William would have been at school together. 'Yes. A very clever copper,' he observed deliberately. As opposed to a good one, he thought, but it hardly seemed the moment to air these doubts. He felt a small pressure from Francesca at his side.

'Very nice to see you both,' she said graciously. 'We had perhaps better go and join the rest of the party.' Francis Lewendon's tight mouth quirked as he nodded to McLeish.

'I expect you had, if Francesca says so,' he said maliciously. 'See you soon. We must go and lose some more money betting on Miranda's favourites.'

'I can't pick them either,' McLeish said equably, and smiled at Miranda. 'Come on, then,' he said to Francesca, took her hand, smiled courteously around him, and withdrew in good order. 'Unkind sod. He rattles you, doesn't he? Did he always?'

She checked, amazed, and walked on soberly considering. 'Yes, I suppose so. Why, do you think?'

'Well, he wants to, doesn't he? Not very nice to his wife, either.'

'Yes, and you were quite unnecessarily civil. Serves her right — she set out to take him off me at a time when we were having trouble. If he is horrid to her, she has only herself to thank.'

McLeish considered her brooding profile. 'Is it all still very painful?'

'Yes. He made me feel dreadful and he can still do it.' She spoke firmly, ending the conversation.

They came up to Mike and Jenny, and McLeish looked at her anxiously, but she shook off her preoccupation and joined smoothly in the conversation, making them all laugh, using what his mother would have called really thoughtful manners — a concept which he had hitherto viewed with mistrust. He was by now used to her ability to do several different things at once, and he noticed that under the easy flow of chat she was thinking hard; in repose she had the inward anxious look of someone trying to add five columns in their head.

The day picked up again, with a couple more good wins thanks to Mike's wholly unexpected knowledge of form. They did so well that they agreed to have supper and champagne. McLeish was just relaxing over his second cup of coffee when Francesca tugged at his jacket, looking anxious and whispered to him.

'Aye aye!' Mike, who was well away and treating Francesca as a sister, beamed at them. 'Trying to take him home, are you? Well, Jenny and I can take a hint.'

'It's not that,' Francesca said with dignity. 'I promised my brother to check on his girlfriend — I told you, Jenny — who is in hospital, and I'm trying to remind John. No need to break the party up, we can go any time, but I don't want John falling down drunk over the uniformed branch.'

'I expect he's not been over-indulging,' Mike said, uproariously. 'I wouldn't be, in his circumstances, but I'm a father three times already.'

Francesca blushed scarlet and Mike let out a smothered cry as his wife kicked him. McLeish, who had been drinking carefully for precisely the reasons Mike had imputed to him, firmly held on to Francesca's hand, said he thought it was time they went anyway, and the party broke up with considerable amity.

He kissed her as they got into the car with the relieved sense of coming home, but despite a very willing response, he realized that at least half her attention was elsewhere. He drove quietly to the hospital and showed his card, which got them straight up to Sheena Byers's room on the third floor. He nodded to the policeman on the door and stood aside to let Francesca through. She stood, silent, considering the beautiful unconscious face, the bruise on the temple now faded to dirty grey.

'How has she been today?' she asked the night sister quietly.

'Oh better. She's coming closer to the surface.'

'What a relief. Did Perry ring?'

'Several times.'

The two women, much of an age McLeish realized, smiled at each other in an understanding that excluded the men in the room.

'Thank you. I'll call Perry anyway, in case he thinks you are not telling him everything. I — we — are picking him up from the airport tomorrow.'

She glanced anxiously at McLeish, plainly feeling that he might not want to do this chore, but he smiled at her reassuringly and the sister looked at them wistfully. McLeish watched with the same detachment as Francesca rushed him out of the hospital, back to her house so she could ring Perry. Lovers take second place round here, he thought, but was mollified by listening to Francesca on the phone.

'Yes, he is here. He took me up to the hospital. Yes, he is coming with me to collect you and Jamie. Yes. No. Yes. Mind your own business. See you tomorrow.'

He took her to bed immediately she put the phone down, firmly unplugging the phone by the bed as he helped her undress. He was very tired, having previously struggled through a long Friday evening shift, and after they had made love, he shifted his fourteen stone over, kissed her neck and went out like a light. He woke three hours later with his head clear and the exhaustion gone. Francesca had moved over to her side of the bed and was lying curled up. He woke her unapologetically.

'That wasn't any good to you, was it, my sweet?' He felt her tense and turned her towards him. 'Close your eyes, I'm going to put a light on.'

He flipped on one of the small reading lights and looked down at his love, who was watching him defensively.

'You have to tell me if it isn't working for you,' he stated, firmly.

'I knew you were going to turn out to be bossy.'

'That's right,' he agreed, and then, his eyes adjusting to the light, '*What* are you wearing? No, don't tell me . . . one of the boys grew out of it.' She clutched the shrunken striped pyjama-jacket round her, wide-eyed. 'Take it off and we'll give it to Oxfam in the morning, if they'll accept it. Oh my God, it comes with legs as well!'

He divested her firmly of both, and, wide awake and feeling perfectly in control of the situation, proceeded to deploy all his considerable experience. He felt her relax, then tense again in concentration, and he waited until he was quite, quite sure she had come, before he did.

He lay beside her, both of them sweating lightly, and as he pushed her fringe back from her eyes, he realized she was crying.

'Fran, darling. Wasn't it alright?' He was momentarily appalled and she reached urgently for him.

'It was lovely, darling John. It's just relief.' She kissed him in reassurance and scrubbed her eyes with the sleeve of the discarded pyjamas.

'I love you. Go to sleep and we'll try again later. No, don't put that object on, stay here.'

* * *

Five hours later he was sitting in the kitchen watching Francesca cook a huge breakfast, which she did with the neatness and dispatch of a short-order chef, confirming McLeish's view that she was only clumsy when her mind was not on the job. He was extremely happy.

He had made love to her again two hours earlier and it had been an undoubted, unqualified success. Francesca, to his admittedly prejudiced eye, was glowing with it. He had understood from what she had left unsaid that he had given her pleasure in a way which her previous lovers and her husband had not, twice in one night, and he was feeling a pure, primitive satisfaction about that, too.

She gave him a huge, beautifully laid-out plate of bacon, eggs, tomatoes, fried potatoes and sausages, and they held hands in the intervals of eating the lot. It was quite the best breakfast he had ever had.

'When do we pick Perry up?' he asked, over his third cup of coffee.

'Two o'clock.' She hesitated. 'I promised to take the Roller rather than my Mini, since we have Perry, plus Jamie, plus all their kit; but I'm frightened of driving it.'

'If it's insured for me, I'll drive. Doesn't Perry know you're frightened of it?'

'All the boys assume I can do anything.'

'Time you disillusioned them, my sweet.' He put his arm around her comfortably, but she was not prepared to be teased and he noted he was on uneasy ground.

He had no difficulty with the huge, beautifully engineered machine and managed to park it without incident at the airport. He followed Francesca into the VIP lounge and nodded to a Special Branch officer whom he recognized. Francesca noticed and asked with interest whether he was recognized everywhere.

'Nine years in the Met does get your face known, yes.'

'There are Perry and James,' she observed. 'Better hang back a bit.'

They waited while Perry dealt patiently and courteously with the waiting reporters. McLeish realized that he had not grasped the extent to which Perry and young James were news. As he watched, Perry listened to a question about his love life addressed in fractured English, and replied briskly in German, making the questioner laugh.

'He said he couldn't remember when he first went out with girls,' Francesca translated. 'Probably true — he can't have been more than four when the little girl next door offered for him. In my calmer moments I try to remember that Sheena is the latest of a very, very long string.'

'Is his German good?'

'Oh very. So is his French, Spanish and Italian. His Portuguese and Russian are less fluent. He has a marvellous ear, and can pick up any language in about twenty minutes — it's just a trick, unattached to intelligence as far as I can see.' She caught him looking at her doubtfully, and laughed. 'When he was interviewed for Cambridge, one poor chap realized what a fantastic linguist he is — Perry was probably telling jokes in Welsh, or similar — and suggested that he read Oriental Languages rather than music. He was totally boggled by Perry who told him, quite truthfully, that he liked languages, but he absolutely couldn't be bothered with Literature. Mercifully the chap was too horror-stricken to ask Perry just how he learns all these languages.'

'How does he?'

'He reads, with occasional reference to a dictionary, any three of the James Bond books translated into whichever language it is. At the end of this he has the language. He is too idle to bother with any more demanding text. He is lazy; he just has these useful gifts.'

'And you love him.'

'And I love him,' she agreed, resignedly.

Perry finally emerged from the press of reporters, kissed his sister and greeted McLeish kindly. In the hiatus of collecting the luggage, McLeish just saw Perry ask Francesca something, grinning broadly, his eyebrows peaking as hers did.

'How did you manage with The Car?' Perry asked amicably as they caught up with McLeish.

'Very well. John drove it.'

'Ah.' Perry touched his sister's arm smiling, plainly having been given the answer to his question. 'Do you hate being driven, John, or can I drive it back?'

McLeish signified that he had no objection to Perry's driving his own car, and stowed the luggage, wondering whether Francesca only ever allowed a man to drive if he was sleeping with her and whether she always told her brothers. Probably, he decided detachedly; which would be something he would have to stop.

Perry moved the big car smoothly out of the carpark and slid into the traffic stream. He drove as he sang, beautifully, concentrated but relaxed.

'How did it go?' asked Francesca, in the back with James.

'"The Apple Tree" went very well,' James volunteered, 'but the alto was not as good as you, Frannie.'

McLeish focused on young James promptly and the boy smiled back at him without self-consciousness. Small for his age, at thirteen he was uncannily grown-up and self-contained. His blond hair was expensively cut and swept up from his forehead. A serious child — or maybe it was just the long neck and high cheekbones, like a blond version of Perry. McLeish remembered that James's mother, like Mary Wilson, was a Scot.

'Let's do it,' Fran suggested and the child nodded to her gravely, focused his eyes on the back of the seat and sang a note. Then he started to sing the old carol, the only sound in the car the true high treble. He was obviously and endearingly a boy who sang as naturally as he breathed. There was none of the controlled, rather nasal, ethereal cathedral treble about this one; he was belting it out. On the second verse Francesca and Perry came in singing the alto and tenor parts, and McLeish listened with real pleasure to Francesca. In any other family, he thought, one not containing the dazzling Perry, her voice would have been considered worth training.

Perry was tactfully under-singing, using only some of that marvellous voice, but all three of them articulated beautifully, so every word and note of the odd rhythmic plainsong was clear. In perfect and well-trained unison they swept into the last three verses, and took the penultimate verse fortissimo, McLeish noting without surprise that James could make his treble heard above both grown-ups. He watched Perry's long hands moving lightly on the wheel in counterpart to the music, and stiffened as a lorry pulled out, forcing a car in front of them into their lane. McLeish braced himself for the collision, deciding with another part of his mind that if he died now, listening to the country's finest treble, the best young tenor he had ever heard and his darling Francesca, it would hardly matter. Perry, without missing a beat, moved his hands and the big car shifted sideways, sliding into a gap behind the lorry, missing it by a coat of paint, and through into a gap which was just opening up in the inner lane. McLeish let out a long breath, and into the silence came James's pure, hard-edged treble from the back seat, singing the last verse by himself, every word clear and separate.

'Nicely driven,' McLeish said and Perry nodded, without taking his eyes off the road.

'Where are we going Perry?'

'I'm going to put Jamie on a train at King's Cross, then I'm going to see Sheena in hospital, then I'm going out.'

'Where out?'

'Just out.' His sister looked at him sharply, and McLeish decided Perry was going off with a girl and wasn't about to confess. He felt a moment's pang for the beautiful, unconscious Sheena but decided she must know how to cope with the likes of Perry.

'Do you sing, John?' Perry was watching his sister in the rear view mirror.

'Not enough to sing with you lot. Rugger-club standard.'

'Can't have everything,' Perry said, grinning at his sister who, thinking herself unobserved, made a horrible face at him. He laughed at her and started softly to sing 'The Lost Chord', and she and Jamie joined in. She wound down the windows as they came round Shepherd's Bush roundabout, so that as they came past the Edgware Road police station and halted in a traffic jam, McLeish found himself with a fascinated audience of half a dozen of the uniformed branch, just as the singers arrived at the final stanza and death's bright angel.

Bruce Davidson signalled them in, grinning. 'I thought you were the radio, John. Afternoon Miss Wilson, Mr Wilson. Since you've dropped by, there's a call from Doncaster. Inspector Brady — will you call him ASAP? Says he has something on that enquiry and it's urgent.'

CHAPTER 15

'It's not a lot to go on, is it?' Bruce Davidson observed as he reached the end of McLeish's notes of his telephone conversation with Brady.

'Mostly gossip. Where did he get it?'

McLeish read his notes again carefully. He had talked to Brady at some length the day before, dictated a note, and decided to sleep on it, this being his natural inclination when faced with new evidence.

Since he would be sleeping with Francesca, the decision had admittedly been easy to take, but he had worried away at the problem in the intervals of spending Sunday evening and Sunday night with her.

'What do we have in this wee note of yours? That Peter Hampton, who is separated from his wife and earns £40,000 a year plus perks, is never short of cash and has his suits made for him. I suppose the suits are a fact.'

'So's his wife's maintenance. Factually, she and the kids are getting about 40 per cent of his gross salary, which doesn't leave an enormous amount of take-home pay.'

'Who says he is never short of a few bob? The note doesnae suggest a source.'

'The source is Brady's wife. I thought when I was there that she'd been having a walk-out with Hampton, but Brady isn't admitting it. He's got her to talk about Hampton, but neither of them is saying to the other or to me that she was pretty close to him. Still, it's a lead.'

He was not about to tell Davidson that at the very end of this conversation Brady had said, with some hesitation, that Francesca and Hampton's display of dancing at the Grand had been widely talked of. Indeed, his wife had heard all about it when they were in a local pub for a Sunday drink. Not difficult to see the sequence of events, McLeish thought grimly: Julie Brady, understanding that Hampton really was looking elsewhere, had decided to make trouble for him.

Still, Brady was reliable and would have looked for proper evidence.

He sat brooding; then after a bit looked longingly at the telephone. If he could find another lead, if Henry Blackshaw's own recommendation as to the best method of taking money from a company was right, then he might find something from the suppliers. He decided to try it, telephoned Henry and explained succinctly that one of the Britex people seemed to have a bit more cash about than seemed consistent with his salary and commitments. Could Henry let him have a list of suppliers in case it came from there?

'No, I can't,' said Henry on consideration. 'But there is a complete list at the company. You can ask for it.'

'Not without alerting our man, if he exists. Don't want him to run. If you're right, he'll have funds outside the country.'

'You'll alert him anyway if you start talking to suppliers.'

'True,' McLeish acknowledged and listened to the thoughtful silence at the other end of the line.

'I can ask around a bit, without including Britex. I know a lot of these suppliers. If the company is being sold — remember *you* don't know that — it'll be the purchasers' job to talk to suppliers, not mine; but I can do it under the old pals' act.'

McLeish thanked him warmly, being clear that Henry would get a better lead than he would and without disturbing the game. If there were a murderer at Britex, then he should be caught, not enabled to sit in Brazil thumbing his nose at all attempts to bring him back and getting himself in women's magazines. He sat, trying to work out whether he really thought something was going on at Britex.

* * *

At the Department, Henry, Francesca by his side, had welcomed Hal Guadareschi and Ed Patello and was listening with pleasure as they did a practised double act. Hal was playing the nice guy, expressing keenness to take over the Britex assets and to make the business work. Ed was apparently sunk in gloom, rousing himself at intervals to make one telling point after another about the difficulties involved in coaxing a phoenix from the ashes of Britex. They were perfectly capable of reversing the roles if it suited them, and Henry wondered idly on what basis they had decided that today Ed should be the hard man. Perhaps they tossed for it. He was recalled from this line of speculation by Ed's changing position slightly in his chair as Hal observed cheerfully that where the business was attractive, then, gee, the financials could always be arranged. Ed, without altering expression, opined that the financials here did look exceptionally difficult.

'Do you have a ball-park figure?' Henry decided they had better get on. Hal and Ed did not even glance at each other, but Ed roused himself to say that no man of sense would pay a receiver more than £10m for the assets, but working capital requirements could easily be another £10m.

'So, the way we see it, Henry, is that the total project that you have here could be of the order of twenty million of your pounds, and I guess that is a major problem for you,' Hal said, with undiminished cheerfulness. Henry mentally saluted the negotiating competence that stated the whole issue as a problem for him rather than an opportunity for them.

'We are constrained by the rules of the European Community as to the level of assistance that can be offered,' he began smoothly.

'Francesca is the expert here, and I will ask her to explain it in more detail.'

He sat back while she explained that 30 per cent of total project costs represented the absolute maximum of assistance that the Department could give and proceeded to a succinct explanation of project costs. The Americans listened to her, smiling indulgently with the air of men listening to an ingenious commercial, but to Henry's pleasure she was not distracted, taking them steadily through the main rules.

'And that means what it says,' he told them firmly as she finished.

'Whatever we do has to be within those parameters. Then we have to persuade a Minister that what we are offering is suitable, and he has to convince the Treasury.'

'I expect Francesca here could convince anyone,' Hal offered gallantly, getting for his pains a long speculative look from those dark-blue eyes and a very brief smile of acknowledgement.

Ed was ignoring all this and thinking hard. 'You are saying, Henry, as I understand it, that one-third of project costs represents the maximum contribution that the British Government is able to make to keep these thousand jobs in existence?'

'And that the Government definition of project costs may not quite sit with yours,' Francesca observed sharply.

Ed, without doing anything particular to his face, gave her his full attention. 'That would be an area in which you might have some flexibility, right, Francesca?'

'Yes. Limited, mark you, but it exists.'

Henry reflected with resignation that expecting Francesca to sit quiet except when spoken to at a meeting was always going to be a doomed exercise. Very well, she could do the work. He formed, promptly, a subgroup of Hal plus a silent, young accountant he had brought with him, Martin and Francesca, to establish what the project costs might be, offered to meet the group again for lunch and banished them from his office. Ed, while agreeing this piece of organization, did not move from his chair as the rest of the group left the office.

'Henry, both Hal and I would appreciate it if you would offer us any, uh, insights of your own that you may have gathered in your researches into the affairs of this company.'

Henry seized his opportunity. 'The management accounts are all right; the stock seems to be reasonably under control — much too much of it, as you know, but they know where it is and they count in. I just have a slight idea that someone may have been on the take.'

'In what area, Henry?'

'It's usually a supplier's fiddle, isn't it? I was going to have a look at the smaller suppliers. Here's the list.'

Ed read silently for two minutes. 'These guys here, Alutex. I've had a problem with them in Birmingham. Just a smell, nothing to get hold of. Who in the company is doing it?'

'Dunno. I don't even know it is happening, but I'd look for it.'

Ed observed, unconsciously echoing Detective Inspector Brady, that when a company was in this much of a problem you often got odd bits of fraudulent behaviour. Meanwhile he had a few more questions if Henry would bear with him? For example, how good was the management below Board level?

'Competent in the main, but no better. The Purchasing Department lost its head six months ago and the acting manager was the chap who was murdered the week before last.'

'That right?' Ed looked up from the suppliers' list slowly. 'Any connection with your doubt about the suppliers?'

Henry cursed inwardly; it was easy, but fatal to underestimate Ed Patello. 'The detective on the case thinks there may be. I should say that he has nothing much to go on; it looks like a simple mugging and it happened in London.'

'OK. If I get shot at, I'll let you know. I'm not going to conduct any inquests, Henry, I'll just make it known that any suppliers offering any, uh, unwarranted incentives, will do no more business with any of our companies.' He heaved himself to his feet and observed that he guessed he would just join the rest of the group. Henry thankfully called his secretary and attacked his In tray, putting the affairs of Britex out of his mind for the moment.

A couple of hours later he walked down to collect the group, who looked up at him as if he were a visitor from outer space. Papers covered the table, all the men had their jackets off, and Francesca's hair looked as if she had backed into a wind machine. She and Ed greeted him and went straight back to an argument about removal costs. Ed was treating her as a respected equal, which in Ed's terms meant treating her like a middle-aged man.

'Do we have a deal on that?' he was asking, narrow-eyed.

'I have to ask my dad,' she said promptly. 'But, yes, so far as I am concerned.'

Ed, momentarily disoriented, asked what her father's part in this negotiation was. 'Oh Ed. It is a metaphor. I meant Henry has the final say.' She was laughing at him, looking very pretty if rather blue under the eyes, and Ed regarded her fixedly.

'OK,' he said, heavily. 'All right. You want to clear this with Henry right now?'

'No,' said Henry, taking pity on her. 'You all need lunch. We'll clear it this afternoon, Ed, and let you have an answer today.'

'Henry, may I just check my office for phone calls and join you in five minutes?' Francesca was flattening her hair unavailingly with both hands.

'I should comb it, honey,' Hal called after her, all constraint well and truly banished.

Francesca skidded into her office and picked up the expected message that John McLeish had rung. There was also a message from Peter Hampton and a London number. She looked at it, tempted, then rang McLeish who was not there. She called Hampton's number and got him immediately.

'Are you allowed to eat lunch with me yet?' He sounded amused and she blushed. 'I promise not to talk about Britex. Today? Tomorrow?'

'Tomorrow.' She combed her hair quickly as recommended and walked back to join the others, feeling both guilty and triumphant.

She rationalized the guilt by reminding herself that she was seeing dear John that night and on Wednesday, and surely lunch with Peter Hampton did not mean anything, while every instinct told her that John McLeish would mind bitterly, and that he would be entirely justified since she was strongly attracted to Hampton.

She put both of them out of her mind until 6 p.m., when she reported to Henry, who considered her with respect. Somehow in the course of the afternoon, she had reached a provisional deal on assistance with Connecticut Cottons, had put together a full note for the Departmental Committee that would consider it the next afternoon, and had personally organized the committee to meet, which had involved as he knew, persuading most of the members to unscramble prior arrangements.

'Well done, girl. You're looking tired.' They were both disconcerted as she blushed scarlet. 'Perhaps you need an early night,' he added, rattled. There was an awkward pause, then they caught each other's eye and burst out laughing.

'That was the original problem, was it? Go home, girl.'

CHAPTER 16

'Henry? Hal here. You know where I expressed some reservations about the people at Alutex? Well, I talked with an associate this morning and found that Alutex is being taken over by Smith Brothers. Did you know that? Well, of course I know most of the fellows at Smith, and just between us, the first thing they did on Wednesday was to get rid of one salesman, who happened to have responsibility for servicing Britex. Name of Ketterick.'

'Because he was on the take at Britex?'

'Not necessarily. The guy was fired because he couldn't make his accounts tie up, and there is no particular proof that Britex is involved. He was passing a lot of expenses for which there was no clear business purpose. He was responsible for Britex, though.'

'Did they call the police?'

Hal pointed out that in business takeovers no one bothered to do that; you got rid of the bad apple and got on with the job. Not your problem. Henry agreed.

He put down the phone and thought, narrowing his eyes against the bright morning light. 'Martin!' he shouted, seeing him go by along the corridor. 'Why does the name Alutex ring a bell?'

'It's a Britex supplier. No, hang on Henry, it's that table that Francesca reconstructed for us on the train. You remember?'

Henry sent him off for a copy. 'Not to mention to Francesca, please,' he said, without attempting to explain, confident that the well trained but incurious Martin would do exactly as he was told.

He had fixed to meet McLeish for lunch and was waiting for the lift when Francesca joined him. 'Where are you going, then?'

'Lunch with a lover.'

Henry, who had assumed he was having lunch with her lover, waved her ahead of him. She avoided his eye in the lift and he decided she was up to something. Perhaps she had seduced Hal or Ed — although, come to think of it, they were peacefully deployed in Yorkshire. He gave it up and joined McLeish in a quiet pub in a street behind Victoria Street. They ordered drinks and food, and Henry handed McLeish the Alutex table.

'It's a bit difficult, but we didn't acquire this just in the ordinary way of business.' He watched as the policeman worked his way through it.

'Whose handwriting is it?'

'Martin Bailey wrote it down to Fran's dictation.' He explained Francesca's remarkable photographic trick, and McLeish smiled.

'She told me she could do that. I knew it wasn't her writing, though; too neat. How did they get it — I mean, who was there?'

'Just Francesca from our side. I understand she walked in on William Blackett and one of his salesmen — Ketterick, and that Hampton arrived later.' He hesitated. 'I'm being indiscreet and telling you all this because I'm beginning to feel you may have something here. The word is that Ketterick just got fired from Alutex who have been taken over, because the new owners thought he might be offering cash to get orders. You could ask Fran exactly what happened. I'd forbidden her to discuss the case with you, but if murder is in issue then I think she has to.'

'I've got a difficulty there,' McLeish observed, not lifting his eyes from the paper. 'I think she's got a bit of a soft spot for Hampton, so I don't want to ask her unless I have to.'

'More of a soft spot for you, surely?' Henry said, remembering the blue shadows under her eyes after the weekend, and McLeish's eyes flickered. 'I'm not sure Francesca will know much more than this — she was amused, you know, and showing off a bit. I think she probably told us everything she remembered there and then. You could talk to Hal Guadareschi; I'm sure he'd put you in touch with the people who took over Alutex.'

'I'll do that, I'll go up there myself.'

Henry considered him. 'There is something there, isn't there?'

'Oh, there's something there, all right.' He spoke with perfect confidence. 'I'm worried about this table, — I mean it *could* just be salesmen's commission, except that the two people who worked for Alutex, Blackett and Ketterick, didn't want Fran to see it. Hampton was openly cross with her, and given that he fancies her, that tells me something. And both he and Blackett have a use for cash. William Blackett lives high, and if Alutex is down the tube too he can't go on doing that.' He looked at Henry. 'That's my indiscretion, but you did tell me to look for people living beyond their visible means. His dad has a chalet in Verbier, and Blackett went there last week. And my Yorkshire mate says Hampton's never short of cash, and you'd think he'd be a bit strapped with a wife and two kids in a separate home to support, wouldn't you?'

'Tell you what,' Henry observed, 'it wouldn't surprise me if Hampton's prospective partner in the burglar-alarm business was expecting him to put up some cash.'

'I didn't interview him myself but I'll look at Davidson's notes.'

McLeish fished out a notebook, and methodically made a note. 'The chap confirmed that Hampton was with him at the time Sheena Byers was attacked, though, and my sergeant is sure he was telling the truth. Hampton wasn't at all fussed about that night, and I interviewed him myself.'

Both men stopped talking to eat, but McLeish paused with a sausage suspended on his fork, and put it down to make another note. 'I was just reminding myself to check on Ketterick. He nearly jumped out of his skin when he saw me at the funeral — I'd like to know what *he* was doing both nights. Thing is, none of this may have anything to do with Fireman's death. A lot of police work is like that: you turn up all sorts of different things, some of them criminal, that have nothing to do with what you're looking for.'

Henry bought them both another drink and they talked of other things, including Henry's involvement with the Aquarius Choir. 'She pressganged you?' McLeish said, amused. 'Actually, it may be worth it to hear young Peregrine sing. He is something else. I'll see you tomorrow, then; I'm picking Francesca up from rehearsal, with two more of her brothers whom she has managed to insert into the ranks.'

'Do you have to take them all out?' Henry enquired, seriously.

'I've just managed to exclude them so far.' McLeish was laughing.

'Thank you for this.' He stuffed the paper into an overloaded briefcase and went off, smiling to himself.

* * *

Francesca, eating lunch three streets away, was not thinking about either of them, her whole attention being concentrated on Peter Hampton to whom she was finding herself violently and inconveniently attracted. He had put an arm round her and kissed her when she arrived, and for a moment she had relaxed against him, wanting him to go on. He was ordering for both of them and put a hand on hers while he checked which sauce she was having on the steak. She felt a wave of pure lust and momentarily closed her eyes, wondering dizzily whether she really could manage to run two lovers at once.

She recovered her hand and her voice, and heard herself ask courteously about progress at Britex.

'I've left the Americans to it.' He was sitting very close to her, his full attention concentrated on her. 'They are seeing suppliers today and customers tomorrow. I'm just churning out figures down here as they ask for them. Francesca . . .' he stopped.

'Yes, Peter?' She looked up and found he was watching her and that she did not want to look away. It was Hampton who looked away, deliberately, and fiddled with a spoon. Their soup arrived and there was a momentary bustle of activity while rolls and butter were produced and wine poured, giving Francesca time to get herself in hand.

'I'm going to Geneva for the weekend, to see friends. Can you have a drink on Friday just before I go to the airport, or is that difficult?'

Francesca, even disorientated by overwhelming sexual attraction, noted appreciatively the care with which he had picked his words, leaving her free to indicate, if she needed to, the prior demands of a current husband or lover. 'I am going out later in the evening, but I'd like to see you,' she said, striking the best balance between various conflicting wishes that she could achieve. 'Would 6-ish suit?'

'Beautifully. My plane is at 8.30. I couldn't wish for a better send-off.'

They chatted easily through the main course, Francesca recovering her habitual poise.

'Sweet, Francesca? Do you want the menu?'

'No, I can remember it. I'd love a raspberry sorbet.'

'What else do they have, then?'

She closed her eyes, aware she was showing off, and recited the full, rather pretentious, list of twelve. She opened them to find Hampton had commandeered a menu and was following it. 'That's quite a party trick,' he said, amused and admiring as she had intended.

'Did you learn them off?'

'No, I don't have to if I only want it for a short time. It's called a photographic memory.'

'I've read about that,' he assured her, and they finished lunch, discussing examinations and methods of passing them, Francesca unnervingly conscious of his every movement. He helped her on with her coat at the end and she had to fight the urge to lean back against him. He bundled them both into a taxi and placed a hand lightly over hers. 'I'll drop you off.' He leant forward, still holding her hand, to tell the taxi where to stop.

'Thank you for lunch.'

'A pleasure.' He kissed her lightly, but deliberately on the lips. 'See you Friday.'

* * *

Henry Blackshaw, returning to the Department after buying some shirts, checked as he recognized Hampton and scowled at Francesca's back. He couldn't now really complain about her having lunch with him, but it was indiscreet, and rather hard on the man he had just been lunching with.

No sign of any of these distractions showed in Francesca's manner at the Departmental Committee meeting that afternoon. Henry, whose natural inclination was to delegate to the lowest sensible level, had wanted Martin and Francesca to present the case, but had been strongly advised by both Rajiv and Francesca that this would be impolitic. 'It's £6m of assistance, our biggest case so far, Henry. There will be opposition, and you have to be seen to be in charge,' Rajiv had urged, while Francesca had pointed out that the only way to get this one through was on the basis that nothing less would be effective to produce a long-term commercial solution.

'And consequently, Henry, I do not open my mouth and we depend entirely on you to carry the case. You are the only person among the twenty or so there assembled who has ever entered a textile factory in anger, as it were.'

Henry had been impressed by the theory but doubtful about the practice, not least about the idea of Francesca's getting through a meeting in silence. He presented the case and let Martin deal with the detailed questions, which he did extremely competently. To his amazement, Francesca did not speak at all, leaving Rajiv to make it delicately clear to the Civil Service audience that Henry and Martin had not been allowed, as he put it afterwards, to blunder about making ridiculous offers to all and sundry, but had been accompanied at all points by a respectful but authoritative Civil Service acolyte in the person of Francesca. It hardly gave the flavour of the negotiations, in which Francesca had taken a leading part, but it appeared to be reassuring. After an hour and a half, the committee agreed that assistance, at this level, should be recommended to Ministers and all filed out, Francesca keeping a little distance from Martin and Henry.

'That went pretty easily,' Henry observed to Martin. 'You had all the answers too; well done.'

'Ah. That was Francesca. She gave me a list this morning and told me all questions were please to be attempted, however lunatic I thought them. Most of them came up.'

Henry nodded, enlightened. She and Rajiv arrived together in his office, grinning.

'Brilliant, Henry. Lovely job. I'd have bought several dozen myself.'

She beamed at him. 'And you were great, Martin. Not a hole in the defence. I'll do the paper for Ministers; it won't get into the Box tonight, of course, but I'll give it to the late-night pool and we'll have it first thing tomorrow.'

'You were pretty good, too,' Henry said drily and got a sharp glance of acknowledgement from her.

Rajiv patted her shoulder lazily and said that he also had been impressed. 'However, we are not out of the wood. We still have to persuade Ministers that Connecticut Cottons are acceptable despite being foreign.'

'Oh come on, Rajiv. They are American, East Coast, at that. And they wear tweed suits. Almost English,' Francesca pointed out. 'It's not as if they were dressed in terylene and came from some Punjabi hill village.'

'You are not to be being disrespectful of my Uncle Sanjay or my many distinguished cousins,' Rajiv said severely, with the Punjabi lilt, crossing one well-tailored leg over the other. 'All of them are owning at least two suits each.'

Henry and Martin breathed again and Henry remembered that Uncle Sanjay was one of the richest men in modern India.

'I think the Directors may need to meet the Minister, Henry,' Rajiv said thoughtfully, reverting to his normal drawl. 'As Francesca says, they do look all right. They are about his own age.'

'I was going to suggest that Hal and Ed at some point will insist on meeting the Minister. They will want to be sure they are dealing with the top man,' Henry said mildly.

Both civil servants regarded him fixedly.

'I suppose we do tend to forget we aren't the top man as far as the outside world is concerned,' Francesca observed. 'We feel, you see Henry, that it is us with whom Hal and Ed are doing business, not the Minister.'

Henry wondered aloud whether the Minister necessarily concurred with this view, and his Civil Service colleagues agreed, after careful consideration and with some wonderment, that it was quite possible Ministers, despite their brief tenure, did feel that they were the centre of the world. They left to organize the submission, leaving Henry and Martin struck dumb.

'They're right, of course,' Martin said, rising to go. 'I can see Francesca running us and the rest of the country as a senior civil servant.'

Yes, well, Henry thought soberly; but her private life may be going to give her trouble. He shook his head in exasperation and answered his telephone.

'John McLeish. I'm sorry to call you at work. The Yorkshire chap who is working on this has found that Hampton goes to

Geneva about once a month. Said to have a girlfriend there. I wondered, you see, because of the banking angle.'

'That is the textbook pattern,' Henry confirmed. 'Lots of banks in Geneva, however. You'll get nothing out of a Swiss bank by way of evidence.'

'I know that.' McLeish sounded momentarily weary. 'But it's all a matter of accumulating bits and pieces. People sometimes collapse if they find you know a lot, and let you have the rest.'

Henry nodded in confirmation and in respect for the patient hunter at the other end of the line. Why could Francesca not see her own best interests? Ingrained Yorkshire distaste for minding other people's business intervened to prevent him telling McLeish that Francesca had lunched with Hampton, but after he had put the phone down he wondered, uneasily, whether he was right.

CHAPTER 17

'*Hallelujah. Halle-e-e-lujah.*' Henry was standing next to Charlie Wilson and they were both singing their hearts out. He could hear, for the first time, the Aquarius Choir tenors, specifically Jeremy Wilson who was holding the motley group together. They all came to an end, simultaneously for once, and the conductor beamed.

'Much, much better,' he said, his glance flickering over the Wilson clan who were tactfully avoiding his eye. He ended the rehearsal, and nodded to Bill Westland, who as Principal Establishment Officer also inherited the mantle of President of the Choir and had felt it right to turn up for this rehearsal.

'Aquarius Choir and friends, I see,' Bill Westland observed, *sotto voce,* nodding to the Wilson boys. 'Good of you to volunteer Charlie — oh, you didn't? I see. Where is she?'

They were by now in the main entrance hall of the Department.

'Who is that?' Westland watched Francesca greeting John McLeish.

'That's Frannie's new boyfriend. He's a policeman.'

Bill Westland bore purposefully down on them and was introduced to John McLeish. Henry joined the group to say hello and managed to take McLeish aside for a minute. 'That bad girl had lunch with Hampton yesterday. After I warned her off.'

'I'd heard. They ate at a restaurant where one of the waiters does a bit for us on the side. Leave it, Henry; I'll cope.'

'Is she embarrassing you?'

The hazel eyes flickered. 'Only a little. I reminded the informant that she was a senior negotiator for the Department and spent her time having lunch with men in the line of business.'

* * *

Despite his brave words to Henry, John McLeish found himself unable to cope with the Hampton issue. That evening Francesca greeted him with affection and fell into bed with him with obvious pleasure, and he simply did not feel like disturbing the atmosphere. He stayed the night, as had become a habit, and was eating breakfast with her on Thursday morning when he heard a double blip on the bell, followed by the sound of a key turning in the front door.

'That'll be Perry,' Francesca said, unperturbed. 'He has a key.'

Perry sauntered in, greeting McLeish without surprise, and made himself coffee, very much at home. McLeish decided to take Francesca back to his flat for the night next time, before he turned into an adjunct of the Wilson family.

'Frannie, the party. Is Jamie coming or do you have to sing the page?'

'Jamie is coming. He's staying with Mum and I'm going round a bit early to do some practice with him. I did explain, didn't I, John?'

'You did. I've taken late duty Friday instead, so I've got Saturday free. I can make time to eat with you on Friday, if you'd like?'

There was a fractional pause, which just caught his ear.

'Oh damn! I've fixed to have a drink at 6 p.m. with a chum who is on the way to Heathrow.'

She picked up both plates to put them into the dishwasher, and he saw Perry look at her thoughtfully under his eyelashes.

'So it doesn't fit,' McLeish said into the silence, calmly. 'I'll see you Saturday.' He felt some wordless communion pass between brother and sister and Perry disappeared upstairs while Francesca came up behind him and wound her arms round his neck.

'You could come on when late duty is finished. I'm only having a drink for an hour, the chum is catching the 8.30 to Geneva.'

McLeish leant back against her, gravelled for speech. He suddenly noticed the time and realized he was going to be late for the station meeting and had no time to tackle the issue presented to him. Nor very much inclination to, either, he admitted to himself as he got into his car. If she was going to see Hampton on his way to Geneva, what did it matter? He drove away, cursing, knowing it mattered very much.

He was still in a state of indecision on Friday morning, to the point where he was relieved not to be able to speak to Francesca for any length of time. She was on her way in to a meeting and obviously tense. He had arranged for a CID Sergeant at Heathrow to report Hampton's movements, after a difficult time with his immediate superior who was obviously finding the connection between a possible fraud at Britex and the death of Fireman tenuous at best. Only McLeish's good record and confidence in his own abilities carried the day, and he came out of the meeting well aware that he had drawn heavily on his credit balance. 'Just as well you've got friends in high places,' his Chief Inspector had observed irritably. 'I had to talk to the Commissioner about you the other day.'

McLeish had looked blank. 'Why?'

'I've no idea. He was asking all about you . . . moral character, marital status. Are you trying to seduce his daughter, John?'

McLeish had denied all knowledge of any daughters the Commissioner might possess and gone back to work, thinking about Francesca. He would, he decided, have it out with her on Saturday or Sunday. Or sometime. But he was unable to resist turning up at her house after working late on Friday. She was playing the piano as he rang the bell at ten o'clock and greeted him with all the warmth he could have wished, so that he was wholly distracted. He woke next morning, late, to find her quietly getting dressed.

'John? Darling, I have to go and help my poor mother organize supper for forty for the party; she'll never manage without me. And practise "My Heart Ever Joyful" with Jamie. You don't need to be early if it's difficult.'

McLeish sat up in bed, slowly sorting out this stream of information.

'I'll come at seven. Forty for supper? Who are they all?'

'Mixed oldies — Mum's friends — plus their children, plus all of us. It's probably more like fifty, but Mum can't count beyond thirty. After that it just becomes "many people" to her. I'll probably have to come back and fetch all my plates.'

McLeish, child of two elementary schoolteachers who had never been known to entertain more than six visitors, and that only with enormous strain, marvelled at the confidence with which she expected to deal with fifty. He noted also the indulgence with which Francesca spoke of her mother, as if referring to some dotty blonde rather than the obviously capable Mary Wilson.

* * *

It was Mary Wilson who let him in at 7 p.m. that evening and he stopped for a minute, breathing in the smells of food. In a room above he could hear the piano and Jamie's soaring treble. 'Do go and listen. Neither of them will notice you. And no, there is nothing left to do.'

He moved quietly up the stairs and into a large living-room, very much the same in design as the one in Perry's and Francesca's houses, and like theirs with a grand piano at one end, the lid propped open.

'Jamie, it's not a quaver there. Listen.'

James Miles Brett peered over her shoulder at the music. 'Yes', he said. 'From 14 then.'

Francesca played two chords and he started again, the sharp treble like a trumpet in the Bach cantata. They got to the end and smiled at each other in a moment of perfect understanding and pleasure. Jamie moved closer and riffled back through the music. 'I wasn't quite right at 11,' he said. 'Can you play those three bars again, with the top line?'

Francesca obliged, with the boy watching the music, counting under his breath, then starting to sing, then going back over it, nagging at the phrase, totally absorbed and professional. Francesca, equally absorbed, worked with him on the piano, biting her tongue with concentration.

'Thank you, Fran,' the boy said at last, very small and light under the quiff of blond hair. She smiled at him, and McLeish thought with longing of coming home to a wife and child of his own.

An hour later the big room was full of people. McLeish found himself deserted by Francesca, drinking a glass of mulled wine and trying to hold an intelligent conversation with an elderly lady about the Sherlock Holmes Society. He had just listened to her account of last summer's expedition to Switzerland where members of the Society had dressed up as Moriarty and Holmes and re-enacted the scene at the Reichenbach Falls, and was struggling for some sensible comment, when Francesca appeared and warmly embraced the elderly lady, greeting her as dearest Phyllis.

'Laddie,' dearest Phyllis said to her, confusingly, 'this young man of yours does not appear to have read much of Sherlock Holmes.'

'Darling, I am sorry. The thing is, he is a real modern detective and may not have that much time for reading fiction. John, come and see Charlie who longs to talk to you.'

McLeish allowed himself to be led away and placed in the middle of the Wilson boys. Charlie grinned at him. 'I saw you talking to Phyllis. Mother of Fran's best friend at school. Did she press you to join the White Boar Society?'

'Does that have something to do with Sherlock Holmes.'

'No, no. The White Boar Society exists to prove that Richard III was innocent of the murder of the Little Princes. Phyllis is on the committee.'

McLeish considered Charlie carefully to see if he was pulling the leg of an outsider, but he appeared to be wholly serious. As he arrived at that view, Perry appeared at his elbow with another formidable middle-aged lady in tow. 'Lady Sybil, this is John McLeish — Detective Inspector in real life. John, the Lady Sybil Cole.'

'How very nice.' This particular Lady, McLeish noted carefully was thin and distinguished rather than plump and cheerful. 'And you are a friend of Francesca's.' She considered him speculatively, while he resisted an urge to hide behind the curtains. 'Dear Francesca. She has given us all a great deal of entertainment over the years.'

Out of the corner of his eye McLeish saw Perry blench, but neither of them was a match for Lady Sybil who extracted ruthlessly the details of McLeish's background, education and training before drifting away to talk to Francesca.

'God, I am sorry John.' Perry was genuinely shaken. 'I hoped I was doing you a favour — she's married to some frightfully high-up policeman and was a friend of Mum's at university. She's an earl's daughter, though, and I suppose she does still have the style.'

McLeish looked at him, speechless for a moment. 'She's married to Sir Francis Cole? Commissioner of the Met?'

'That's right. He is singing the Good King this year.'

'What?'

'As in Wenceslas. It's a tradition. We sing carols later and we always do that one. One of us used to do the page till the twins' voices broke, and one of Mum's ancient mates always does the King. This year she has resuscitated this Sir Francis from somewhere and Jamie will sing the page. Fran won't let him over-use his voice, that's why he isn't doing the rest of the carols. Jamie, I mean, not Sir Francis.'

The crowd round them opened, the familiar, diminutive figure of his Commissioner advanced on them, and McLeish found himself coming to attention.

'Sir Francis, this is Detective Inspector John McLeish,' Perry said promptly.

'Thank you, Peregrine. Would you be good enough to find me a weak whisky with plenty of soda? Come and sit down, McLeish, I'm too old to stand long.'

A passage cleared for them miraculously and McLeish sank uneasily on to a corner of the sofa, the small man perched up beside him. He found himself put through a detailed catechism of his experience in the force, and understood, as his mind recovered from temporary paralysis, that the Commissioner was better briefed than was reasonable on the career of one out of the hundreds of Detective-Inspectors in his command. He saw in the background, just for a few seconds, Mary Wilson watching them consideringly, and very nearly failed to reply to a question, occupied as he was with the revelation that this nice woman, whom her children treated so indulgently, had quietly arranged to take up a reference on him and had gone straight to the top for it.

Peregrine had come back and was hovering with a weak whisky — held at a ten-foot distance, McLeish decided, by the force of Sir Francis's personality alone. Sir Francis finished his questions and observed, with a needle-sharp sideways look, that he had heard McLeish well spoken of, in particular from colleagues at Edgware Road, then indicated to Perry that he might approach.

'Sir Francis, I am also to tell you that if you are ready, my mother would like to start the carols.'

'I'll come, Peregrine. You'll be wanted yourself, McLeish.'

Dismissed, McLeish struggled to his feet and arranged himself beside Charlie, as the party swept into the first verse of 'Good King Wenceslas'.

'Hither page and stand by me', Sir Francis sang decisively, revealing a fine bass voice. Jamie, standing beside Sir Francis, came in smoothly as the page. The rest of the party sang the next verse and the clear sharp treble came again, frightened that the night was growing colder and the wind stronger. Another communicator like Perry, McLeish thought, and understood Francesca's evident affection for this slight, golden child. Like Perry, he made you feel the cold and the wind and the fear. He listened with pleasure to Sir Francis's bluff, kingly reassurance, much more suited to calming several hundred nervous policemen than one anxious boy.

They all sang two more carols together, then Francesca took over the piano. Jamie sang flawlessly the Bach cantata that McLeish had heard them practising and there was a slight pause before the party applauded. McLeish observed that the Lady Sybil was wiping away tears.

'Shall we try "The Lost Chord", laddie?' It seemed to be Perry who was being addressed but several people agreed cordially, and McLeish backed away towards the curtains, knowing his own limitations.

'We just accompany Perry,' Phyllis said firmly to the assembled group, who nodded obediently. McLeish noted with respect that it seemed to matter to Perry not at all whether he was accompanied by a motley collection of family and friends or by the Bach Choir — he sang just as beautifully, and timed the crescendo at the end in exactly the same way.

'Makes you see the bright angel, doesn't he?' Sir Francis observed to McLeish. 'A stunning voice. Rocks ahead there, though, I would have thought. It's a lot to cope with, a talent like that.'

McLeish blinked at him, lost for comment, but Sir Francis appeared to have said all he had to say. 'Time to go home for me, but I wouldn't have missed that for anything. Or young Miles Brett.' He collected his lady with one swift authoritative nod and went over to say goodnight to Mary Wilson.

'Bit of a golden oldie, that one,' Perry observed companionably to McLeish, watching as Sir Francis said goodnight to Francesca. 'Not a bad voice at all. Choir-trained, one imagines. Right then, let's get them all out — I am due somewhere else.'

'And thank you for giving an old man the pleasure of singing with you,' Sir Francis said, beaming generally on the assembled Wilsons.

'What old man is this?' Francesca was laughing, and Sir Francis smiled at her.

'A baggage,' he observed to McLeish. 'I'll be seeing you again, young man, I don't doubt.' He wheeled himself and the Lady Sybil out of the door, signalling a general break-up of the party. McLeish under Francesca's direction helped with the clearing up, and not long afterwards managed to get her as far as the door.

'Where did Perry get to?' she asked crossly. 'He ducked the washing up as usual.'

'I thought he was probably meeting a girl,' McLeish said firmly.

'No! Honestly, and with poor Sheena still unconscious.' She brooded her way down the steps, then remembered her manners.

'Good night for a run,' she observed conversationally. 'Look at the stars.'

McLeish gazed obediently at the bright sky, his attention elsewhere.

'Who runs with you at night? Perry?'

'No, of course not. I run by myself. I'm much better than I was, I can do two miles.' She caught sight of his face. 'But John, I don't run in Hyde Park at night, just round my own streets.'

'Frannie,' he put his arm round her, 'there are more than enough villains on the streets where you live to do you a lot of damage.'

'Oh nonsense! I've lived here or hereabouts all my life and I've always gone out at night by myself.'

'I'm a policeman, remember. Night after night we get girls in the station who have been robbed or raped or frightened. Why should you be immune?'

She hunched her shoulders, obviously deeply irritated. 'I'm hardly a seven-stone weakling, and I don't hang around when I run. You told me yourself that the average drug addict isn't strong enough to rob anything more ambitious than a little old lady. And a rapist can surely find an easier target than me sprinting through the streets, seductively dressed in Charlie's old tracksuit.'

'Rubbish.' He tightened his arm round her shoulders, but she pulled away from him. He looked at her, amazed. 'Frannie, don't be so bloody silly — I'm only trying to look after you.'

He pulled her towards him and kissed her, but she was still looking thunderous so he decided to leave the subject and wait for her native common sense to reassert itself. 'I'll never forget Jamie singing the Bach,' he said, and was relieved to see her relax and smile.

'He's lovely.'

'He's very fond of you.'

'And I of him.' She smiled to herself, her face soft.

'You could marry me, you know. We could have a Jamie of our own.'

He had spoken on impulse, carried away by the memory of her and Jamie practising in perfect understanding in her mother's living-room, and he glanced anxiously down at her to see how she was taking the idea. In the sodium light she was pale and pinched and plain, staring straight ahead at some spiritual desert.

'I can't,' she said, not looking at him. 'Never again. We were so happy when we first met, and then somehow, very quickly after we married, it all went dark and he hated me, and we were enemies. I mean, I hated him too.'

'Wrong man,' McLeish said, steadily, holding her firmly. 'I've met him, remember. He put you down; he needed to make you feel bad for some reason. And he is doing the same to the next girl along.'

She still would not look at him but some of the tension eased.

'Possibly,' she said carefully. 'But what was so awful was that I was stuck in the situation. I couldn't do anything else. And if there had been children I could never have left. Not fair on them.'

McLeish considered her serious, driven face. 'I'm nicer than he is.'

She smiled, briefly. 'He wasn't even my first love you know; I had had some experience, and even so the whole marriage turned out to be a catastrophe. You aren't the only person who cannot imagine why we ever got married. But if I can make a crashing mistake like that once, I can do it again. Easily. So what I decided was not to settle down with anyone, even to go out with, but to try a lot of relationships and see what suited.' She glanced up at him cautiously. 'I knew you wouldn't like it, but I do mean it. I'm not ready just to stick to one relationship, never mind marry anyone.'

She was tense with the effort to communicate, and he laughed involuntarily.

'John, don't be so patronizing. Listen, will you — or go away.'

McLeish looked at her incredulously, not quite able to believe in the storm that had arrived from a clear sky.

'What is all this, Frannie? Look, darling, with our schedules if we are going to manage to see each other at all, neither of us has time to have it off with other people as well. I don't want to, anyway.'

Francesca had removed herself pointedly from his protective arm, and was standing under a streetlight, her hair spiking up, with exactly the same expression of miserable ten-year-old stubbornness that he had provoked by trying to stop her running at night. He stood in scowling consideration of her, his temper rapidly growing in the face of this apparently causeless intransigence, and was suddenly assailed by a particularly unwelcome suspicion.

'That bloke Hampton — is that what this is about? You stay clear of him, Francesca, whatever else you do. I'm warning you!'

Her eyebrows peaked up and a flush appeared across her cheekbones.

'This is exactly what I object to. I'm not prepared to be told what to do. By anyone.'

'You need telling when you are making a fool of yourself.' He stopped, and took a breath. 'Frannie. Darling. Have some sense. Come home.'

He moved towards her, but she backed away, shaking with temper.

'Leave me alone.'

He stopped in his tracks, almost too angry to speak. 'All right I will. There is your car; get into it and let me see that it starts. Then you can go home and do what you like. I give up.'

Francesca, white with temper, slammed her way into her car, started it noisily and made to pull out, forgetting to put on her lights. Grimly he indicated the problem and she flicked them on, dazzling him, and pulled away, missing the car parked in front of her by a coat of paint.

He found his own car and sat down in it heavily, miserable with rage and disappointment, and incredulity at the way the quarrel had got out of hand. He turned on the radio to soothe himself and managed to listen to ten minutes of a discussion on St Luke's Gospel before deciding that he would drive round and sort this out with Francesca, preferably in bed, rather than let the sun go down on so comprehensive a quarrel.

Full of virtuous determination he drove to her house, and nearly ran her over as she shot across the road in front of him dressed in Charlie's tracksuit, plainly in too much of a temper to notice him or anyone else. He turned the car, swearing, and followed her at a discreet distance, grinding his teeth as he drove down the poorly lit streets through which she was so defiantly pounding. Pindar Street, for heaven's sake, where Fireman had been murdered. Chatterton Street, which had been the scene of a gang rape the week before, and Arnold Terrace which contained three squats, each a nest of addicts of one sort and another. He sat in the car, watching her sprint to her own door, and realized for the first time that the phrase about blood boiling might not be a metaphor after all. Deciding reluctantly that he was too angry to cope sensibly with her, and that he would have to leave any reconciliation till the next day, he turned sadly for his flat.

CHAPTER 18

'Francesca? It's Peter Hampton. Did I wake you?'

'No, no,' Francesca lied groggily, fighting clear of the thick sleep she had finally achieved at 6 a.m. 'Are you in Geneva?'

'Yes, I am, but I am getting the 4 o'clock plane. Can you have dinner with me — I know it's short notice. We could go dancing at the Hammersmith Palais.'

'Yes, I'm sure I could.' She sounded fractionally hesitant, and Hampton said easily, not to worry if it was difficult, another day . . .

'No, it's not difficult, I'm just not awake. Seven o'clock? Fine.'

She put the phone down, and to her own amazement burst into tears and wept painfully for several minutes. She considered her reddened, blotchy face in the mirror, along with the unnerving conviction that she had made an almighty fool of herself the night before with John McLeish. She made coffee, her lips moving as she rehearsed what she might say, but stopped as she realized she was in no position to open negotiations, having just agreed to go out with Peter Hampton that night. She realized also that John, being a generous man, was likely to decide to reopen negotiations himself, and hastily arranged to have lunch with her mother.

She had been gone five minutes when McLeish rang from Edgware Road where he had gone to finish some work. He listened to the phone ring, angered by not being able to find her, and decided she could stew in her own juice. He had more than enough to do if he was to find Ketterick and persuade him to talk. He hesitated momentarily, and decided to ruin Brady's Sunday by ringing him in Doncaster, and getting him to find an address. Brady promised obligingly to go into his station and find the address, and McLeish decided while he was waiting to read the whole file again: in fact, he acknowledged to himself as he worked through the file, his affair with Francesca had been getting in the way of his work. Hampton and Blackett had each had the opportunity to attack both Fireman and Sheena Byers, and they were in key positions in Britex and Alutex: he needed to check their statements very carefully. The phone rang, and he reached for it, expecting it to be Brady; it took him a few seconds to recognize the duty sergeant from Heathrow.

'A Peter D. Hampton is confirmed on the 2 p.m. Swissair flight from Geneva,' the voice was saying in his ear. He thanked his informant grimly and looked at his watch, hoping very hard that the reason Francesca was not answering her phone was not because she was meeting that plane. As he was deciding to give her the benefit of the doubt and call her again later, Brady rang him.

'Simon Ketterick is away,' he said, without preamble. 'He lives quite near the station so I ran round there — literally, I mean. I've lost eight pounds since you saw me, just from running.' McLeish, mentally dancing with impatience, congratulated him. 'Anyway, so I turned up on his doorstep, along with four pints of milk and three days' newspapers. Neighbours don't know where he is either. But I did see something interesting. An old acquaintance, you might say, chap we had in on a charge of supplying dangerous substances, but didn't prosecute — not quite enough evidence, witnesses vanished, you know, the usual — he was hanging about, though he faded pretty fast when he saw me. The neighbours said he had just asked all the same questions as me, saying he was a friend of Ketterick's. I didn't quite remember who he was until he had gone, or I would have asked him a few questions myself. Sorry. But it would be interesting if Ketterick was a user, wouldn't it? I mean, come to think of it, he looks terrible.'

'Shit!' McLeish, who rarely swore, sounded appalled. 'Too right he looks terrible; I even wondered myself if he'd been ill. No, I didn't think of that. I wanted to talk to him because he was very jumpy when he saw me at the funeral and I knew he'd been in London the night Fireman was killed. If he's a user, he really needs cash and that puts him right in the frame to be running a fiddle with someone at Britex. Look, can you get his bank account checked, too? And will Julie know where he'll be — I mean, he is her cousin? I'm sorry, this isn't doing much for your Sunday.'

'Say no more, John. Did me a lot of good seeing you again. I'm off for lunch with the mother-in-law but I'll start the hunt there, all right? How's your young lady?'

McLeish made lying and non-committal noises down the phone, and rang off with renewed thanks, wondering what it was that was stopping him from telling the friendly and sympathetic soul at the other end of the telephone the full strength of his worries. He decided it was simple, idiotic, masculine pride: he was just not prepared to admit to Brady that he, too, was having trouble with his girl and Peter Hampton. At that moment he was distracted by the realization that he had not checked where Ketterick had been on the night Sheena Byers was attacked, and started sifting through statements to see if he had been with Blackett, or was placed somewhere else.

* * *

Two miles away, and two hours later, Francesca was saying goodbye to her mother. She had explained McLeish's absence by saying, more truthfully than she knew, that he was working. Her mother had not been deceived. 'A good man, darling.'

Francesca had agreed with her, sadly, both of them knowing exactly what they meant. 'Too bossy, though.'

'Darling, all the good men are. John seems to me to know what he is doing, and to want to look after you. A man like that is going to suit you much better than Francis, whom you had to mother. Don't drive him away.'

'I may just have done so,' Francesca confessed.

'I wondered. I'm sure you can get him back, but don't leave it too long if you want him. Don't chew your finger-nails, darling.'

Francesca guiltily sat on her hands, looking miserable. 'I don't know if I do want him.' She looked at her mother, daring her to comment, then rose and kissed her goodbye. 'I'll let you know.'

* * *

Three miles away in the Glengarry hotel, Simon Ketterick was fidgeting round his room, unable to sit down or to settle to anything.

He picked up the Sunday papers, read two paragraphs, and put them down again. He made himself a cup of tea, finding a surviving teabag among the debris on the tray, and drank it, gazing out of the window, crunching four aspirin as he drank. He put the tea down half drunk, and made two phone calls, neither of which was answered. He took another turn round the room, rubbing both hands up and down his face and yawning, every moment eloquent of acute physical irritation. The phone rang, and he snatched at it, spilling the half-drunk tea.

'About fucking time. I waited in for you and I need to go out. Yes, I bloody do. You have some? Well blessings on your name, and get up here, quick.' He banged down the phone, and rushed into the poky bathroom, carved inadequately out of a corner of a room which had been none too big to start with, and opened a sponge bag, needing several tries to get his hands to work the zip. Lovingly he spread out the hotel's bright blue flannel, and laid on it a syringe, a spoon, silver paper and matches. He looked at himself in the mirror above the basin, eyes huge above thin cheeks and a lined neck, and made a face.

In response to a quiet knock, he rushed to the door. 'Welcome friend. Where's the stuff?'

'Here. Get one in, Ketterick, then we can talk.'

The visitor sat down in the only chair and picked up the *Sunday Times* which he read in a desultory way, flicking restlessly through the pages and looking uneasily at his watch. After ten minutes, Ketterick appeared from the bathroom, looking a stone heavier, smiling and with his hands under control.

'OK now?'

'Yes, bless you. Good stuff, and it'll keep me going till tomorrow, then I'll need to score. Trouble is, I couldn't leave a forwarding address. I rang the chap who usually gets it for me, to see if he had a contact, and he told me the police were there this morning. Time I took a little holiday.'

'I brought enough more of the stuff to make sure you didn't need to score in London where you don't know what you are buying. It's a present. You got money?'

'Yes, but it won't last all that long, and then I'll be looking for more.'

Ketterick was watching his visitor carefully but the man seemed unmoved by the implied threat.

'Cross that bridge when we come to it. For the moment you need to go away.'

Ketterick nodded and yawned hugely. 'Right now I have to sleep a bit, I had a fucking awful night. I'll go tomorrow. Where's the rest of the stuff?' He closed his eyes briefly, swaying slightly on his feet.

The visitor took a paper bag out of the capacious pocket of his overcoat, and tipped out of it a small plastic bag, stuffing the paper bag back in his pocket. 'Here you are. I guess that it's three days' supply.'

'More.' Ketterick was holding it lovingly, and his visitor rose to go.

Ketterick stretched himself on the bed with a deep exhausted sigh, and turned on his side, the plastic bag clutched tightly in his right hand. The visitor watched him for a minute, expressionlessly, then went quietly out of the room, tucking the key into his pocket.

* * *

At Edgware Road, McLeish had finished an inadequate and nasty lunch, and was talking to Detective Sergeant Green. He was noticing with interest that Green's long blond locks had just been retouched at the roots, but what he was saying made sense, as usual. 'Depends what he is on, John. It's most likely heroin, because you can function quite well if you keep up the dose, and you told me he was employed, right? In a senior job? Well, could be costing him anything from £70 a day up. That's £350 a week, or was when I went to school.'

McLeish nodded, considering Francesca's table which he had spread out in front of him. If this was the documentation for a racket, rather than commission, then three people were splitting £5,000 odd a month, and two of them were getting £2,000 plus. Any of them could just about fund a heroin habit. He considered Blackett and Hampton, and decided that neither of them was a likely candidate for drug addiction, though Blackett was probably an alcoholic.

'How do you catch an addict, then, Doug?'

The steady, shrewd country face that matched so oddly with the fashionable hair turned to him in surprise. 'We don't. We don't even try — I assumed you knew that, John. For a start we want to get the bastards who are making fortunes out of supplying, and we don't have time to waste on users unless we've got one who is willing to turn in his supplier. But the thing is, if we have a user who can afford his habit, we never see him. We only catch the ones who get involved with crime — either pushing the stuff or thieving — to pay for their habit. While your man has cash, we won't find him.'

'Yes, I see.' McLeish sat in silence, accepting the unpalatable fact that he had been negligent in not following up the Alutex lead earlier, and that both luck and good police work would be needed to enable him to cover this mistake. If Ketterick had saved some cash it might be weeks before he was found, and by then Britex would be in receivership and staff probably scattered in other firms, so it would be that much more difficult to establish that Ketterick or his associate in Britex had ever been near London the night Fireman was killed. It all rested on a pretty delicate set of hypotheses which needed to be established quickly or not at all.

'Win a few, lose a few,' Green offered, watching him with sympathy, and McLeish nodded, unconsoled.

'Should have got on to this one before, Doug. Thanks for your help.'

* * *

Francesca, a mile away as the crow flew, had spread her entire wardrobe on the bed and decided that it was all far too serious and conventional for an evening at the Palais, and that she would very much rather not be going anyway. She stood uneasily, eyeing her clothes, and was suddenly visited by inspiration. She unpicked speedily the side seams of a long velvet skirt, originally bought as part of a defensive strategy for dealing with the ferocious draughts that whistled round the house of her husband's father and his third wife, and chipped two feet off the bottom, converting it into a knee length skirt that split to the thigh whenever she moved. She added a tunic-type silk shirt and a heavy leather belt, long earrings and a lot of make-up, and danced to the front door as the bell rang, feeling successful, cheerful, and disposed to take the evening as it came, including Peter Hampton if she felt like it.

'Wow,' he said, stepping back slightly. 'You look marvellous.' He hesitated on the doorstep, satisfactorily disconcerted, and she beamed at him.

'You look nice, too. That's a very good suit.' She considered him, smiling, liking the look of his long legs and broad shoulders in the conventional dark grey.

'Made for me by a little man in the backstreets of Doncaster.'

'Who uses a very expensive Reid and Taylor cloth,' Francesca observed, peering at it. 'Henry Blackshaw has been teaching me that sort of thing,' she explained, seeing him look disconcerted.

'Aren't you the clever one,' he said drily, and Francesca, aware that she had been a bit over-intelligent, hastily offered him a drink, giving him the bottle to pour his own when he asked for whisky, and courteously enquiring after his flight.

'That was OK. It landed a bit late, so I came straight here. Smashing house this is — did you live here with your husband?'

'Briefly, but it was always my house. I bought it years ago with a legacy when property round here was cheap.' Francesca spoke firmly, and blushed as Hampton looked openly amused.

'Come up to the living-room,' she offered hastily, and led the way, very conscious of her split skirt. She disposed herself on the sofa, and admired the cool with which Hampton took an armchair rather than sitting beside her. Watching his long fingers curl round the glass, she suddenly wanted him very much. He was watching her, too, and unhurriedly put his glass down and came over and knelt on the sofa beside her, sliding an arm behind her head as he kissed her.

She kissed him back, opening her mouth against his, and felt him jerk the tunic blouse clear of her skirt at the back and then his hand on the skin of her back.

The front doorbell rang twice, sharply, and she pulled away. 'Ignore it,' Hampton suggested into her neck.

'I can't. It's my brother, he has a key, the bell is only a signal. I'll have to go.' She scrambled to her feet, tucking her shirt in.

'Frannie?' Perry sounded absolutely confident of his welcome as he called from the hall below. 'I just want my jacket, I left it in the living-room sometime last week.' Francesca gave Hampton a harassed look, and he got easily to his feet and picked up his glass, just as Perry clattered up the stairs.

'You could have rung up and asked for it back,' his sister said, sharply, in greeting. 'I don't think you know Peter Hampton.'

The look of pure, wounded astonishment that Perry turned on her said more clearly than any words that he had not been expecting to disturb his sister in a tender scene with a man unknown to him, and Francesca blushed uncomfortably. It was Perry who recovered first.

'No, I don't think we have met. Nice to see you,' he said, punctiliously shaking hands with Hampton. 'I am sorry to barge in like this, but I did need this jacket.' He brandished it demonstratively, and refused the drink that his sister belatedly managed to offer him. Shaking hands again with Hampton, and giving his sister a long, wondering, reproachful look by way of farewell, he left behind him a marked silence which endured until the front door slammed behind him.

'I must change the system and get that key back,' she said, ruffled and apologetic, but Hampton laughed.

'Come on. We'll go dancing and get some food.' She followed him downstairs, amused in her turn by his apparent lightness of touch, and unwillingness to resuscitate a scene that had gone wrong. She got in his car, very conscious of him, but he kept both hands on the wheel and chatted easily as they arrived at the Palais. Dancing together was as great a pleasure as it had been in Doncaster, and she said as much as they sat down after a long session, both breathing hard.

'Good, isn't it?' he agreed. 'We might have been practising for months.'

He raised his glass to her and smiled but she noticed that he was looking tired and said so.

'Yes. Well, it's not an easy day tomorrow.'

'Oh dear. It isn't, is it?' She looked into her glass. 'I can't really think the Minister is going to overrule the advice Henry told you we had given.'

'Oh, nor do I. Not your fault, beautiful. It's just gone on rather a long time. Don't let's talk about it.'

'OK. I think you and your lot have been very steady and good-tempered through it all, and that can't be common.' She smiled at him. 'You only got ratty once.' He looked at her blankly, and she was embarrassed but decided it was better to go on. 'You know — when I was roaming the corridors at the factory trying to find a ledger for Martin, and ran into William Blackett and one of his salesmen allegedly tidying up.'

'I'd forgotten that. Yes, they weren't really helping, were they? What were they doing there, anyway?'

'Oh, they were looking for something. I rather think I found it for them, quite by accident, because it had got tangled with the ledger, only everybody was so cross I never stopped to ask, just crept out.'

'What was it?'

'Something like the discount on purchases from Alutex — I mean it was headed Alutex and appeared to be about commission paid. What a very boring subject, Peter, I'm sorry I introduced it. Well may you look fed up.'

'Doesn't sound terribly important, either way. I was just remembering you had a photographic memory. Not much use keeping things from you.' There was a slight edge to his voice, and she said hastily that she didn't really think anyone had been trying to keep it from her particularly, and asked if she might have another drink, deciding that she would really have to stop showing off. They had another drink and a hamburger, and danced together again, amity restored.

He kissed her as they reached the car, and drove her back sedately.

She watched his profile, confident now of the evening's likely outcome and hoping she had tidied up the bedroom properly.

'It's still a fairly rough district, isn't it?' he observed as he drove cautiously past the crowd spilling out of a pub.

'Oh no,' she said, firmly. 'I've lived round here for ages and it's perfectly safe. I run round here at night.'

'By yourself?' he asked, scandalized, and sounding so like John McLeish that she was taken aback.

'Yes, of course — absent anyone else living with me.'

'That can't be a good idea, can it? You could easily get mugged.'

'Don't you start.' She spoke warningly, and was immediately and uneasily conscious that she had told him rather more than she meant to. They arrived at her door and she invited him in demurely for coffee, and made them both some. As she had confidently expected, he finished his coffee in a business-like way, standing in the kitchen, and reached for her. She slid her arms round him under his jacket, and was without warning assailed by an exact memory of the feel of John McLeish's heavily muscled, comforting shape. She put this thought resolutely and irritably from her and settled to the business in hand.

'Sweetie,' Hampton pulled gently away from her, 'listen — I've got to meet my potential partner. He flew in tonight from his holiday, and it's the only time I can see him. I didn't tell you before because I wanted as much time with you as possible, but I've run out of rope. I have to talk to him.' He touched her cheek. 'Can I see you tomorrow, assuming the day ever ends? I have to go up to Doncaster tomorrow night to be at the factory when the news breaks, but I could get the late train.'

Francesca considered him, disconcerted but realizing that something had not gone quite right; and wondered if he had sensed her momentary qualms.

'Tomorrow has its difficulties because I've got a rehearsal of the *Messiah*. It starts at 3 o'clock, and only God and the leader of the choir know when it will finish. We could have a quick meal or a drink — I'm never hungry when I've been singing.'

'I'd like to see you, even just for a little while tomorrow.' He stood, looking down at her intently. 'If I'd met someone like you ten years ago, everything might have been rather different.'

'I'd have been eighteen and head girl of my school,' she pointed out, in the interests of reality, and he laughed, and put an arm round her, shepherding her towards the door. He collected his coat and the two of them stood for a moment on the doorstep, agreeing precisely where they would meet next day. He bent and kissed her lightly, and went off to his car with a backward wave. Watching the car out of sight, she failed absolutely to notice John McLeish's car hastily accelerate past her.

* * *

McLeish, who had found himself driving past her door on his normal route home from the station had seen Peter Hampton bend to kiss her, the whole vignette brightly illuminated by the light over her door, and had been concerned only to get out of the way. As he drove on, he found himself so gripped by rage and desolation that he had to stop the car in order to recover. He sat, with the engine running, staring unseeingly through the windscreen, totally winded. It was less than twenty-four hours ago that he and Francesca had been on their way home to bed together, and after one fierce quarrel there was already another bloke on the scene. He sat, getting steadily angrier and more miserable, deciding bitterly that he ought to have taken some warning from earlier history when she had apparently switched so easily from O'Brien to him. At least the bastard wasn't staying the night, he thought savagely — but then perhaps he had already had what he came for? At all events, there was nothing for him to do but cut his losses and go home.

He glanced automatically in the mirror before pulling out and froze at the sight of Francesca pounding along the pavement. He shrank in his seat, but she was past him, unseeing, and he remembered that she never noticed cars unless they were about to run her down in the street. He watched as she turned left at the top of the road, Charlie's tracksuit flopping round her, and remembered, from what seemed many weeks ago, that one evening when they had made love she had refused to run with him on the basis that her knees were no good afterwards. So either Hampton had not got her to bed, or the experience had been such as to leave her knees unimpaired.

He cruised after her at a safe distance, determined to see her safe home, if only for the sake of his station's crime statistics, and watched her in through her own door before turning the car back towards his flat, entirely unconscious of the other man who had also been following Francesca's course.

CHAPTER 19

'So what you are telling me, Henry, is that Britex in its present form cannot be rescued?'

Henry Blackshaw, who had spent some time going over Francesca's admirably concise two-page submission to the Minister, suffered a moment's paralysing irritation at the thought that David Llewellyn had apparently not read any of it. Francesca, in obedience to his edict on the conduct of meetings, sat admirably silent.

'That's right, Minister,' he said, patiently. 'Also that we have a credible purchaser for the assets who will preserve some two-thirds of the jobs.' David Llewellyn nodded, looking uncomfortable and aggrieved, and Henry mentally apologized to Rajiv, who was looking sleek and unperturbed, and to Francesca who had both predicted exactly this reaction. 'No politician can bear to use the word "no",' Francesca had explained authoritatively, and this one was certainly having trouble even when 'no' was the only possible response.

'A receiver will always try and preserve the jobs, though, won't he?' the Minister asked hopefully. 'I met Ian Fraser last night at some reception and he told me that he would always try and cooperate with Government in saving jobs.'

Henry blinked at this unexpected view of a corporate undertaker's work, particularly considering that it came from the senior vulture of them all. He cast about for some alternative to telling the Minister outright that this statement was a load of old cobblers and Ian Fraser a conniving liar trying to get some business put his way by innocent Department of Trade and Industry Ministers, and the delay gave Francesca a chance to seize the baton.

'Minister, I am not sure that we have ever briefed you on the legal duties of a receiver.'

Llewellyn, nobody's fool, looked at her suspiciously.

'Does this mean I am going to hear something I would rather not?'

Henry laughed aloud, and Francesca, grinning apologetically, nodded to him to continue. 'A receiver, Minister, can only be appointed by a secured creditor. That is, a creditor who has a charge on the assets of the business. Once appointed, a receiver's primary duty is to ensure that the creditor who appointed him gets paid. He has only the most rudimentary duty to any other creditor — it boils down to avoiding kicking them in the nuts — and no duty at all to anyone else.'

Llewellyn's face was a study in reluctant enlightenment. 'So if the best offer from his creditor's point of view involves throwing the whole of the workforce on the streets, that is just too bad?'

Henry opened his mouth, but Francesca leapt in with the answer.

'Theoretically you are absolutely right, Minister, but in practice the best offer for the business usually comes from someone who wants to keep it going, and needs the workforce. Typically, a receiver will try and keep the business going in order to attract the best offer. But if push comes to shove, he has indeed to take the best financial offer.'

She hesitated, watching Llewellyn carefully to see if he had understood, and opened her mouth to speak again, but Henry gently kicked her under the table. She glanced at him under her eyelashes and subsided, while the more experienced Henry waited patiently for Llewellyn's question to formulate itself.

'Might the best financial offer come from some other textile firm who just want the order book, and who would let the workforce go?'

Henry, who had been waiting for him to get there, agreed that there was a risk of this but not, he thought, a serious one. That part of the textile trade engaged in making sheets and thermal underwear was fragmented, and no UK firm was really big enough to outbid a purchaser who wanted to manufacture here. Nor indeed would the Britex order book be very valuable, since it was both short and skimpy.

'Like their sheets,' Rajiv was heard to murmur, disruptively.

'What about these Americans?' Henry now understood that the Minister had in fact read the papers carefully, and was working through the key points.

'Sound businessmen,' he said, firmly, 'and well able to deal with a receiver. Perhaps it would help your thinking to meet them?'

Llewellyn looked towards Rajiv and Francesca enquiringly, and Henry understood that a political judgement was being sought.

'You need to meet them, Minister.' It was Rajiv who answered, taking, as senior adviser there present, responsibility for the serious business of political advice. 'If you decide to recommend assistance to your colleagues, the amount involved will be over £6m. There could, I would have thought, be some criticism if Departmental Ministers had not insisted on meeting prospective management when taxpayers' money at that level was involved.' Henry realized from Llewellyn's alarmed jerk of the head that 'taxpayers' money' must be a shorthand method of indicating every kind of trouble, from a row with backbench MP members of the powerful Public Accounts Committee to leaders in the heavier papers.

They left the Minister's office with his agreement that the current Britex management should be told that Ministers had now agreed that assistance would not be forthcoming.

The Americans should be told that, in principle, assistance would be considered for their plans, up to a maximum of £6.3m. Henry was pleased with the way the meeting had gone, and told Francesca that she had behaved well.

She smiled at him with affection, and he noticed that she was looking pale and tired.

'Burning the candle at both ends?' he asked bluntly when Rajiv had left them.

'No. Precisely not. I just slept badly.' She looked at her feet. 'I seem to be in a muddle.'

'Can I help?'

She hesitated, tempted, and then recalled the absolute impossibility of confessing to going out with Peter Hampton in the teeth of Henry's warning.

'How is your nice policeman?'

'Part of the problem. I'll just have to sort it,' she said, firmly and dismissively. 'Listen, Henry, someone — like you — needs to ring Sir James Blackett at Britex and tell him that the Minister has agreed no assistance. I'll ring the good Hal and tell him and Ed to parade tomorrow to meet the Minister. You and I have the *Messiah* orchestra rehearsal at 3 p.m. so we'd better get on.'

Henry agreed meekly to do his part of the task, and took her with him to listen while he failed to locate Sir James.

'I must call someone there,' he said. 'I'll talk to Hampton.'

'He's at the London office with Blackett *fils.*'

Henry accepted without a blink this unconscious betrayal, and rang the London office, flipping over the loud-speaker switch as he was connected and punctiliously telling Peter Hampton that he had Francesca with him. He delivered his message, added civil regrets that he had not felt able to recommend otherwise, and thanked Hampton for his help and cooperation, his eyes on Francesca who was openly soaking up the technique of delivering a difficult message.

'And I'd like to thank you — and Francesca and Martin — for the way you have handled this case,' Peter Hampton said, civilly, the slight northern accent emphasized by the phone. 'I can't pretend the decision is unexpected since you warned us what you were recommending. All the directors are here, except Sir James who is on his way — he telephoned from his car — and I expect we will be asking the bank to put in a receiver as soon as possible.'

Henry rang off after a further exchange of civilities, and looked across at Francesca. 'Nothing else to be done but tell them, Frannie. Don't look so anxious.'

'I'm not — I mean, I thought you did that very well, and now I know how to do it. I'm just tired. What can I usefully do for you apart from organize Hal?'

For a few minutes they discussed and divided up the various tasks, Francesca taking part with every evidence of intelligence while her emotional and intellectual energy was entirely deployed, as it had been all night, in trying to decide whether she really wanted Peter Hampton enough to risk the loss of John McLeish whom she wanted very much and was missing painfully. Or whether there was some way she could have her cake and eat it. Having considered all the angles, she decided that whatever she did long term she could not in decency cancel a date with Peter Hampton on the evening of a day in which he and fellow directors had been forced to ask for a receiver to be appointed to his company.

She returned to the business at hand and contemplated the list of tasks that had appeared under her hand, bent her mind to it, asked one key question, and went away.

Henry reached over to switch the phone back to his secretary, but picked it up as it rang to find John McLeish on the line, sounding over-tired and harassed.

'Mr Blackshaw — Henry — sorry, but I can't find Francesca. Peregrine's girlfriend, Sheena, has recovered consciousness.'

'That's marvellous. I'll tell Fran, she was just here. Hey up — does Perry's girl know who attacked her?'

'Oh yes. Yes, she does.'

Henry waited for a count of five before losing patience. 'So who was it then, lad?'

'Her brother-in-law. Her husband's brother, moved by indignation and drink, most probably. He has a lot of form. Mrs Byers is quite clear about it, and I don't doubt she's right. We went looking for him straightaway of course, and he's in Marbella. Has been since last Tuesday, the day after she was attacked.'

'That buggers it,' Henry observed, realizing that any expression of sympathy would be hopelessly inadequate.

'Makes me wonder whether I haven't gone right over the top on this case.' McLeish sounded both sour and despondent, and Henry sought for some way of cheering him up. 'Had you got any further with any of the likely candidates, though?' he enquired cautiously.

'Yes a bit.' The policeman's voice warmed and strengthened, and Henry grinned to himself. 'You know that salesman you tipped me off about — Ketterick? Well, I have a whisper that he might be a user — hard drugs. That'd take money, wouldn't it? — and he is a supplier to Britex.'

'Oh yes. Have you asked him to assist with your enquiries?'

'Not even invited him for a friendly chat down the station.' McLeish sounded ferocious. 'No, the trouble is, Henry, the bastard's gone missing, and no one knows where to find him.'

'That table Frannie memorized could be very important,' Henry commented, getting the point with his usual speed. 'Does she know?'

'No.' Henry waited patiently so that he was forced to continue. 'I haven't talked to her since Saturday.'

Henry waited out another silence, then took pity on him. 'How can I help you, John?'

'You can tell me where to find Ketterick, when I ought never to have lost him.'

Henry considered the blotter in front of him wonderingly, but decided to try. 'He's looking for another job, isn't he? Being interviewed somewhere, perhaps in Europe or even in the States. It's an international trade at managerial level.'

'I didn't think of that.' McLeish sounded unhopeful, and Henry sighed.

'What are you worried about, lad? I mean, as you say yourself, now that the attack on Perry's piece of fluff turns out not to be related to Britex, perhaps you are making too much of this.'

'I know, but I don't like Ketterick going missing. If he is an addict, he's got a motive for being involved in theft from Britex. He could be a murderer or an accessory. And for various reasons, although you tipped me off I didn't get on to it quickly enough. If the firm goes into receivership, it's going to be more difficult to find any evidence.'

Henry considered. 'In confidence, lad, precisely that is going to happen, and fairly quickly. I told Hampton this morning that the Minister had accepted our advice. That leaves them nothing else to do but to ask the bank to put in a receiver.'

'What's the form there? Does Hampton just leave when the receiver comes in?' The question was desperately over-casual, and Henry decided to help.

'Tell you what, lad. I'll make a few phone calls, find out if any of my mates in the trade have been seeing Ketterick. I'm in meetings here until 3 p.m., then I have to go straight to a rehearsal. Why don't you pick me up at St Margaret's, Westminster around 7.30? I'll buy you a drink and tell you what I've found. Frannie is singing too — we'll maybe buy her a drink if she's a good girl.' He grinned sardonically at the receiver.

'I'd like that, thanks . . . I'll be there, 7.30.'

Henry put the phone down, pleased that his judgement of McLeish as a determined character, not one to let opportunities pass, was confirmed. He rang a colleague in personnel at Allied Textiles, and asked him as a favour to find out in the trade whether anything had been heard of Ketterick, so that he would have something to report to McLeish should it prove necessary to adhere to the convention that it was he whom the policeman had come to see. Beaming evilly on

Francesca, who put her head in with a question, he decided to make this whole arrangement a surprise for her.

* * *

McLeish settled back to work, cheered by Henry's invitation. Brady rang in an hour later to report that Ketterick banked with a local Barclays and ran a model account, never overdrawn — a circumstance suspicious in itself, Brady opined. Like Hampton he was paying a lot of maintenance to an ex-wife and children, and like Hampton he paid regularly via a standing order from the bank. Would McLeish like someone to have a word with the wife who could presumably be readily traced via her bank in Birmingham? McLeish thanked him, and said he could perfectly well call Birmingham himself and would do so. He considered the piece of paper in front of him and remembered William Blackett. Since Alutex had been taken over he was presumably on his way out, but he might know where Ketterick was. He tried the London office to be told that Mr Blackett had just left; and then rang Blackett's house in Yorkshire, to his relief getting the housekeeper rather than Mrs Blackett, who told him that Blackett had spent the previous night in London at the Glengarry Hotel. At the Glengarry, there was some confusion as to whether Blackett had or had not checked out, so he left a message there too, and decided to get some lunch.

* * *

In a small room, on the fifth floor of the Glengarry Hotel, Simon Ketterick stirred and blearily opened his eyes, rubbing them to get rid of the grit. He focused on the bright light showing through the Glengarry's fashionable but translucent curtains, then, more slowly, realized someone was standing silently by his bed. He moved his head sharply, feeling as usual the lurking pain at the back of his neck, but relaxed as he recognized his visitor. He felt congestion in his arm;

then the sharp stab of a needle in the vein in the crook of the elbow; then the golden warming glow filled his body, killing the pain in his neck.

'Bless you,' he murmured, as his whole body relaxed, one arm falling away over the edge of the bed and his chin slumping on to his chest.

His visitor dropped the syringe on the floor, carelessly, and reached with his gloved hand for a second syringe. He plunged its contents into the vein in the same site as the first, dropping the syringe on the floor as well. He glanced round the room, then slid out of the door, locking it and making sure that the 'Do Not Disturb' sign was still in place on the outside.

* * *

McLeish came back from lunch and found himself drawn off the affairs of Britex by a summons to New Scotland Yard to talk to the man who had been his boss in the Flying Squad. He was offering McLeish a job at the Yard on promotion to Chief Inspector in CI, the division which deals with murders. Cheered by this prospect, which would make him one of the youngest of this rank in the Met, McLeish drove away, noting automatically a concentration of uniformed police and realizing that they were controlling the entrance to St Margaret's, Westminster.

As he pulled off the road into the tiny parking-space, two constables converged politely on him. He snowed his warrant card and asked, innocently, what was happening.

'Some pop star in there, singing. We're here to keep the fans out. Waste of time — the only really dodgy characters turned out to be his driver and his agent.' The young constable was laughing, and McLeish said he knew exactly what he meant, but he knew the singer and would pop in for a moment. Leaving his car keys with the uniformed branch he edged into the ill-lit church, sliding into an pew at the back under cover of the Aquarius Choir's desperately uneven rendering of *'All we like sheep have gone astray/We have turned every one to his own way.'* Indeed, McLeish thought, that was exactly what it sounded like. The conductor stopped them and made another attempt at a particularly ragged entrance, and McLeish was sure he could pick out Francesca's steady contralto.

The choir struggled through the chorus again; it was still uneven, and the conductor said as much, but added that he would have to move on if they were to complete the orchestra rehearsal before 8 o'clock.

'Mr Wilson please,' he called, and Perry rose from a chair at the front of the choir, looking contained and unself-conscious as he always did.

The violins played the introduction to the tenor recitative which describes the sufferings of Christ, and Perry started to sing. The hairs rose on McLeish's neck as he sat bolt upright in the uncomfortable pew. Perry was using a harsh dry edge to his voice that McLeish had never heard before, rather than the mellifluous tones usually adopted by a tenor singing Handel. He ended the short passage and the choir came in with real feeling on the chorus, *'He trusted in God that he would deliver him.'* That too was a bit ragged, but the conductor plunged straight on to Perry's next recitative, which leads into the tenor aria, *'Behold and see if there be any sorrow like unto his sorrow'*. McLeish felt a horrified sense of desolation as the marvellous voice, deliberately hard-edged, sang on, and for a moment he felt the weight of the cross, heard the mockery of the soldiers and the night wind blowing cold over Golgotha.

He listened transfixed, among a silent and unmoving audience as the magnificent, chill voice ended the second recitative.

The conductor, absolutely concentrated, with no more than a glance at Perry, went straight on with the orchestral opening to the second tenor aria, *'But Thou didst not leave His soul in hell'* and Perry came in joyfully, using the fat of his voice, golden and mellow, the hard edge gone, in an affirmation of faith that could not, McLeish thought, covertly blowing his nose, have left a dry eye in the house. For the first time he observed that Perry was not using a score but was singing from memory, head slightly back, looking like something off a stained glass window. The Aquarius Choir, listening trance-like, muffed completely the entrance to *'Lift up your heads, oh ye gates'*, and ground to a ragged halt four bars later.

'Right,' the conductor said, on an exhaled breath. 'Thank you, Perry. Will you give us the last twelve bars so we can get that entry right?'

Perry, who had remained on his feet, nodded without a change of expression and gave them the last twelve bars, with all the joy and the steady faith and triumph over death sounding exactly the same.

But this time the choir was ready for him, and crashed in together on *'Lift up your heads'*. Perry waited to make sure they were launched, and sat down again, gazing into space. Just at that moment one of the uniformed constables slid into the pew beside McLeish to say that they had answered his car radio for him, and would he please ring Detective Inspector Brady in Doncaster?

* * *

'Ketterick's wife reported him missing this morning.' Brady was sounding tense. 'I phoned Birmingham for you — I've got an ex-sergeant of mine there — and the name rang a bell. They are divorced, but she had expected him on Sunday to see the boys. She reported him missing because he never fails to turn up for the boys, and his neighbours could not find him. She was worried, she said, because she knew he had lost his job.'

'Unusually decent behaviour for an ex-wife,' McLeish observed, drily.

'She's remarried. Looks as if she walked out on him, so she feels badly. She's expecting a call.'

McLeish thanked him, fixed himself a date with ex-Mrs Ketterick, now Mrs Laing, for the next day, then dropped back into his office and sorted out more paperwork.

He arrived back at St Margaret's, just in time to hear the choir and orchestra taking the 'Amen Chorus' at top speed and at top volume.

They were sounding a great deal better than earlier in the afternoon, and the conductor was grinning as he pushed them through. He beamed round him at the end, observing that if they could do it that well tomorrow, it would all be a great success. John McLeish watched from the back as the Wilson boys coalesced into a little group with Henry Blackshaw and Francesca, and, picking his moment, strolled to the front to join them, placing himself between Perry and Henry.

Perry greeted him with obvious pleasure and told him that Sheena really was all right, as evidenced by the fact that she had asked for a mirror and, after one horror-stricken look, for all her make-up.

Francesca was deep in conversation with Henry and took a moment to surface. 'Hello,' she said cautiously, and glanced round involuntarily.

Henry looked up, sharply. 'Ah, it's you, lad. Yes, you do owe me a drink: I have something for you from one of my mates. Let's all go. Come on, Francesca.'

'I can't. I was due somewhere else twenty minutes ago.' She avoided looking at McLeish. 'I really am sorry,' she said, earnestly to Henry, who was so clearly not the real target of this apology that McLeish was torn between hope and exasperation. She gave him a hunted sideways look, closed her mouth firmly on all further explanation, and started to look for her coat. McLeish, feeling himself being sharply pushed at waist-level, looked down surprised on a very small, plump girl, surely not more than fourteen, gelled hair spiked straight up from her skull, eyes fixed worshipfully on Perry, as she pushed an autograph book at him, temporarily struck dumb by his physical presence. When he looked round again, he saw only Francesca's straight back as she hurried to an exit, shrugging herself into her coat as she ran.

CHAPTER 20

'Come for a drink, John?' Charlie turned to him, amicably. 'What have you done with Frannie?'

'She's gone,' McLeish said as neutrally as he could, but Charlie's alarmed look at Perry said it all.

'Oh dear. Then particularly come and have a drink.' McLeish hesitated but found himself swept along by the boys and Henry Blackshaw. Perry turned his coat collar up and pulled a peaked cap down over his eyes as they went out into the night air, and McLeish saw Biff, the resident bodyguard, and the Wilson boys close round him protectively. 'Perry can just about still go to a pub, but if he does this film they are talking about that'll be an end of it. It's a curse,' Charlie observed.

They arrived at the pub, and McLeish found a whisky appearing in front of him, organized by Biff who was pointedly nursing an orange juice. Charlie settled himself on a bar stool beside him, and ordered sandwiches on the basis that he was likely to be carried out if he drank on top of all that singing.

'Over four hours' rehearsal,' he pointed out. 'And except for Perry, it's not very good yet.'

McLeish agreed that Perry would have been ranked as outstanding in any company and against the background of the Aquarius Choir was ridiculously out of his class.

'Perry will do nearly anything for Francesca, and quite a lot for the rest of us. It may not be the same, of course, if he marries Sheena.' He paused, and took a long swallow of his whisky, while McLeish thought that this was a sensible one, this dark blond changeling, unlike the rest of his damned family.

'John. Are your intentions towards my sister honourable?'

McLeish choked on his whisky, totally taken aback. 'I've only known her three weeks.'

'When did that ever make any difference?'

'No, all right. Yes they are; or they were, I suppose.'

'And you somehow indicated this to her?' Charlie, embarrassed but dogged, was watching his drink.

'Yes.' McLeish finished his drink, and looked round for the barman but found Perry at his side who forestalled him. 'I suppose that was a mistake?' he observed, feeling a double whisky start to take effect on an empty stomach and too little sleep. The brothers gazed sadly into their glasses.

'I blame the television,' Perry said suddenly to his tonic, and both McLeish and Charlie blinked at him. 'I've read books you know — I know you don't believe I can read, but I can — and before we had television women used all sorts of wiles to get men to marry them, and men spent all their time worrying about being trapped into matrimony.' He glanced slyly at McLeish. 'Chance would be a fine thing, wouldn't it, these days? Where have all these women gone? Mine tells me she is never going to marry anyone again. My own sister is rejecting good offers out of hand. We chaps are going to be reduced to desperate measures like tricking them into getting pregnant, or going off with other women to make them jealous, until finally they give in, and we can drag them kicking and screaming to a registry office.' He shook his head, sadly, sparkling with amusement, his audience laughing with him. McLeish decided he could see the point of Perry; he was the family clown, the one who could take the sting out of a situation with a joke.

'Was it like that when you were young, Henry?' Perry was demanding of his sister's boss.

'Oh aye.' Henry, heaving with laughter, was prepared to play along.

'Mothers gave dinner parties and tried to lure young men who had got into decent accountancy firms. All of us with Prospects were very much courted.'

'Mind you, this is 1863 we are talking about here,' Charlie observed with privileged cheek, and McLeish found himself laughing along with the rest, his bruised feelings considerably soothed.

'Where's Francesca?' Jeremy, appearing innocently from further down the bar, was nearly annihilated by the battery of scowls, and Charlie told him testily that no one knew. John McLeish, observing the sudden, instantly checked, turn of Perry's head, decided that he probably did know, and, whatever he felt about it, was not going to give her away.

'Mind you, Frannie and Sheena both had one bad marriage, and that puts them off,' Perry said lazily, catching his thoughtful look.

'As John may not know, her first husband turned out to be a real shit. Sapped her confidence completely,' Charlie offered.

'I've met him. He still rattles her.'

'Poor Frannie,' Perry said, dreamily. 'She had to go everywhere in the three-piece suite — you know, suit, matching hat, gloves. None of it worked, she still didn't fit in with all those army people.'

'Some of her clothes still look rather like that,' John McLeish, half-way down his third whisky, observed. To his surprise and pleasure, Jeremy, who had been sitting silent and crushed, burst out laughing, showering peanuts over the bar.

'Anyway,' Charlie said, quellingly, 'she once said to me she was never going to bend herself out of her natural shape for anyone, and it seemed to her that all marriages involved women taking up ridiculous postures in relation to very ordinary men, and never again for her.'

John McLeish contemplated the vision of Francesca trying anxiously to fit herself into an alien military society, pushed on by a man who undermined her with every word, and despaired. 'Why ever did you let her marry him?'

The Wilson boys gaped at him, then looked at each other helplessly, much as if they had been asked to explain the rules of cricket in Russian.

'There were only four of them to stop her?' Henry suggested, watching them with grim amusement.

The brothers slanted resentful looks at him. 'Well, she's our elder sister,' Charlie said, glancing to Perry for support. 'Yes, all right, John, I suppose it sounds pretty wet but she was twenty-two, I was twenty, Perry eighteen and the twins sixteen. I mean, she had always been the one who knew what to do. It never occurred to any of us that she had no idea what he was like and was just marrying a pretty face.'

'She would never have taken any notice of what we said anyway.'

The other twin, Tristram, had arrived from his Bach Choir rehearsal.

McLeish sighed and finished his third whisky, which was going down grateful, in Bruce Davidson's parlance. He realized he was swaying on his feet, and said as much to Perry who, without apparently doing more than murmur something to Biff, moved the whole party to an inner room where they were served steak and chips in an amazingly short time. He found himself sitting with Henry Blackshaw and Martin Bailey, as well as the Wilson boys. He pushed his plate aside with some chips left on it.

'If Francesca were here, she'd finish those for you,' Martin Bailey observed, grinning, then blushed as he realized from the concerted expression of disapproval round the table that he had been less than tactful. McLeish's sense of the ridiculous reasserted itself as he looked round at the four Wilson boys scowling at poor Martin; and he said easily that he was perfectly right, one was simply not safe eating with Francesca.

'Any luck with finding Ketterick?' Henry asked *sotto voce* as three different conversations started up awkwardly round the table.

'None at all. He's completely vanished — his ex-wife just reported him missing, as well. Did you find any trace?'

'Yes,' Henry said, smugly. 'He is seeing a sales director at Allied — my old firm — tomorrow.'

'Oh, great!' McLeish felt suddenly rejuvenated. 'Marvellous. I do feel better for that. Thank you very much, Henry — I'll catch up with him now.'

'You still worrying about that table, then?'

'Francesca's table?' Martin Bailey, somewhat cowed by his previous *faux pas,* brightened up, and they looked at him enquiringly. 'I had an idea, you see. You remember those letters at the top of the column? They must be initials, mustn't they? — only we couldn't think of anyone whose surnames matched. Well, what if they were Christian names?'

McLeish felt a faint ringing in his ears, and hoped it was the whisky, as he fished out the table from his top pocket.

'Bloody hell!'

'P. for Peter Hampton you see, perhaps?' Martin suggested stolidly, looking tidy, clean-cut and indefatigable as he always did. 'And W. for William Blackett. I don't know who S. is for, though.'

'Simon Ketterick.' McLeish and Henry spoke together, and both of them glared at Martin.

'I didn't think of it before,' he protested.

'I didn't think of it at all,' acknowledged McLeish, shaken.

'That would mean they were all three in it, John.' Henry was bouncing with excitement. 'It's the classic supplier fiddle. Hampton places orders with Ketterick at Alutex, and Ketterick gives him an envelope of used fivers at the end of the month. Ketterick keeps some cash for himself, and Blackett is cut in as well, presumably because he is the chap who authorizes the cash going out of Alutex.'

'So Fireman wasn't in it?' McLeish felt as if his brain was made of high-quality cotton wool.

'Well, he could have been, but that table doesn't suggest it. No, I think you were right first time, John, he wasn't that sort of chap.'

'But one of those three topped him because he found out about it. Jesus!'

'Well it was a lot of money. If that table is right, Blackett and Hampton were getting £2,000 a month each, tax free, and Ketterick £1,000 odd — I wonder why he got less? I suppose the other two reckoned they were directors, and entitled.'

Martin, uninterested in this reflection on salary differentials, was methodically grossing up for tax. 'That's the equivalent of about £50,000 a year in gross salary for Hampton and Blackett and £25,000 for Ketterick. More than double their existing gross salaries,' he observed, and then visibly thought about the numbers, and looked up, astonished, at McLeish. A silence had fallen round them. Charlie and Perry were listening, fascinated.

'Well, if Ketterick's an addict we know what he's doing with the cash, but what are the other two spending it on?' Henry asked rhetorically. 'It could all be current expenditure but it seems too much — my guess is they are stashing it somewhere.'

'Oh, they are.' McLeish sounded savage. 'Both of them took trips to Switzerland recently. You were right, too, Henry, about Hampton needing money to put in with his new partner: the bloke wanted £20,000, and Hampton had told him he'd be able to borrow that on his house. He could have too, I understand.'

'Easier still to steal it, though,' Henry pointed out. 'You don't need to repay it.'

McLeish shook his head to clear it. 'I must get back. Can I have some coffee — a lot of coffee?' He looked enquiringly at Charlie who seemed to be in charge, and was struck by the way the four boys were watching him for guidance, much like baby monkeys with their mother, and felt very old. They were all so alike, and he longed for the missing Francesca as Jeremy tentatively smiled at him, with exactly her smile when she was not quite sure of her ground.

Jeremy's face changed suddenly as he looked at a point behind McLeish's head, and he turned to see a uniformed sergeant looking doubtfully at the assembled group.

'Inspector McLeish, can I have a word?'

McLeish got up and joined him in a corner of the room, conscious of the effects of three whiskies and two glasses of wine, but reminding himself that he was off duty. 'Sergeant Davidson rang through, sir. Says to tell you a Simon Ketterick has been found dead in the Glengarry — you know, that big hotel near Euston. Drug overdose. Been dead since lunchtime, likely, but the body's only just been found. Euston Road CID have got it.'

McLeish felt the shock down to his bones, and stood staring at the sergeant who fidgeted uncomfortably, visibly wondering whether this particular ornament of the CID was actually understanding what was being said to him.

'Telephone,' McLeish said, recovering with an enormous effort. 'No, wait a minute.' He strode back to the table and lent over the back of his discarded chair, both hands flat. Everyone stopped eating or drinking. 'Henry. Ketterick's dead; said to be a drug overdose.'

Henry and he looked at each other.

'Could be carelessness,' Henry suggested, unhopefully.

'Or one of the other two tidying up.' McLeish sounded, and felt, grim. He drank down his own coffee, commandeered Charlie's and finished that as well. Reaching for his jacket, he stood up straight, wishing he had drunk at least one less of everything.

'Any bets, Henry? Or Martin?'

'Well, Peter Hampton's got a nasty temper,' Martin volunteered. 'I mean, if that means anything. I mean, he needn't be a murderer . . .'

He stopped, horror-stricken.

'What are you thinking of, Martin?' Henry's completely matter-of-fact manner defused the question, and Martin relaxed.

'Well, when we were doing the suppliers' lists that day, I also disorganized a cupboard in the room where we were working — Fran wanted a biscuit, you know what she's like.

She was brought in from down the corridor by Peter, and he was already in rather a paddy, but he was *furious* when he saw me at the cupboard.'

'What was in the cupboard?' The whole table froze in their places as McLeish came back into the conversation, leaning over towards Martin.

'No biscuits. Some odd papers, draft accounts for three years back, cups for swimming, a box of biros, some of those giant paperclips.'

Martin's eyes were narrowed with effort. 'Ah. And a little flat box.'

'What sort of box?'

'A blue one. It said Britex dash forty years.'

McLeish stared at him, and Martin quailed. 'How do you know?'

'I noticed, I mean I remembered, I mean I was there.' He took a deep breath, and calmed down. 'About this big.' He set his hands down on the table about nine inches apart, and McLeish tore off his watch and laid it between Martin's hands where it fitted neatly.

'That's right,' Martin said, plainly relieved. 'A presentation box.'

McLeish felt the table sway, and Martin's face changed. 'What have I said?'

'The murdered Britex Purchasing Manager was not wearing a watch. This surprised everyone because he had last been seen wearing one presented to him by Britex for forty years' service. He had been presented with it, in a box, the Friday before. We have never found either the watch or the box.'

Martin and Henry looked at each other in horror. 'You think the watch was in the box, John? Why did he keep it?'

McLeish straightened up, his mind finally working. 'I had better not drive. Sergeant will you get me to Edgware Road, please, and I'll use your radio on the way.'

'The Car is here,' Charlie volunteered. 'Biff could take you, couldn't he, Perry?'

Perry, absolutely white-faced and his eyes looking huge, looked back at him, speechless, and his brother was on him in a flash.

'Perry. Where is Fran? Tell me this minute.'

'You don't need to shout. I don't know where she is but she is with this Hampton.' His eyes flicked towards McLeish and instantly away again. 'I saw him waiting for her after the rehearsal, and said hello. He was apparently going to have a drink with her and go back to Yorkshire tonight.'

'How did you know it was Hampton?' Charlie asked, puzzled. 'I've never met him?'

'I went round to collect a jacket from Fran's house before supper last night. He was there having a drink.' He kept his eyes fixed on his brother's face, avoiding McLeish. Charlie's mouth tightened, and McLeish understood that a message had been passed.

'Oh, but that is naughty of her,' Henry said, seriously annoyed. 'I mean, dammit, she'd been told not to mix socially with the customers.'

He blinked as he considered the implications. 'What do we do, John?'

'I don't know whether Blackett or Hampton murdered Fireman, and possibly Ketterick. We find her.'

The whole table stared at him, aghast, and he remembered that they dealt with paper, not violent people. It was Perry, whom his family thought barely intelligent, who recovered first.

'I'll drive for you, John. I hardly drink, and we have a car telephone. Two, in fact. Let's go. She may be home, if he was catching a train tonight. Do we ring up?'

Jeremy appeared at his elbow. 'I did. No answer.'

McLeish nodded to him, and he and Perry raced for the door, McLeish instructing the uniformed sergeant to get on to Edgware Road and get Davidson and a police car round to Wellcome Street to meet them. He hurled himself into the front seat of the Rolls as Perry took off, observing as he did so that Charlie, Jeremy and Henry Blackshaw had somehow got into the back.

'I have come in order to tell her that the next time she does something I tell her not to, in professional terms, I'll see her posted to the Wigan branch of the Department of Health and Social Security,' Henry said, grimly, in answer to his unspoken question, but McLeish was not fooled. Henry Blackshaw had come out of love, to try to protect her from the full consequences of her idiocy.

'The others are behind us with Biff,' Perry noted, and McLeish, with the bit of his mind not occupied in putting out a general alarm for Hampton and Blackett, marvelled at the ease with which Perry was flicking the big car through heavy traffic. He organized Brady to get a search warrant and to go for the Britex safe. He put the car phone down, but it rang again, sharply. Charlie snatched it up, prepared to blast any of Perry's associates off the other end, but handed it over immediately to McLeish.

'It's Bruce. I have yon Blackett, or I will in ten minutes. Ye mind that lassie he had spent the evening with when Mrs Byers was attacked? A business girl? She rang me ten minutes ago because she had Blackett on her hands, insensible with drink since lunch-time. What time he was not loading more in he was screaming his head off about someone whom he'd found dead in bed at his hotel.'

'In bed?'

'Ketterick was found in bed, seemingly asleep, until the wee girl who was cleaning the room tried to rouse him and frightened herself out of a year's growth.'

'Get Blackett, Bruce, and sober him up.' The concentrated ferocity in McLeish's voice silenced the background chatter in the car, and Henry raised his eyebrows, wordlessly. McLeish explained, tersely, and swung round to urge Perry on, but held his tongue as he realized Perry was doing sixty down the outer lane in the narrowest part of the Edgware Road, headlights full on, his hand on the horn, clearing a path for the big car.

'John, does that mean Blackett killed him?' Charlie was shaking his shoulder to get his attention.

'No, I don't think so. I think it was Hampton. Perry, for God's sake!'

He threw up his right arm to protect his face as a motor cyclist hurled himself bodily out of their way, taking out the Rolls's right-hand headlight and buckling the bonnet, sending himself ricocheting off the Rover he had incautiously being trying to overtake.

'At least he didn't come through the windscreen,' Perry observed, slamming down the accelerator so that the big car leapt across the road to turn right down Wellcome Street under the bonnet of a giant articulated lorry, whose air brakes sounded like an explosion as the driver brought it up all standing.

'There!' He slid the car into a space twelve inches longer than its length outside Francesca's door.

'I have a key. I'll do the usual signal and go in.' Perry was half out of the car. 'Wouldn't that be less awkward for you, John?'

'We're long past all that, Perry.' The big man spoke dismissively as he ran up the front steps, Perry at his heels.

Perry unlocked the door and Charlie pushed past him and ran upstairs, shouting for his sister. McLeish and Henry both stopped in the hall, staring at a crumpled skirt and leather shoes dumped in the middle of the hall.

'She's running, John,' Perry spoke over the nightmare. 'She does that, puts on the tracksuit and trainers she keeps in the hall, and just takes off whatever she can't force under a tracksuit. It's all right. He must have gone, and we can just wait for her.' He sat down, heavily on the floor, and breathed out carefully. McLeish swung round to go upstairs but stopped.

'Who is singing?'

'Me,' said Perry from the floor. 'It's a recording,' he added redundantly.

'In fact it's the tape of the BBC thing.' He started to sing quietly with the tape. *'It may be that Death's bright angel, Will speak in that chord again . . .'* He was plainly not thinking about the words, but McLeish and Henry stared at each other, appalled. Charlie crashed down the stairs.

'She's not there,' he reported. 'I looked in the cupboards, too.' He sat down, equally heavily, and quite unselfconsciously rested his head momentarily on Perry's shoulder. 'I'll kill her when we find her,' he observed, simply.

'Not if I find her first,' Henry said, grimly. 'And I expect we'll all have competition from John, here.'

They looked round for McLeish who had gone into the street. 'Her car's here,' he said, from the doorstep. 'At least she isn't running in Holland Park.' He hesitated, looking at Perry. 'I know a circuit she does run, though, and we must find her. You OK to drive?'

'Of course,' Perry, still very white, got to his feet, and they all went out to the car, meeting Biff and his carload on the way.

'We'll take Pindar Street. And hurry.'

Perry looked at him sideways as they left. 'You're still worried? Surely he's gone?'

'Just drive, Perry.'

The car hurtled round three sides of a square, cutting off a corner, and emerged at the end of Pindar Street, long, ill-lit and apparently deserted. Perry checked his speed. 'There. Left-hand side, right at the top.'

McLeish, who had until then thought he had perfect eyesight, squinted into the night and saw, just, a flicker of movement.

'It's Charlie's old tracksuit, you can see it.' Perry slowed the car further.

'I'll have to take your word for it.' McLeish felt torn between relief, rage and real apprehension about confronting Francesca with the news that she had either been having or considering an affair with a man who was probably a thief and possibly a double murderer.

'Look out!' Perry had never taken his eyes off the distant figure, and as he shouted the car leapt forward, its headlights flashed on, and his hand came down hard on the horn. In the powerful Rolls lights all of them saw the tall shadow, arm upraised, barring Francesca's path.

* * *

Francesca was counting aloud as she ran, making sure that she was putting her feet down evenly as John McLeish had taught her, watching the ground ahead of her. She checked as a dark shadow fell across her path, and lifted her head to see a tall figure standing in her way, dressed entirely in black. The man moved to intercept her and she saw him clear, the blond head haloed in the streetlight, very bright against the dark mackintosh. She saw his arm go up, the hammer in his right hand glinting silver in the light, and she threw herself violently sideways, hearing her wrist crack like a piece of wood as she fell, twisting to face her attacker who was silhouetted against the light like the bright angel of death himself.

'No, Peter,' she screamed, as he threw himself on her and the world went dark.

* * *

McLeish saw her swerve, trip clumsily over the kerb and fall, spreadeagled, in the road, throwing out an arm to save herself. Then he was out of the car in a flying tackle, flattening a man nearly as tall as himself who fought like several demons. A blow on his collarbone momentarily paralysed his right arm and turned him sick, but he hung on grimly, and his assailant suddenly went limp and terribly heavy. McLeish shifted the weight painfully and laboriously and struggled to his knees, feeling extremely ill, to find Charlie squatting anxiously beside him, clasping a half brick.

'I hit him over the head, John — do you think I've killed him? *John?*'

McLeish, concentrating hard, turned over the body, and felt inside the mouth for any obstructions. He put two fingers to the pulse in the neck, and the man's eyelids creased. Charlie's explosive gasp of relief echoed in the dark street.

'Is that him? Is that Hampton, I mean?'

'Yes.' McLeish got slowly to his feet and greeted Bruce Davidson, who had arrived with two squad cars and half a dozen police. 'Cuff him, but he needs to go to the hospital.'

He waited, Charlie anxiously fidgeting beside him, while his head cleared and the attendant police dealt with the spectators who had arrived from nowhere, as they always do in London, then turned reluctantly and slowly to find out what had happened to the others.

The first thing he saw was the Rolls, slewed diagonally across the road as Perry had swung it to avoid running down his sister, bonnet buckled and the wing on the driver's side beaten in. He looked for Francesca in a fever of anxiety, and saw her on the other side of the builder's skip that had provided Charlie's providential half brick. She was standing in the middle of a tight group of Perry, both twins and Henry Blackshaw, and whatever they had privately threatened they were grouped round her in a defensive formation, prepared to repel the world. He could just see her profile as she watched Peter Hampton being loaded on to a stretcher, handcuffed, his head lolling to one side. She was terribly pale but dry-eyed and expressionless, nursing her left elbow in her right hand, leaning on Henry who had wrapped his jacket round her. McLeish found it impossible to look away from her as she absorbed, steadily, the full depth of the situation, and he found himself praying for her sake that Hampton had not actually been her lover.

Davidson arrived at his side and stood silently; McLeish realized, touched, that he was there to offer what support he could in McLeish's own difficulties. Hopeless, he thought dispassionately, and managed to turn away from Francesca and concentrate his mind on the formalities of arrest.

* * *

Henry, supporting the shivering Francesca, was equally realistic in his assessment and started to concern himself with getting her into a police car and off to hospital. She checked him as he gently pushed at her.

'What do I do, Henry?'

'About what?'

'About John.'

'You could try apologizing. There'll never be a better moment, lass, if you can do it.'

'John!' The clear voice cut through the general background noise, and McLeish turned reluctantly back towards her. She was shivering uncontrollably, her eyes enormous, and he felt a dreadful pang of loss. He moved towards her, noticing how her brothers bunched closer to protect her.

'She is in shock, John,' Perry said anxiously. 'And I think her wrist is broken.'

'Perry, I need two minutes with John. Go away.' She pushed at him gently, and the crowd around her melted. Henry carefully withdrew his supporting arm, and she swayed slightly, finally causing McLeish's temper to snap.

'If you want to talk, come and sit in a car like a Christian.' He hustled her to the nearest police car Biff had driven, whose occupants abandoned it as if it were on fire, and sat her down in the front seat, conscious of four wide-eyed Wilson boys left standing on the pavement and an equally wide-eyed Davidson pretending to adjust a radio aerial on another car.

He shut the doors firmly, and glared at her. 'All right. Let's have it.'

Her head came up and she gave him a long look which reminded him that although down she was not out, and that there was a functioning intelligence at work. 'I am here to apologize. I nearly got myself killed, and I have made a fool of both of us in front of your colleagues. I'm sorry.'

McLeish, the wind taken out of him, sat and looked at her. She was using everything she knew not to cry, where any other girl he had ever known would have made it easier for both of them by weeping.

'Just before the boys and Henry take me away, I want you to know I didn't go to bed with him. I wanted to once, but Perry arrived at a key moment.' Only Francesca, he thought, would have added that rider.

She stared out of the windscreen, the long nose and the strong jaw looking particularly stark. 'Then I found I missed you very much, and I wanted you back. But Peter's company was put into receivership this morning and it didn't seem the moment to tell him so.' She swallowed, painfully, and eased her right shoulder carefully. 'I don't want you to go away. I don't know if that will do. Now, I mean, after all this.' The lifted chin indicated comprehensively the crowded scene outside the car, two other police cars with flashing lights, two ambulances, into one of which Peter Hampton was being lifted, and some forty assorted policemen, members of the Wilson family, and general spectators.

The silence in the car deepened, as John McLeish decided what he had to say, win, lose or draw.

'It's not on if you want to sleep with other blokes. I can't cope with it.'

'I understand that. I found I couldn't cope with it, either.' Tears of strain finally started to pour down her cheeks, as she bowed her head and with a huge sigh of tension released he hooked his arm round her and turned her face to kiss her.

'You're freezing. You've gone blue,' he discovered. 'Why didn't you say?' He reached across her, wound her window down, and paused for a second at the sight of Perry, standing contemplating his wrecked car with simple interest and studiously avoiding looking in the direction of his sister.

'Peregrine! Come here, and go with Frannie to St Mary's immediately. She's in shock.' He looked again at her left hand, awkwardly angled in her lap. 'Your wrist. Christ, it is broken.'

'I told you,' Perry pointed out from the driver's side. 'If you get out, John, I can get in.' McLeish blinked up at him, as Charlie and Henry scrambled into the back and leant over to pat the weeping Francesca on the shoulders, and the twins appeared anxiously at Francesca's side of the car and peered in, stroking the bits of her they could reach. He realized that all four of the boys were watching him carefully, caught Henry's sardonic eye, and took a grip on the situation.

'Listen boys,' he said firmly. 'Charles and Perry, take your sister to St Mary's, don't follow the ambulance because it and I are going somewhere else. They'll want to keep her in for the night, and you are to see they do.' He put a firm protective arm around Francesca, dislodging Charlie as he did so, and heard a faint, collective sigh of relief from her brothers. 'I want her somewhere where I don't have to worry about her getting properly looked after, because it is going to be a long night for me. Frannie, I'll come when I can.' He leant over and kissed her on the lips, in a deliberate signal to all observers. She touched his cheek, painfully freeing the unbroken arm, tears still pouring down her face.

'Off you go, Perry,' he said, getting out of the car, and stood for a moment to watch its departure, before turning to the night's business.

EPILOGUE

Francesca woke, and lay cautiously still in the blessed absence of pain, wrapped in a warm cocoon of blankets. She considered the ceiling and the decor and realized she must be in a hospital but no longer in Casualty, which she did dimly remember; watched the light, and decided it must be late afternoon. She felt a twinge from her right arm, and moved it cautiously before realizing that it was attached to a tube into which an elevated bottle of clear liquid was dripping. Her left arm seemed to be outside the bedclothes and curiously rigid, and she peered at a clumsy white plaster.

Then suddenly she realized there was someone else in the room, and lifted her head carefully to see John McLeish asleep in a chair in the corner, awkwardly folded into rather too small a space, and with his left arm in a large khaki sling. He looked utterly exhausted, and she watched him, remembering that she had seen him like this before after a very long shift. Even abandoned in sleep he looked formidable and not at all childlike. She fidgeted her left arm which rewarded her with a sharp painful twinge that brought tears to her eyes. She must have made a noise because he was awake, straight from a sound sleep, and beside her instantly.

'Mind that drip,' he said, warningly.

'What's it for?' she asked, teeth gritted against a recurrence of the pain from her wrist.

'In case they have to get your blood pressure up in a hurry.'

'It's always low. Didn't the boys tell them?'

'Many times, apparently, but it wasn't just low last night, it disappeared. Your mum was here, but she went off to get some sleep when I got here about eleven this morning. Henry Blackshaw was here half the night, too. To keep order, he said.'

They smiled momentarily at each other, but she was watching his face. 'What is it John?' The faint colour vanished from her cheeks, and he cast a harassed look at the drip, before pulling a chair close to her.

'Darling, Hampton is dead. I'm sorry, but I must tell you because the evening papers have it.'

'Because Charlie hit him?' She started to shiver, and McLeish, swearing, leaned over her and pressed the buzzer.

'No, no, no. Nothing to do with Charlie.' He looked apologetically at the arriving Sister, who glanced at the drip and stood, hand on Francesca's wrist, counting her pulse rate.

'Go on, John,' Francesca urged, shivering, 'I promise not to die, but I must know that it wasn't Charlie.' One might, McLeish thought, with exasperated love, have remembered that brothers outranked lovers in Francesca's world.

'He killed himself. Took an enormous overdose of heroin which no one spotted until too late.'

'But where . . . I mean, how . . .' her voice tailed off, and he nodded.

'Yes, we slipped up there. I was with him in the ambulance, and we took the cuffs off so the ambulance men could handle him more easily. Then I distracted them by passing out — I've got a chipped collarbone, it turns out — and he must have taken it then. No one spotted the overdose in the prison hospital because they were looking for a skull fracture, and another bloke in there ran amok, and they had to X-ray my shoulder; and one way and another he was dead three hours later before anyone did anything sensible. No skull fracture, by the way.'

She was staring at him, absolutely white, her eyes very blue and narrowed with concentration, and the Sister looked up, sharply, in warning.

'Was he a murderer?'

'Yes. At least once, and possibly twice. He killed William Fireman all right. Bruce found the presentation watch with Fireman's name on it in Hampton's car. I imagine he took it to try and delay Fireman's identification and give himself a chance to get clear away to Yorkshire but he must have been distracted, and he left Fireman's card case on him. Then he took the watch up to Yorkshire with him and couldn't dump it anywhere there because, if found, it would have told us there *was* a Britex connection and that it wasn't just a London mugging. He moved it after you and Martin found it in a cupboard.'

'He did it for money? I mean because he was on the take and Fireman had found out?'

'I'd not be able to prove it very easily, but yes. In fact, but for that watch, and of course for the fact that he attacked you, I'm not sure we could have made the case stand up. There were two others in the fiddle, William Blackett and Simon Ketterick — you met him once. He was a heroin addict.'

'Was?'

'Oh God, you don't know about him either.' He looked anxiously at the Sister who scowled at him warningly, but he decided to ignore her. 'He died of an overdose yesterday.'

Francesca looked up at him intently. 'Did Peter kill him too?'

'Probably, but I couldn't prove it. No fingerprints on the three syringes in the room, but smudges as if someone were wearing gloves. Blackett swears he found him dead, and I believe him. Too frightened to do anything but go and get hopelessly pissed and weep all over a tart he'd only met once before. But even if I didn't believe him we'd never get a conviction now, with Hampton dead.'

'Was Peter an addict?'

'Forensic say no, that's why what he took killed him.'

He realized as he spoke that she had suddenly turned even paler, and her wrist went limp in the Sister's hand. The Sister reached across him without apology and pressed a bell, and within ten seconds a young doctor had banged unceremoniously into the room.

'That's much too low,' he said briskly. 'Inspector, sorry, but out. Change the drip please, Sister.'

McLeish moved reluctantly back from the bed.

'No, please.' Francesca opened her eyes with an enormous effort of will. 'Please don't go, I must know what happened, I'll be worse if I don't.'

The medical help, struggling with the drip, ignored them both, and McLeish moved quietly back to her side, stroking her cheek. The doctor stood back, and the Sister picked up Francesca's wrist again while they watched. She nodded to the doctor after a couple of minutes.

'All right,' he said to McLeish. 'But don't do anything exciting.'

Francesca's eyes opened. 'Why did Peter try to kill me?'

'He knew that you had seen the Alutex table and the presentation box. I don't know how he realized you were dangerous to him. Did you suspect him?' He was acutely aware of the young doctor and the sister, both obviously fascinated.

'No, I didn't,' she said, flatly, 'I'd never make a detective.' Then she looked up, eyes widening, and a faint pink blush crept over her cheekbones. 'Oh God. I know.'

'What, Frannie?'

'I told him I'd seen the Alutex table — I was teasing him about losing his temper. And he knows I have a photographic memory.'

'And he *didn't* know you'd written it all down and passed it on to Martin and Henry.'

'No. God, what a fool I am.' She looked at him. 'And, as you are not saying, I made it easy for him by going running by myself.'

McLeish managed, he thought commendably, not to move his face at all, contenting himself with stroking her cheek. 'Would you have caught him if it hadn't been for me?' she asked, hesitantly, but McLeish, even knowing her overdeveloped sense of responsibility, was unwilling to equivocate.

'No. If it hadn't been for your being involved with Britex, I expect I'd have called it a mugging in the end. Would you rather he had got away with it?'

'No. No, of course not. Don't be silly.'

'Don't you be silly, then. That's what my job's about.'

Both of them glanced at the hovering medical help. 'She's all right.'

The young doctor self-consciously made a minor adjustment to the drip, and took himself and the Sister reluctantly out of the room.

'I know what would help my blood pressure, but I can't move either arm,' Francesca said apologetically, and he leant over her and kissed her till they were both out of breath.

'Oh, darling John. What a time to break my wrist.'

'We'll manage,' he said, with love.

He sat down in the chair beside the bed, totally at peace with the world, watching while she drifted back into sleep.

THE END

THE JOFFE BOOKS STORY

We began in 2014 when Jasper agreed to publish his mum's much-rejected romance novel and it became a bestseller.

Since then we've grown into the largest independent publisher in the UK. We're extremely proud to publish some of the very best writers in the world, including Joy Ellis, Faith Martin, Caro Ramsay, Helen Forrester, Simon Brett and Robert Goddard. Everyone at Joffe Books loves reading and we never forget that it all begins with the magic of an author telling a story.

We are proud to publish talented first-time authors, as well as established writers whose books we love introducing to a new generation of readers.

We won Trade Publisher of the Year at the Independent Publishing Awards in 2023. We have been shortlisted for Independent Publisher of the Year at the British Book Awards for the last four years, and were shortlisted for the Diversity and Inclusivity Award at the 2022 Independent Publishing Awards. In 2023 we were shortlisted for Publisher of the Year at the RNA Industry Awards.

We built this company with your help, and we love to hear from you, so please email us about absolutely anything bookish at feedback@joffebooks.com

If you want to receive free books every Friday and hear about all our new releases, join our mailing list: www.joffebooks.com/contact

And when you tell your friends about us, just remember: it's pronounced Joffe as in coffee or toffee!

ALSO BY JANET NEEL

WILSON & McLEISH MYSTERIES
Book 1: A FATAL BLOW

Printed in Great Britain
by Amazon

37151464R00152